For Ellie

Kerry Hancock

THE TASK

AUSTIN MACAULEY PUBLISHERS™

LONDON • CAMBRIDGE • NEW YORK • SHARJAH

A CIP catalogue record for this title is available from the British Library.

ISBN 9781528909754 (Paperback)
ISBN 9781528909761 (Hardback)
ISBN 9781528959377 (ePub e-book)

www.austinmacauley.com

First Published (2019)
Austin Macauley Publishers Ltd
25 Canada Square
Canary Wharf
London
E14 5LQ

A big thank you to Mel for his time and patience.

Chapter 1
Dax

This is a story above all others. The story of Meridien. The city that grew from the ashes. It is a story all know well. Monmoo, the volcano of the north, had ceased to erupt but still boiled with activity. It was the foundation of the city, allowing metals to be mined and forged within its belly. With toil and tool the city was built, and it grew, and it grew, and it grew. King Maximilian ruled with leadership of steel and had two fine sons to follow in his footsteps. The riches of the city were massed from the crafting of weapons. Its gems, jewellery and finery were made from the rarest of metals, all forged inside the volcano itself. The king knew his time as leader would soon come to an end and his son Lexion was to take his place. The boy had lived and breathed in his father's footsteps from the day he was born, ready and willing to step up. But Daxion, his second son, was about to start his own path, a path the king feared would take his son's life.

Lex strode out onto the balcony behind his father, every step snip and sharp, every arm swing made with purpose. This was to be Dax's hair-cutting day. The whole city was out to see the king and his two sons. Most had waited for hours in the blistering heat to see the two boys. Both sons were dressed in the red and gold uniform of the Meridien army, stiff and crisp. Their father wore his general's uniform. The three were a royal sight for peasant eyes.

"Daxion, come now, don't drag your feet. You know it irritates me." The king hated these occasions. It made him feel humble and that would not do, it simply would not do.

"Yes, father, sorry." Young Dax hurried his step and fell in behind his brother.

The king took his place on the balcony and Lex and Dax stood either side of their father. The crowd hushed, and hundreds of ears strained excitedly for their king's voice. Maximilian cleared his throat and bellowed as regally as he could.

"Subjects of Meridien! Loyal servants to the crown! Welcome here today! I present to you my Sworn Son, Prince Daxion the third." The king swept his arm towards Dax and the whole crowd erupted into cheers. Dax, at only ten years old, tried to shy away from the greedy eyes and whooping crowds, but a firm, fatherly hand on his back held him in place. He raised a tentative arm and gave a tiny wave. This whipped up the crowd again, the noise was deafening.

The king spoke once more, "As you all know, today is Daxion's hair-cutting ceremony and I have invited you all here to bear witness." Tiny beads of sweat ran down the king's forehead as Daxion started to fidget. The thought of having his hair cut in front of hundreds of people made him want to flee. "Let us delay no longer. Bring forth the box." An old and honoured soldier of the royal guard stepped onto the balcony carrying a gem-encrusted box. He bowed to the king and held out the box at arm's length. "Behold, citizens of Meridien, the Sworn scissors!" Dax's father lifted the lid with purpose and withdrew a tiny pair of silver scissors. A rich, red piece of ribbon was tied to the handle. The king turned to Dax and gestured for him to turn his head. They had practised this day a hundred times but the greedy eyes of the people made the whole thing seem dark and foreboding. Dax stared across at Lex but he faced the crowd, no muscle moving, no hair out of place. Slowly and with the face of a doomed boy Dax turned his head.

His father once more addressed the crowd.

"With one snip we shall see to what Prince Daxion has been Sworn and what his future and the future of this, the greatest of all cities, holds."

King Max gently clasped a lock of Dax's hair, held up the scissors and snipped. A long tendril of brown and red hair fell to the floor and everyone held their nerve and their breath, none so deeply as The King. Dax closed his eyes and wished. He wished for one thing only, a royal Fire Dragon of his own. This was the only way he would get to have one. Dax's neck started to burn but he endured it as he was taught. It prickled and stung, but still he didn't move.

His father's gasp brought him back to the present. A deep, red and gold pattern of flames spread across the back of Dax's neck.

"Praise be!" his father shouted. "Praise be, celebrate and rejoice! Prince Daxion is Fire Sworn, Fire Sworn!"

Dax released the small breath he held and smiled deeply.

"Now I shall have my dragon."

Chapter 2

Five Years Later

Dax dug his toes into the warm, volcanic sand and crouched low behind the rocks. The old egg-hatcher had been looking for him for hours and was tutting and shuffling his way towards Dax's hiding place.

"I know you're out here, boy. Lazy, idle fool. Show yourself." The egg-hatcher had had enough of his arrogant, royal charge. Five years he had trained him and taught him, only to be repaid with such shenanigans.

Dax picked up a tiny rock and threw it behind the hatcher. The hatcher chuckled loudly.

"Do you think me stupid? I have taught many a royal brat, now come out from there!" The hatcher was losing patience.

Dax knew he'd had his fun and lounging in the sunshine all day was worth the sting of the hatcher's stick. He rose and swaggered over to his teacher.

"I see lying in the sunshine agrees with you, Prince Dax."

"Well, a prince needs his rest time." Before the last word left his lips, the hatcher whipped him across the arm with his stick so quickly Dax squealed and jumped back, stunned.

"Your test is tonight, stupid boy; you know it is a test you must not fail." The hatcher frowned and shook his head. "Your father will not accept failure, boy, you know that." The hatcher softened his face and nodded for Dax to follow him. "You shall start after sunset. You know where to begin?" Dax looked way up to the top of the volcano and shrugged. "This is not a joke, Dax. I will not be there to guide or save you."

"I know. It's just that it all seems so real now. I'm not ready."

"Oh, but you are young, Dax. More ready than you know."

That Evening

Dax and Master Hatcher Kef stood on a flat outcrop at the top of Monmoo. Hot, blistering wind whipped up their hair.

"You've come a long way, boy." Master Kef was proud of his young charge. Dax shrugged and turned towards the volcano's edge. "Dax, look at me. This is not a test to be sniffed at. You must do this alone." Kef wished Dax would take this seriously. "There are three parts to this test, Dax. First, you must descend the outside of the volcano without being seen. Then you must select and steal away an egg from the Hatching Grounds. Now, you know the keepers will be on high alert and thirdly you must take your egg to the river of fire, deep below Monmoo, and bathe it until it hatches," Kef stopped speaking abruptly. "Dax! Are you listening?" Kef grabbed Dax's shoulder and drew him close. "If you fail to capture the dragon's first breath, all you have been through, will have been for nothing and your father will show no mercy for either of us." Kef lowered his hands and slumped his shoulders. Still Dax said nothing. "I will return to this spot in the morning at first light. May the Merfolk bless you, young Dax." With that Kef turned and made his way down the narrow, rock steps that led down to Meridien.

"Wait! Please, Master Kef." Dax didn't want to do this alone. His training had all been done in pairs or with his teacher. This was the first time he had doubted his skills.

Kef turned and smiled at Dax before turning a corner in the steps. Dax was now alone.

Dax sank to the floor and ran his fingers through his thick hair. *First things first*, he thought. He pulled the long piece of red ribbon, he had been given on his cutting day, from his pocket and bound his hair back. The hot wind tried to whip a few strands from him, but it was soon all slicked back and tamed. Dax looked at his open hands, a thick layer, like scales, covered his palms. He checked his feet and roughed up the scaly layer that covered his soles also.

"Time to climb," he shouted to no one. Dax rose to his feet and studied the ground around him. He had done this a thousand times, but never alone and never undetected. He knew the guards would be on full alert, for to catch out The Prince on his trial would encourage great bragging rights amongst the men. He would take the cold side of the volcano. It was a longer and more treacherous path but there were more nooks and crannies. Dax rubbed his hands together to ruffle up the scales, then stepped over the edge of the outcrop and was gone.

"So, Master Dax, the cold side is your choice. We will see how that serves you," Kef muttered to himself, the long, thin spy lens gripped close to his eye. Kef had been Master Hatcher for many years and Dax would be his last royal charge. The rest his retirement would bring would be most welcome. Kef knew The Mistress would be on her way soon and he prayed to the Merfolk that Dax would pass his test and be able to claim the prize that The Mistress would deliver.

Dax skimmed and clawed his way down the cold side of Monmoo. Keeping himself small, checking for lose shale and rocks, it was slow going but worth it. He would not give the guards the satisfaction of sounding their horns and beating their chests at his capture. The scaly layer on his hands and feet gripped and clung to the rocks surface allowing him freedom of movement that no rope or glove could. He needed to feel his way. Monmoo was a live beast and had to be treated like one. Half way down he heard the heavy feet and deep voices of a patrol. Two thickset men carrying spy lenses and alarm horns scaled just below him. Dax pulled in his legs and anchored his arm around a large boulder. He buried his face into his chest and let his body relax. He was no more than a ripple of rock blending into the volcano's landscape.

"You see anything up there?" one guard called to the other.

"Not a thing."

"Give it here. Let me look. You're as blind as my gran." The smaller of the two guards snatched the spy lens from the other and held it to his eye.

"Oi, give that back, you stupid, fat fool. You are on horn duty."

"What did you call me?" The smaller guard had lowered the lens and had turned to face the other. "If you had just kept your mouth shut we wouldn't be up here before sunrise. But oh no. We volunteer, sir, we'll catch the young prince, sir," the small guard mocked in a squeaky voice. "Now look! We're half way up the volcano. No supper and no prince to catch. Why I call you my friend I'll never know!" The two guards carried on snapping at each other as they passed underneath their prize and shambled up another ledge.

Dax let out a slow, long breath and smirked at the guard's foolishness. He released the rock and carried on scaling down his chosen path. After what seemed like an age he felt the ground even out and the floor starting to warm. He turned his head to look back where he had come from and bit his lip. *I must make up time. That has taken me twice as long as the hot side would have and stealing an egg will be slow business*, he thought as he scurried down the last of the out-crops. Dax paused for breath to get his bearings, trying to remember his lessons with Master Kef. The three moons had reached mid-height and Dax knew he could not linger.

Kef lowered his spy lens and stroked his thin, grey beard.

"Easy, boy, easy. The Hatching Grounds will be tough. Merfolk bless you."

Dax crouched low behind the hot springs. One false move and he would be caught or worse, boiled alive.

I need to distract the watchers, he thought. Dax scrutinised the ground for answers. Tiny, red flame bugs were scurrying across the spring potholes, collecting minuscule pieces of volcanic rock to make their homes. *Now all I need is a slingshot*. Dax quickly back-tracked to the volcano's base and searched around the stony soil for dead roots. Having collected an armful, he began plaiting them into a long, thin rope. He ripped a ragged piece of cloth from his shirt and set about tying each end of the rope to the cloth to make a swing-ing pouch.

This should do the job, he thought, as he swung the empty sling shot over his head to practise. Now to collect the ammunition.

Dax made his way back to the springs and searched the ground for his unsuspecting allies.

"There you are, my hot, little beauties." Dax reached out and scooped up a handful of hot fire-bugs and loaded them into his sling. One quick look to see where the watchers were, then he launched them. Glowing, red, little angry bugs landed all over two of the watchers and had them leaping to their feet.

"What in the name of Mer is going on here?" the Head Watcher shouted, seeing two of his men dancing and raking at their clothes.

"Fire-bugs sir. Lots of them."

Dax let fly his next load and watched as three more watchers hollered and jumped around.

"Take hold of yourselves, men," the Head Watcher screeched. "Do not lose your focus."

Dax let fly one more bug surprise and as his luck held they hit the Head Watcher full in the face.

"Mer, have mercy! They burn!" Dax couldn't help but snigger at the scene before him. The usually calm and passive watchers all running and screaming towards the waterhole to wash off their burn-ing little friends, was quite a sight.

Dax crept out onto the bed of hot springs and carefully tiptoed around the spring mounds. He knew the Hatching Grounds were just

14

around the corner. He slipped into the shadows and crouched down to get a better view. There before him were the Hatching Grounds. The boiling water from the springs flowed underneath the beds of hot sand. Here the dragon eggs were nested. Dax lay down on his belly and slithered towards the eggs, all the time listening for any signs that the watchers had returned. The hot sand made his skin tingle and his eyes scratchy, but still he slithered on. After what seemed like an age, he reached the first of the eggs.

"No, not these ones. They will take an age to hatch. They are small and not yet hot enough," he slithered on. Dax gently wriggled his way through the eggs, a slow and time-consuming task. At last he came to the larger eggs, smooth and warm. He selected one and slid it close to him. "Now to get us out of here," he whispered to his mute prize.

Dax could hear the low grumblings of the watchers returning, no doubt rubbing their stings and scalds. He slithered backwards along the path he had made in the hot sand until he felt the cooler earth underneath himself. He risked rising to a crouch and turned for the springs. WHOOSH. Dax staggered backwards as the hot, wet spray of the springs hit him. He tripped over his own feet and fell to the ground, clutching the egg.

"Merfolk be blessed! That was good timing, little fellow! A few more steps and we would have been done for." Dax waited for the spring to finish its impressive blast and hurried across the spring mounds, his breath held and prayers a-plenty, Dax and his egg made it across unharmed.

Kef lowered his spy lens and wiped the heavy sweat from his brow.

"For the love of the Merfolk, luck has you on his side, my boy. That was a close one." Kef returned to his spying with shaky hands and dry throat.

Dax cowered low underneath a large overhang and caught his breath.

"Well, that was a close call, my friend," Dax spoke softly to his egg. "Just one more part to complete and your first breath will be mine." Dax peered up to the sky and saw that the moons had started to dip. He knew he would have to hurry if he was to make it back up the mountain to see the three suns first rays.

The small, narrow path that led to the river of fire was well hidden and guarded. Dax knew he needed a disguise, but what? He would have to ambush a guard and steal his clothes. After slipping into the shadows he waited. He was not very good at being patient and started to doubt his choice when he heard the soft whistle of a passer-by. He crouched low and readied himself, small stones sweaty in his hands.

The tired guard was heading home, his duties for the night complete. He whistled a soft tune to himself as he thought of his comfy bed. He was just about to turn the corner when he heard a small knocking noise from the shadows.

"Hello! Anyone there?" Dax threw another stone. "Henry, if this is your idea of a joke, I'm way too tired for your foolishness. Come out now, lad." Dax threw the rest of his stones and waited. "OK, you asked for it. I'm going to give you a good thrashing for this and wait till I tell your mother! Oh boy, she'll be mad…" Before he could say another word, Dax had him. He wrapped his legs around his waist and his arms around his neck and face. The guard caught by sheer surprise, thrashed and stumbled around, flailing farther from the path until his head went dizzy and he passed out through lack of breath.

"Sleep well, my friend. And thanks for the clothes." Dax stripped him of his cloak and wriggled his way into it. *A little on the large size,* Dax thought. *But beggars can't be choosers now, can they?* He knew the guard would wake soon and sound the alarm, so he took up a fast pace along the path. Head down. Just another guard heading for an early start. Three or four guards passed him in a huddle. They just nodded and Dax nodded back. His egg clutched under his stolen cloak. He reached the fire-river cave covered in sweat, his hand cramped from holding the egg. "Now I just need to reach the river's edge, dip in the egg and wait."

The cave had four entrances and if memory served him right the one farthest to his right was the passage he wanted. Dax slipped into the dark, hot cave and breathed a huge sigh of relief. *We've made it so far, Kef, I hope you are praying for me*, he thought as he sneaked his way down the winding passage. At last he came to an opening. He carefully kept his back to the wall as he rounded into the huge cavern that held the river of fire, the heart of Monmoo. The heat that blew up from the river was so intense, Dax had trouble opening his eyes. He could feel his skin begin to dry and his throat was on fire with every breath he took. He peered through slitted eyes. At the river's edge six guards were patrolling, large horns and sticks hooked to their belts.

No way I'm getting to the river down that way, he thought. He scanned the river all the way back to its farthest point. There in the shadows a small rivulet of fire broke off and trickled away under the rock.

"There! That's the only point that's not guarded and my only chance."

Dax skirted his way around the edges of the cavern keeping to the shadows, slow step by slow step. Soon he reached the little rivulet and slowly eased himself to the floor. With shaking hands, he withdrew the egg from his cloak.

"Now, my little companion, it's time to hatch." The heat that was coming from the rivulet was almost too much to bear. Sheets of sweat were running down Dax's face and he was finding it harder and harder to breath. He leant forward and dipped the egg into the liquid fire, its hot molten sticking to the egg like glue. Dax withdrew the egg and placed it on the ground beside him. He felt light-headed and had to fight to keep himself awake. He started to drift into sleep, dreaming of life in the palace, cool water in his cup, the laughter of his brother, the softness of his bed, the sharp crack of Kef's stick across his arm. *Wait! That's not right,* Dax thought. *That's not a comfort.* Dax shook himself awake and realised the crack of Kef's stick was the crack of the egg beside him. Dax shot upright then remembered where he was and hunkered back down.

A large crack made its way from the top to the bottom of the egg and something moved inside. Dax knew he must inhale the dragon's first breath or he would have no chance of ever owning his own dragon. Slowly and with tender hands he placed the egg on his lap. Smaller cracks bled from the main one and patterned the shell. Small fragments fell away and Dax could just make out a greenish colour inside. The little dragon clawed and scratched his way out from his shell and stared at Dax with large emerald eyes. Mirror like scales covered its body and Dax had to hold it tight as it whipped its long dagger like tail from side to side.

"Hello," Dax ventured. The Dragon just stared. Dax picked the few remaining pieces of shell from his head and cradled him in his arms. He knew he would not release his first breath unless he felt safe. Dax slid himself away from the burning rivulet and deeper into the shadows. The dragon snuggled closer to Dax's chest. "Come now, little fellow. We can be friends, can't we?" The beautiful dragon just blinked. Dax held the dragon away from himself and looked deep into its eyes, for it is said a dragon can see into your soul and judge you to be worthy. The little dragon started to cough and splutter, he opened his tiny mouth and croaked out his first hot breath and Dax was there right in front of him, drawing in the magical air. He felt it fill his lungs and enter his blood. The hot, tingly magic made his heart pound and his hands and feet shook.

"Hey, you! There, in the shadows! Show yourself!" A half-naked guard had stumbled into the cavern and raised the alarm.

"No time to lose, my friend," Dax whispered to the dragon as he lowered it to the floor and started to climb. All he had to do now was make it to the volcano top and he would pass.

"STOP! By order of the guards, STOP!" The Head Guard was starting to make his way to where Dax had been hiding, the five others close behind. But the small dragon had waddled out from the shadows and was squawking his displeasure at having been left behind. "What in Mer's name is going on here?" the Head Guard declared, leaning down and scooping up the dragon.

Dax was gone. A quick and nimble climber, he scurried and scrabbled his way back to the passage and burst out into the last of the weak moonlight. Down the narrow path he ran. No care now for disguises. He flung the guard's robe over the ledge and into the rocks. On he ran, he had no need for the Hatching Grounds now so up he went. Up and up and up, not pausing for breath; no heed for cuts and bruises, on he went.

Kef had been standing on the outcrop for a good half hour before he heard Dax's desperate gasps as he pulled himself up onto the flat rock next to him. Dax lay on his back and took huge, deep breaths, trying to talk at the same time.

"Easy, young Dax, I'm here. We have time. The dawn is just about to break." Dax sat up and rubbed his face. The fire river had burnt his skin and his eyes were weeping and blurry.

"I did it, Master Kef! I did it!" Dax laughed great bellowing laughs.

Kef stepped forward and took Dax's hands.

"Let me see, boy. Let me see." Kef turned his hands over and saw the gentle pulsing of dragon magic pump itself through Dax's veins. "Praise be, Prince Daxion the third! We will make a Dragon Master of you yet."

Chapter 3
Malya

This is a story unlike any other; a village, a hut and a tribal witch. Koiya was head of her tribe, all tribes in the Marshlands had a leader, but a woman leader was rare. Koiya's knowledge of beast and plant was unrivalled. Her herb work, sought after and respected. She was quiet and humble. But Koiya knew that the time for being timid was over. Her eldest daughter had a path to follow and follow it she would. The village depended on it.

Koiya watched her eldest daughter from a distance. She loved to watch the children play. Malya was teaching the youngsters to play with small, glass balls and tiny holes poked into the earth. The idea was to flick the balls into the holes with the fewest attempts, but she was having no luck calming the little ones enough for them to concentrate.

"Come now, Zenara, just a little flick," Malya encouraged. Zenara rolled her eyes and flicked the little ball half way across the small, earth pitch. "Never mind, try again." Malya chuckled, handing the tiny girl another glass ball.

Koiya stepped out from the tree line and beckoned to her daughter to join her. Malya ruffled Zenara's hair and rose from the little pitch.

"Soon you'll get it, small one, I promise." The small girl smiled up at Malya. She was Zenara's hero. "Yes, mother, do you need my help?" Malya offered. She knew her mother's health was failing her.

"No, my beautiful one, just walk with me. I have a tale to tell." Koiya lent heavily on Malya's arm as they headed into the marshes. "You see all that is around us, Malya?" Koiya swept a hand across the horizon.

"Yes, Mother."

"You know it is ours to protect, yes?" Koiya stopped and turned to her daughter.

Malya frowned at her mother.

19

"Is there something wrong?"

"Not wrong, Malya, but written. There is a darkness coming, my beautiful one, a darkness that will end our way of life." Malya struggled to take in what her mother was saying.

"Darkness. What do you mean? Is there a storm coming?"

Koiya smiled softly at her daughter's innocence.

"No, Malya, there is an evil in this world that has to be faced, an evil that can only be stopped by a few." Koiya led her daughter to a cluster of rocks and encouraged her to sit. "There are lots of cities in this world, Malya, as you know. Some strange and far away; all the head families of these cities have a gift passed down through generations." Koiya could see the confusion in Malya's face. She would need to be truthful. Only the truth is called for now. "You know of the head shaving ceremonies, yes?" Koiya raised her eyebrows at Malya waiting for an answer.

"Yes, mother, but what does that have to do with the evil that is coming?" Malya felt her heart breaking. She could feel the tension coming from her mother, her rock, she was fearful of her mother's next words.

"Well the head is shaved to see if the child is Sworn. If a dark patch appears at the back of the child's neck, then a further hair cutting is required at age ten." Koiya closed her mouth, slowly waiting for Malya to put all the pieces together.

Malya slowly reached behind her head and ran her fingers through her thick, black hair, her eyes flew open and she leapt from the rock.

"What do you mean Sworn? I'm ten. What happens now mother? Do I have to go away? Please, mother, no, I cannot leave you." Malya was beside herself as tears flowed down her soft, brown cheeks and dripped from her chin.

Koiya struggled up from the rock and gently placed her arms around her daughter.

"We will cut your hair now, Malya. If a symbol appears on the back of your neck, my child, you are Sworn. You have been blessed with a gift, a gift that will save us all."

Malya sniffed and looked deep into her mother's gentle, brown eyes. Love and reassurance shone there.

"Okay, I am ready." Koiya new her daughter would not let her down, she would take this responsibility with calm strength. She had an inner quiet like all the women before her.

"Come, beautiful one, let us sit, it will make the cutting a little easier." Malya helped her mother to sit once more and calmed her fear. Koiya drew from her knapsack a pair of small, silver scissors, a small, red ribbon was tied to one of the handles. Malya stared with awe. The sunlight caught the blades and they shone like precious metal. "Are you ready, Malya, ready to know your destiny? Are you ready to know to what you have been sworn?"

"Yes, mother, I am ready." Malya turned her head so Koiya could reach and with one swift snip Koiya cut away a long, thick, black lock of Malya's hair.

"Now, stay calm, child. Let us pray together. Pray to the mother of all nature that you will be sworn to her domain." Koiya clasped Malya's hands and gently rocked them both from side to side. Malya started to feel warmth on her neck, then an itching feeling.

"It burns, mother, please look."

Koiya turned Malya's head and gasped. "For the love of the Merfolk, Malya, you are Serpent Sworn. Praise be to the Holy Mother."

Chapter 4
Five Years Later

Malya rose from the soft grass where she had been sitting for the best part of an hour. She removed her blindfold and stretched out her cramping legs. For the past five years Malya had worked with her mother closely to learn the nature of beast and plant. She had trained and mastered the close combat fighting style called Teknaa and she had mastered tracking from the old man. This was her final test and it felt good to finally be close to beating the master himself.

She steadied herself and gently sniffed the breeze. Nothing. She closed her eyes and listened. Birds are the first ones to give away a hiding place, or an intruder, in their midst. She heard nothing. She crouched down on one knee and studied the grass and plants around her. Still nothing.

"Well done, old man," she whispered to herself. She rose and studied the outer bushes surrounding the grass. *You sly old fox,* she thought. Just to her left grew a patch of scarlet blossom bushes, their petals small and bright red. She knew they didn't drop their petals till late July and it was mid-May. There on the grass beside them was a handful of fallen petals. Someone had brushed past.

Malya crept forward, her breathing and movements as slow as a predator stalking prey. She bent down and studied the flowers. *The old man had passed through here*, she smiled as she thought. She brushed past the bush herself, causing a few more petals to fall and gently eased herself through the bushes. She continued through the undergrowth as soft as rain, seeing no more signs that anyone had been this way. After a few minutes the bushes thinned and Malya stepped out onto the harsh, bare nesting grounds of the koonoo birds. Nesting was in full swing and the whole area was covered in little twiggy nests. She listened closely, hearing the soft cooing and bustling of the birds, but no distressed squawking. She swept her eyes over the hundreds of nests, looking for anything that looked out of place. Each nest housed a small black and white bird. Competition for these nests was fierce, she knew, and all were occupied. All accept one. Malya crept slowly between the nests, being careful not to tread too closely to the birds and set them to fussing. It seemed to take an age to reach the empty nest. As she approached the barren stick home she heard the faint rush of the river. She paused for a moment and scanned the horizon. The nesting ground continued down a gentle slope that led to the soft, black sand of the river's edge.

When she reached the empty nest, she peered in. No bird. No eggs. She slowly reached down to feel inside. The nest was still slightly warm. *Gathering a bit extra for your pot tonight, old man?* Malya thought to herself. She straightened up and headed for the river, still padding lightly. Haste now would scare the birds and give away her distance from the old man.

Malya dug her toes into the warm, soft, sandy soil of the riverbank and scanned the river's edge. No prints. She watched the river for a few moments and judged its speed and depth. "There's no way he could have swum it, not at his age."

She chuckled to herself. Malya walked to the river's edge and scanned the shoreline. Something caught her eye. There, just starting to get washed away was a series of small, deep holes leading out into the river.

"Clever." She smiled to herself again. "He really is inventive." Malya knew if she was to catch him, she would have to swim. She tightened the strap that held her wooden staff to her back and lowered herself into the river. The cold, sharp shock of the ice-cold water almost had her gasping, but she had to bear it in silence. She walked as far as she could and then pushed off, taking gentle, slow sweeps of her arms to glide herself across. Of course she could swim with vigour and strength but that would make too much noise and alert the wildlife into a panic.

When she reached the opposite shore she pulled herself onto the river's bank and lay still, trying to control her breathing before getting to her feet. Her hands and feet were frozen and the once warm breeze was chilling her with every gust. She checked the suns positions. She had a few hours of daylight left and she had to find him before the evening meal was served or she would have to do this again tomorrow. *I will not fail, I will not fail myself,* Malya thought, easing herself to a sitting position. She scanned the river's edge and found more small, deep holes leading into the tree line where the Marshlands started to turn into the dark forest. Remnants of the Black Road poked up through the sand, Malya avoided them, they brought bad luck. She knew she would be safe in the forest during the day but at night it would be teaming with hunting packs of wolves and bears. Malya stood and sniffed the breeze once more. Still nothing. She slowly followed the line of holes into the tree line and felt the change of temperature immediately.

The forest was cool and damp. The floor was covered in thick, decaying leaves and twigs. She listened though the layers of sounds. First the slow, heavy bustling of mammals. Then the soft tweeting of the birds. Right down to the high pitch of the insects. Malya could hear that something was wrong; she could hear the distressed chirping of the little, green cricket.

"They should all be in their wood burrows in the day. Something must have disturbed them." She padded into the forest following the cricket's cacophony of noise. After a while she came to a small clearing where the ground was covered in prickly cones. One step on them would earn you a nasty sting. She crouched lower to study the cones. They seemed to be lying in random spots just as they had fallen from the trees. She was just about to turn and find a different path towards the crickets when she spotted a pine cone that had been turned onto its end to sit upright, then another, then another. Someone had gently turned the cones aside to create just enough room for a small foot, one in front of the other, to pass through. Malya sighed deeply; she could see no footprints. She looked a little closer. Every now and again there was a small round imprint pushed into the forest floor.

"So, old man you have tiptoed through on just your big toe." Malya hesitated before she followed the tiny path made by the old man. He was smaller and lighter than she and she would have to be as steady and light on her feet as he, or suffer a week of painful stings. She set off as quiet and gentle as a falling feather. When she finally reached the edge of the clearing she gulped in a huge breath of air and wiped the sweat from her brow. "Now," she whispered, "let me find those crickets."

Malya knew the crickets made their burrows in rotting wood, so she swept her eyes across the forest floor for old branches and stumps as she walked. The noise of the crickets was getting louder and closer. As the forest became denser, she followed the noise to an old tree stump crawling with disgruntled crickets, their angry little legs busy calling out their displeasure. To the right of the stump was a vast mushroom patch, its bulbous globes of white almost giving off a light of their own. Malya studied the mushrooms. She knew if he had passed through them they would have revealed his passage easily, for even given a gentle brush, the mushrooms would bruise and blacken. She could find no such sign. Even if he could not touch them for fear of giving his path away, she could pick a few, for later. She bent and snapped of a handful of mushroom bulbs and tucked them in her knapsack. *Now,* Malya thought as her eyes searched the surrounding forest, *which way did you go?*

Malya knew the old man would not have ventured further into the forest as he would not like to spend a night there, waiting for her. She knew he would have sought the river again to take him back onto the Marshlands and away from the evening packs. Malya listened for the direction of the river and determined it was away to her right. She rounded the mushroom field and headed back out of the forest. When she reached the black, sandy soil she stopped and sat for a moment to get her bearings. She checked the suns again and determined she hadn't got long until dusk. The river was too deep and wide here for her to cross and she could see no little holes in the river's edge. Upstream looked narrower. If she had learnt anything, it's that man and beast will always chose the easiest and safest route across any water, so, upstream he must have gone. After walking upstream for a while she could see some huge, brown rocks poking up from the rushing water. As she approached them she could see they were covered in wet, green moss and that they led all the way to the other side, but they looked slippery and dangerous. Malya walked to the river's edge and bent down on one knee to study the first rock. No footprints but the moss had been squashed flat by something, something with ridges in it. Malya smiled and turned towards the bushes and small trees that grew at the edge of the forest and ventured down onto the sandy soil. One bush she spotted looked like it had several leaves stripped from it. She hurried towards it and ran her fingers over the leaves. "Of course, the leaves of this river bush are coarse and ridged. Perfect to wrap around your feet to stop you slipping on the moss." Malya stripped some leaves for herself and using some soft roots she dug up from the soil, wrapped her feet and made her way back to the river. She removed her staff to give herself balance and tentatively stepped onto the first rock. The leaves worked, and she moved swiftly from rock to rock. When she reached the other side she removed her leaf shoes and threw them back into the river and they were swept away leaving no trace. Malya checked the suns. Dusk was upon her and now she was back in the Marshlands, she was running out of time. She listened for any suspicious noise but all she could hear was the low hum of the animals getting ready for their night's sleep. She sniffed the air and caught a very faint smudge of smoke. She sniffed a little deeper and it was gone. Malya sat and thought through the situation. She thought about all she had been taught. *Where do animals go at dusk if they are not predators? They make their way home or somewhere safe for the night. No creature puts itself in discomfort. It heads for a familiar place, somewhere warm.* Malya shot up and headed off. She knew where he was, that crafty old man. She trekked through the marshes, past the bamboo, rounding the huge Yok Yok trees. Over the shallow rivulets and streams that web the marshes. She paused and sniffed again. The smoke was stronger now and the suns were setting.

Malya entered her village just as darkness fell. She could see the elders gathered around the fire and she smiled to herself as she recognised the hunched figure of the old man. Malya sidled up to the fire and lowered herself next to her mentor.

"Did you bring the mushrooms child?" the old man asked in a voice as knowing and wise as time.

"They will make a nice extra for your bird stew," Malya replied slipping the mushrooms into the cooking pot upon the fire.

"If you had looked harder you would have seen the two branches I broke from the young tree to make my stilts," the old man smirked. At least he had out-foxed her on something.

Malya smiled. He really was the best tracker in the village. She would let him have his little victory. She had seen the breaks on the trees trunk and had decided to swim anyway. He would never need to know.

"This will be our last meal together, I have nothing more to teach you, Malya, you are ready."

"Thank you, old man," Malya sniffed. She was starting to get cold. She would get a blanket from her mother's hut before she ate.

She rose and stopped for a moment.

"Old man, a question if I may?"

"You may."

"Ready for what?"

Chapter 5
Selena

This story starts as any other, a kingdom, a palace and an old, wise queen, gentle and graceful yet loyal and upstanding. The White Palace has been her family's home for generations spanning back to the beginning of worlds. Carved into the Great White Mountains that divide the kingdom from the sea at its southern edge. It is a wonder to behold and now it was hers: but for how long?

Queen Philamo sat at her mirrored dresser just staring at her face; she knew what was to come: the tears, the firm tone she must use. She counselled herself.

"It is for the good of all." But the words sounded hollow and lack-lustre. The small click of her door handle pulled her attention up. "Selena, my love, come, come." Philamo held out a welcoming hand and the timid princess stepped quietly into The Queen's bed-chamber. "Close the door, my sweet, no prying eyes or bat ears are needed for this."

Selena was tall for her age, like all White Kingdom children, for they were a warrior nation. Courage, strength and heart were their breeding standards and Selena fulfilled them all. Her hair was the colour of pure gold and her eyes crystal blue, the same as every child born inside the White City.

"Grandmother, you wished to see me?" Selena whispered.

"Yes, my dear, I have a telling for you. Come, sit on my lap while I brush your hair. It will make it a little easier." Selena slid gently onto her grandmother's lap and felt the long, soft strokes of her grandmother's brush. "Do you remember your lessons on the history of this world Selena?"

"Yes, Grandmother," Selena answered.

"Do you remember the war stories you have been told?" Philamo asked gently.

"Yes, Grandmother."

"What you haven't been told is how they were won." Selena held her breath for Grandmother's tellings were rare and she didn't want to miss a word. "There is a deep magic in this world Selena, not the magic of tricks and sparkles, of fancies and love potions, but an ancient power only to grace the few." Philamo turned Selena to face her, "Selena have you heard of The Sworn?" Selena felt nervous. Every child in White City had heard tales of The Sworn, the kind that scared small, naughty children to bed, Selena nodded her head.

"Yes, Grandmother." Selena's voice was small and shaky.

"Every generation from all the royal families, from all the kingdoms in this world, have children that are Sworn born." Philamo's voice was soft and even.

Selena felt the cold tingle of fear start in her heart, her hands clenched tight, as she tried to swallow.

"Now don't take fright, child. Listen to my words. Now is not the time for childish terror." Philamo's voice took a sharp edge but seeing the fear in Selena's eyes, she raised her long, pale hand and gently touched Selena's face. "You, my dear are Sworn." Selena let out a tiny gasp as Philamo gripped her shoulders. "War is coming Selena, a war to end all wars. The fate of the White City rests on your shoulders, my girl. You must take courage. You must steel yourself." Selena had heard the words, had felt her grandmother's hand upon her cheek, but now all she could hear were her own sobs, small, childish sobs.

"Selena, Selena!" Philamo's voice was rushed and harsh. Selena raised her eyes to meet her grandmother's. "When every child is born into this family their heads are shaved at one year. If there is dark shading on the base of the skull, they are Sworn." Selena instinctively raised her hand to touch the back of her neck. "No, no, don't. The mark has faded now my dear. Please concentrate, listen to my words. At age ten years, as you are now, the hair will be cut again, after the hair is cut a symbol will appear on the back of the neck on any child that has proved worthy. Many haven't my dear, but a chosen few have. The symbol will tell the family to what you have been Sworn," Philamo paused, swallowed loudly and continued, "There are four Sworn symbols, we always hope for one in particular, it is what we pray for every day at the gathering site, it is what our nation is built on." Philamo snapped her mouth shut, for she knew this would get no easier. Selena just stared opened mouthed at Philamo. "We will waste no more time," Philamo spoke softly now. She reached for the small, silver box that sat on her dresser and carefully lifted the lid. From the box Philamo drew out a pair of silver scissors, they were carved with wonders and had a red ribbon tied to one of the handles. "Are you ready to know Selena? Are you ready to face your destiny with courage, strength and heart?"

Selena couldn't speak. She just blinked wildly. Philamo gently turned Selena's head and with one quick snip cut away a long golden tress from the back of her head. The back of Selena's neck started to burn, to itch, to prickle and a pattern of silver and white started to appear.

Philamo gasped. "Praise be, oh praise be! You are Blade Sworn my child, Blade Sworn! Our prayers have been answered."

Chapter 6
Five Years Later

The suns were high in the sky. Not even a wisp of a cloud and the training circle was hot and dry. The trainee warriors had been at it for hours in full armour, pitting themselves against each other, rank after rank, match after match until only two stood. Most times it was Selena and Jug, but Big Bow had his day every now and again. Selena was spent. She knew Jug was too. She had to end this quickly. This was the last sparring session until trials and then the best would be given a rank in the great White City army. Selena took stock. She had to out manoeuvre him, they were matched in ability, where he was strong, she was quick. They had been fighting each other for years; he knew all her moves, her bluffs.

No, Selena thought, *I must do something unexpected, something quick.* She knew he would always defend against her battle charge, she always feigned right then struck left at the last moment.

"Well, big fella, let's see how you deal with this," Selena chuckled to herself, lent back on her right foot and charged full force, sword held high with both hands, straight for Jug. She let out her battle cry, not yet perfected, but alarming never the less. Jug saw her coming. He knew she was using her last reserve of strength. He thought she had decided to end it quickly but when she flew at him hollering and screaming, it caught him off guard. He saw her lean to the right and in his mind he knew she would lean left at the last moment. He smiled and braced his left foot forward ready to defend the blow, but Selena just kept coming right and before Jug had a chance to adjust his footing Selena had leapt clean into the air, planted her left foot on his leg and thrown herself behind him. She gripped the hilt of her sword with both hands and drove it into the back of Jugs helmet with a horrifying clang. Selena landed behind him with a thud and crouched down to catch her breath.

Now let's see who knows whom, she thought smiling to herself. But as she stood and turned she saw Jug was still lying on the floor, face down.

"Jug, you can get up now." Selena laughed, as she crossed to where he lay. The other warriors were starting to enter the circle and gather round. "Jug, you've had your fun. Come on now, we all knew you would lose today." Selena jested as she walked. Gulguy, who had been watching from the stalls had started to make his way across the training ground. Selena could see his little rotund belly jiggling up and down as he hurried. Even though he was passed his best years, there was no one as qualified in battle and tactics as Gulguy. Selena reached a sprawled-out Jug and crouched by his head; she reached out a hand and shook him. "Come on you big lump, up." Jug didn't move.

"Make way! Come now, let me in." Gulguy was jostling past the other warriors and came to a halt at Jugs feet. "Leave him, Selena, I've seen this before. A whack like that could have him half stupid for weeks." Gulguy was fussing and tutting and giving out instructions to be followed.

Selena swallowed into a dry, sore throat. What had she done? Selena lowered herself to Jug's ear.

"Please, Jug, come on! We've got Rick Rack to play and you've got ale to drink. Please!" Selena sat back on her haunches and dropped her sword. What had she done? Just then Jug moved just a little. Selena jumped back. "Jug! Oh, thank god!" Selena gasped. Jug opened his eyes and winked at Selena.

"Got you, little bird," Jug whispered. Selena went from joy to confusion, then anger in the space of a second. Selena jumped up and stormed off.

"That's not funny, you pig," Selena called over her shoulder. *How could he*, she thought, *I thought I'd sent him stupid or worse, killed him. Some friend he is.* She crossed into the shade of the palace walls and removed her helmet. Selena lent up against the cool, white stone, sweat dripped from her brow, nose and chin.

"Quite a swing you had there, little bird," Jug joked as he approached.

Selena raised her eyes and stared at Jug, he was sweating just as much as she was.

"Well, if you can't keep up, then don't step into the circle," Selena huffed.

Jug pretended to be hurt by her words.

"Beg your pardon, your majesty." He lent forward and gave her a low bow. "No, seriously, Selena you were fast today. In all honesty, I'm really having trouble keeping up," Selena scowled as the suns beamed from her silver armour.

"Okay then, Rick Rack tonight under the old oak. You may have a chance of winning that, without having to fake death at least." Selena offered. Jug smiled back.

"Okay, little bird, prepare to be thrashed."

Selena loved him, he was her best friend in the whole world. Being a princess can be lonely, but as a Sworn princess you become a person others avoid. Not Jug though, he had always fought her as an equal and had always had her back ever since they first stepped into the sparing circle together, five years ago.

"I'm off to the warriors' mess for some tucker; enjoy your fine dining, my lady," Jug shouted over his shoulder as he swaggered off. Selena smiled and nodded as he walked away, with a strut only a warrior has.

"Great! Dinner with Grandmother. More blab, war this and Sworn that, if I can get through dinner then I can fight anyone Sworn or not," Selena muttered to herself. She shook the sweat from her face and with it came a tangle of hair. What once was an intricate weaving of plaits was now a bush only an experienced handmaid could tackle. She raised a hand to flatten the worst of the wisps and caught hold of the little red ribbon that had been plaited into a single lock of her hair. "Blade Sworn, more like blade cursed," Selena spat. She started to walk towards the side entrance to the palace, a place no other warrior would enter. The cool of the doorway was a welcome relief. She looked down at her sword, a fine piece of steel but nothing special, she had out-grown it, she knew. All the other warriors knew too, sparing had become a bore. When this dinner is over, she thought, she would tell her grandmother she was done, no more training, no more being looked at with sideways glances every time she stepped into the circle, no more privileged dinners in the palace. She wanted to eat in the warrior house with the others. To drink ale and stuff down meat and bread without a care for the mess and the spills. After dinner she would have her say. Selena climbed the steps to her bedchambers with heavy feet, for she knew she would not speak a word of what she felt. She would only carry it in her heavy heart. She crept through the doorway like a naughty child, hoping to avoid a scolding for the state of her hair.

"My lady, your hair!" Minn gasped as she startled from her needlework. Selena gave Minn a pleading look.

"Do your best, Minn. You are the only one that has the brush and hand skills to tackle this." With that Selena shook her head like a great, blonde lion. Minn laughed but gave a firm cough.

"In the bath with you, right now miss! The Queen expects you in one hour." Minn clapped her hands as she spoke, a sign that she meant business. Selena was desperate for a long, hot soak. Now her hair would take an age to tame so every second counted. She started to strip off her armour like it was on fire. "Miss, please don't throw it around. You know how much polishing it takes old Leafy to get a shine back on that thing," Minn pleaded; too late. Selena's silver armour laid Strewn around the room like trinkets in a jewellery box.

"Sorry Minn. Couldn't wait." Selena was already at the tub by the time Minn's telling-off had finished. The hot mineral water felt like silk on Selena's hard muscles as she lowered herself in right up to her face. She relaxed and thought about Jug feasting with the other warriors. If only she had the courage to speak up, if only her Sworn symbol hadn't appeared, she'd be over there right now challenging him to an arm wrestle or clashing heads with Big Bow. Selena sighed and slid under the hot soapy water. *Just eat dinner, look interested and nod when needed. Then off to a game of Rick Rack with Jug.* Selena thought, *If I eat quickly and look princessly enough then the lecture should be less stern.* Selena sat up so Minn could unwind and wash her hair.

"Oh my, just look at this, it's going to take all the scented oil in White City to sort this," Minn tutted. Selena smiled, Minn had been her handmaiden for as long as she could remember, soft and warm were the feelings that sprang to mind when ever her name was mentioned. Selena drifted off into thoughts of her own as Minn washed and combed her long, golden hair. She let Minn dress her and fuss over her; she knew it made Minn happy to transform her from warrior to princess.

"There you go, my lady." Selena looked at herself in the long-gilded mirror, she hardly recognised the reflection.

"Minn, you truly are a miracle worker." Selena's hair was oiled and plaited with such small intricate work it really must take a magic touch. Her gown was sapphire blue with silver trim and on her feet soft slippers that felt so fragile. She was used to hard sparring boots. "I'm sure my grandmother will think me an imposter looking this beautiful." Selena held out a hand and Minn squeezed it in hers

"All will be well, little bird, all will be well."

Selena tapped on the door to her grandmother's dining room and hoped there would be no answer.

"Come in." Her grandmother's voice, as stern as ever, could be heard down the corridor. Selena pushed the door open and stepped inside. The room was one of her favourites, warm and cosy, tapestries and hangings covered every wall. There was always a delicious mouthful to be had here, only the best for The Queen. "Come on, come in," Philamo coaxed. "You know how I get when I'm kept waiting." Selena moved to her usual seat and stood to attention. Philamo swept her eyes up and down Selena. "I see Minn has worked her magic again." Selena and Philamo both burst out laughing together.

"Well if anyone can turn me into a princess, it's Minn," Selena said running her hands down the front of her skirts.

"And silk slippers as well! I am honoured," Philamo's face softened as she spoke. Selena swept into her seat with as much grace as she could muster in a gown and slippers. Philamo picked up the tiny, silver bell and gently rang it. Maids and servers hurried in, from who-knows-where and started serving dinner, small heaps of this and liquid pools of that; the colours were those of a rainbow. Selena grabbed a fork and dug in.

"Err excuse me, I thought I was in the presence of a princess," Philamo questioned.

Selena stopped mid chew and stared at her grandmother.

"Oh, yes. Sorry," Selena mumbled. She wiped her mouth with the small, soft napkin from her lap and swallowed loudly.

"Now a little less haste and a lot more grace, dear, please," Philamo advised. Selena smiled at her grandmother and re-adjusted her fork, took a portion of prawns in butter and ate them slowly. "Better! Now, how was training?"

Selena knew her grandmother secretly watched her, so she knew how it had gone.

"Oh, terrible, I had to fight six Fire Dragons and a Merbull. Terrible mess I made of them," Selena said matter-of-factly.

Philamo blinked and held her fork mid mouthful. A small twinkle in her eye began to appear and she smiled, a huge genuine smile. It was rare to see her grandmother smile like that and Selena returned the smile enjoying the warmth and love they shared.

"Little bird, how you tease me."

"You know how it went today, I know you watch me." Selena pretended to be hurt by the fact.

"Well, yes, I do, but I want to know how you feel about the training. It's been five years now, I feel that you have lost your passion for it." Selena swallowed and pursed her lips. Now she would speak; now she would tell her grandmother how she felt.

"No, Grandmother, it's fine" was all she could say. She would not let her grandmother down. Selena's love for her was too strong

"Come, child, you would lie? To me, do you think me a fool?" Philamo snapped.

"No, oh no, Grandmother! It's just that I'm Sworn, it's my duty, my destiny. I will complete the training, of course I will, but…" Philamo raised a hand for silence, put her fork down and swung around in her chair.

"Selena, tell me what troubles you; do not think me old and unreasonable."

Selena stared into her grandmother's stern blue eyes and blew out a long breath.

"No one is a challenge any more, I can out-fight them all, even Gulguy, my trainer. Oh, he gives me a good fight, there's no doubt. But I'm Blade Sworn, the sword just becomes part of me." Selena dropped her fork and slumped her head into her hands.

Philamo pursed her lips, she knew this day would come.

"Do not sulk child, the reason for this dinner is because I have news." Selena looked up, a sly squint in her eyes.

"What news, Grandmother?" Selena asked with a slow control to her voice.

"Your day is now upon us my dear, I have been instructed to prepare you for your challenge." Philamo held her breath. *Too soon, I have spoken to soon, I wanted to explain, reason with her*, Philamo thought, panicking inside.

A challenge? What? Who? Is it a battle? I shall be ready, Grandmother, I shall do us proud. My armour! Selena's thoughts raced back to her battle armour thrown around her room. "I must tell Minn, I must summon Leafy." Selena glanced out of the window, it was dark with a full sky of stars. "Oh, he will be sleeping, shall I wake him?"

"Selena, stop! Please, calm yourself. It's not that sort of challenge. Listen!" Philamo desperately needed to gain control of this conversation, but Selena was too intent on her armour and having it ready in full shine for the battle. She was not listening to a word her grandmother spoke.

"Oh, you wait till I tell Jug. He's going to flip!" Selena squealed.

"Selena, please!" Philamo's voice was harsh and shrill. Selena jolted into silence.

"But, Grandmother, you said a challenge." Selena's voice was ripe with excitement.

"I know dear, but you must listen." Philamo tried to soften her voice to sound almost pleading, but Selena was in her own world.

"There's so much to prepare. My sword, I must sharpen my sword! My boots! Oh, I've needed new ones for a while now. I'll send word into town tonight. A challenge! Is it a battle-warrior, a wizard?" Selena's voice was getting higher and higher, she was pacing the room like a wild thing.

"Selena! Please calm yourself. It's not what you think, there are things that need preparing, yes, but not your armour or new boots. Please listen!" Desperate to stop Selena jabbering Philamo snapped, "Silence!" She shrieked. Selena stopped pacing and turned towards her grandmother.

"What then, what needs to be prepared?" Selena asked a little timidly now.

Philamo slumped her shoulders. *I have already said too much,* she thought, *I cannot give my granddaughter hope of battling a wizard or war-elf. I will have to tell her, there is much to do.*

"Grandmother, what aren't you telling me?" Selena was growing suspicious now. Philamo stepped back and turned towards the grand fireplace. "Grandmother, please! What are you hiding?" Philamo reached for her neck and felt the small, silver key. It had hung there for five years and tomorrow it would be gone. "Grandmother!" Selena's pleading voice brought Philamo back into the room. Philamo's thoughts whirled, *I have messed it all up, a quiet dinner to advise and pass on knowledge is what I hoped for. Now false hope and a false battle is what I have portrayed. The truth would have to be told, my granddaughter deserves that.*

"May the Merfolk forgive me!" Philamo whispered. Selena took the three, small steps towards her grandmother and made a grab for her hand; a small tear ran down Philamo's cheek. "It is The Mistress, Selena. She is coming!"

Chapter 7
The Mistress

"Arieanna, Arieanna." The voice whispered and floated on the breeze.

The Mistress stirred in restless slumber.

Arieanna looked down at her feet. Tiny feet, those of a young child, her toes dug deep into the mud.

"I'm coming, mother," Arieanna called back. Arieanna looked around for her sister. The fog had risen from the lake and the suns were starting to set. Arieanna's feet sunk deeper into the mud.

"Arieanna, where are you, child?" Her mother's voice seemed far away.

"I'm here, mother. Please wait!"

The Mistress thrashed in her blankets, trying to free her dream feet.

Arieanna darted her head around desperately searching for her sister. The fog slowly rolled closer, all engulfing, hushing everything in its path. Arieanna looked again to her feet. The mud was now at her knees.

"Sister, why do you struggle?" The gentle voice seemed so close. Arieanna looked up as a thin, glistening hand reached from the folds of fog. "Take my hand. Come now, don't be afraid." Her sister's voice was ice cold.

Arieanna slowly raised her tiny, frozen hand and felt the thin, icy grip of her sister. The grip was too tight. Bony fingers like twigs dug into her wrist. Sharp, cold flakes began to spread along Arieanna's fingers and hand.

"You're hurting me! Please, Anya! Let go!"

"As you wish." Anya released her hand and sent her sister tumbling backwards. Down, down through the thick, dark mud.

The Mistress awoke with a start, tangled in her blankets, a sheen of sweat coating her face and neck.

"For the love of Merfolk! Thistle! Help me."

Thistle bumbled into The Mistress's bedchamber, sleepy crust blurring her eyes.

The Mistress had removed herself from the cocoon of bedding and was gasping for breath. Thistle recovered her senses and rushed to her aid. A soft cloth was dunked into cold water from the basin and offered to The Mistress.

"Many thanks." The Mistress mumbled, as she wiped sweat from her face with shaky hands. Thistle hadn't moved. "Food, if you will, Thistle. Nothing to be seen here. Just a bad dream." The Mistress shuffled to the edge of her bed and eyed Thistle closely. "Did I cry out while sleeping?" Thistle shook her head sharply. "Are you sure?" Thistle again denied all knowledge. "Good. Then no harm done. Breakfast, Thistle. Long days are ahead. We should both be prepared. I wish to leave at sunrise. Pack what I will need for a day of travelling and wake the rats. They too will need a good breakfast. We have much ground to cover."

Thistle made her way to the kitchen, nudging the pack on her way through. The rantings of The Mistress haunted her, but she would never tell the secrets she heard while The Mistress slept. Much too dangerous to know such secrets. Quiet she would keep and breakfast she would make.

The Mistress rose. The aches in her bones all crying for attention. *A little St John's wort will quieten you down,* she thought. She struggled out of her sleeping gown and wrestled into a clean robe. The Mistress caught a glimpse of her twisted hands as she fastened her belt.

"Not long for this world now. My duties almost fulfilled. Almost." She whispered to herself with a small hint of sadness. Thoughts of what would come after flooded her mind, but the smell of food forced her to think of the hard day ahead and the strength that she would need to succeed. With stiff back but determined mind The Mistress made her way to her chair and picked up her brew from the table. A long, deep slurp warmed her through and set her to thinking. "Now which was the quickest way to Meridien?"

Thistle had spent an age packing and re-packing a small carrying pouch for The Mistress. Everything was essential but not everything would fit.

"Stop fussing with that bag and come help me with my boots!" The Mistress snapped. The worry of what lay ahead was making her short tempered and her pack had felt the end of her cane more than once this morning.

Thistle knelt and eased on the worn boots with care, laced them and smiled up at her Mistress.

"Now don't go all soft on me, fool. I shall need you more than ever these next few weeks, if the prophecy is correct, this shall be my last chance to see all my Sworn children to adulthood, so there is no room for mistakes or sentiment." Thistle, still smiling, rose and patted The Mistress on the shoulder and returned to her pouch stuffing.

The pack returned from their morning rampage through the forest and scratched eagerly at the door.

"Let them in, please, Thistle, then we must be away. The gate to the North is at least two hour's walk from here and time hurries us."

Thistle welcomed home the pack and at last packed the pouch. She fed the fire and gathered up The Mistress's cloak and cane and settled herself by the door ready for goodbyes.

"Where is that blasted crystal? I'm sure I put it in here the last time I visited Meridien!" The Mistress was huffing and puffing around in her bedchamber, heaving open draws and cupboards. Thistle calmly walked to the small spell cupboard and unlatched the smooth, worn doors. Amongst the potions and oddments she found a small rock, nothing special, blue and white granite ran through it. It was the size of a small plum. "Ah, there it is!" The Mistress snapped behind Thistle. Thistle jumped and almost dropped the stone. The Mistress could be as quiet as a mouse if she chose and Thistle's heart skipped a beat when she crept up behind her. "I shall be home in a day or two. I will be tired and hungry and in need of assistance. And remember, Thistle, if I fail we shall all pay the price." Thistle's blood turned cold, memories of what they had endured after the last failure were dark and deeply hidden. "Come now, let us not dwell, let us be away." She turned to her pack and ushered them out the door to where Jengo was waiting. The moons were low. Soon the suns would rise and time would rush on like the wind.

"Mistress, are you well?" Jengo whispered as he took a low bow.

"Quite well, my friend. Shall we be away?" The Mistress felt in her robe and stroked the small pack of fire-dust she had hidden there. *For the love of the Merfolk, please let it still be active,* she thought. The Mistress paused, closed her eyes and sent up a prayer to the Mother of all Nature. "Give me strength and speed for the day ahead, wise one. I do your work with a righteous heart and a willing soul.

May you bless me with your knowledge and grant me your protection." The Mistress opened her eyes and all stared, waiting for her to move first. "To the gate, Jengo. Lead the way."

Small, keen eyes peered from the undergrowth.

"So, Mistress, you are on the move. We shall have our day yet." The tiny, red scorpion scurried away towards the Black Road.

Chapter 8

Jengo padded along in front of The Mistress, sniffing for any dangers, alert to the ebb and flow of the forest noises. They were reaching the edge of their home and the southern boarders of The Drylands. A hot breeze had picked up and rustled the trees, which were brittle and dry this far north. Jengo stopped and waited for The Mistress and her pack to catch up.

"Holy One, we are close. The forest floor is warm beneath my feet and the trees are thin and bare."

"Jengo, we stop for rest and water. Will you scout into the Drylands and check if the path is safe?"

"At once." Jengo bowed and turned, his large paws sinking into the warm, grainy soil. He slunk around the remaining trees and along the barren pathway to the Drylands.

"Rest, my lovelies. Drink a little. This part of our journey will be a hot morning's work, believe me." The Mistress emptied a little water into her hand and allowed her pack to lap up the small offering. Jengo returned shortly and relayed his findings.

"All is clear. No beast or bird stirs near." Jengo was panting but The Mistress offered him no water for this was as far as he would go. It was just she and the pack from now on and the thought played upon her.

"Jengo, thank you for the escort. Now go. Check with Roughwing that The Grey is on his way. And, Jengo, be alert. The events of the next few days are crucial. Nothing must go wrong. I'll have no one interfere."

"Yes, Holy One, you have my word." Jengo turned to leave. He couldn't shake the feeling they were being watched, but he could not place any scent. He returned to the forest and to locate Rough Wing. "Stupid bird. Why she trusts that little pest, I'll never know."

The Mistress and the pack hurried down the dry road. It would take them to the barren riverbed and home to the North Gate. The lush green coolness of the forest was long behind them and the rocky, hot Drylands lay ahead. The path twisted and turned with the land-scape. Around large boulders and through flat empty wasteland, the path wound on.

"There! Look ahead, my friends!" She pointed with her cane and the pack surged forward with The Mistress swiftly behind. Set back into the side of a cliff were the curves and folds of rock only a waterfall could have made. Directly below was the dry bed of what was once a river. The Mistress let her mind wander back. The dry bed had once been a river the colour of the sky. Fresh and flowing, full of fish and flowers. The river's edge had been bursting with life. Great trees had their branches dipped into the water and small mon-keys would jump and play along them. The magnificent waterfall had been called 'Life Giver' back then, always moving, crashing into the river, stopping for no man. The Mistress shook her head and returned to the empty, dead present. She knew time was not her friend, but a moment to grieve the bountiful past was a moment she would take.

"Make way! Come now, move yourself!" The Mistress clumsily waded through the pack, a few crunched tails and trodden-on paws were no concern to her. She made her way to where the waterfall would have once cascaded down the rock and slowly crept along the crumbling edge. She swept her hand over the rock-face. A small bowl shape had been carved out of the stone. It was filled with dirt and sand. She rested her cane against the wall and reached in to scoop it out, blowing out the last few grains. "Stay back, my loves. You know what the static does to your fur." The pack scurried back. The Mistress brought out the blue and white crystal Thistle had found for her that morning and cupped it in her hands. She closed her eyes and began to chant.

"May the light of the heavens heed my plea. I, Mistress of the forest, keeper of all things, wish to pass. Hold back no more your life force. Let me through, oh keeper of the gate!" The crystal started to glow, to almost hum with life. The Mistress was surrounded with a mist of palest blue, swirling her hair and robe. "I offer the crystal as a barter for passage!" She placed the now hot crystal into the small basin and raised her arms. "Open! I demand it!"

At first there was a trickle. Then a dozen trickles till these be-came streams. The waterfall lunged to life, wave after wave of glis-tening water flowed down the rock-face and into the dry river bed. "Quickly now. To me!" The Mistress beckoned, from behind the fall of water, as the thin ledge began to crumble. The pack scurried in a single file towards her. Without warning and to the sound of a great rumble, they were all gone. The waterfall slowed. It trickled and spluttered and then ceased altogether. Every drop left was burnt off by the hot morning sun. Just a barren, dry riverbed and a dusty rock face remained.

Chapter 9

Kef had been pacing the dry crater, that had once been a lake, since first light. Hiccup was also restless inside Kef's pocket. Hiccup was one of only a few fireflies left in this world and Kef treasured her. Dax was safely in his bed exhausted from his nighttime test.

"Where can she be? For the love of Merfolk! This is taking too long." Kef knew if The Mistress didn't arrive, then all would have been for nothing.

As his dry, sandaled feet turned for another pacing across the crater he felt a tremor in the ground.

"She comes, Hiccup. She comes."

With the full force of a giant wave, fresh, sparkling water jetted up from under his feet. Kef fell backwards and scrabbled away from the now rising flood. At last the ground broke and The Mistress and her rats unceremoniously ruptured up into the now, waist high lake.

"Holy One! Please take my hand!" Kef lunged forward and grasped The Mistress and hauled her to her feet. The pack swam to the crumbling edge and scrambled their way out of the flowing torrents.

"Kef, old friend, your presence is a welcome comfort!" The Mistress was soaked and bedraggled, all airs of power gone. She allowed Kef to guide her out of the lake, humbled by her appearance, and onto dry ground.

They sat and watched the lake's water cease to flow and recede back to a muddy puddle, for the North Gate was a secret known to only a few and used by even fewer, so watching its power was a rare thing of beauty.

"I take it all is well? Has Dax passed his test?" The Mistress asked, now recovered from her watery arrival.

"He has, Holy One. He has done well. The dragon magic flows through his veins." Kef puffed his chest slightly, proud of his charge.

"Good. And the firefly, she lives?"

Kef suddenly jolted upright. He had forgotten all about Hiccup in his pocket. Gently he reached in and withdrew the tiny ball.

"It's okay, little friend. The water is all gone." Kef reached out a gentle finger and stroked Hiccup's head.

"Is she well?" The Mistress asked, seeing the scrunched up little ball.

"Quite well. Just a little scared. As you know, fireflies are not that fond of water." Kef lowered his hand and rolled Hiccup into The Mistress's lap.

"Wake now, my child, there is work to be done. No time for childish fears." The little firefly, on hearing The Mistress's stern voice, recoiled a little more.

"Hiccup, my dear. It is time to work your magic." Kef whispered. "You want to impress The Mistress now, don't you?" Hiccup knew that using her magic was a rare thing. Fireflies had been hunted to near extinction and the chance to shine, especially in front of one so holy as The Mistress was an honour she could not miss. Hiccup slowly unfurled her wings and lifted her minuscule head.

"Now, that's better. Shall we begin?" The Mistress whispered in a softer tone, for she knew scaring the little creature would only hinder her task.

"Mistress, shall we make our way to my cabin? I have made ready all that we need." Kef stood and offered The Mistress his hand.

"A chair and a little refreshment will be offered, I take it, old friend?" The Mistress was hungry and thirsty and needed to finish up here and head for the Marshlands as quickly as she could. But honest friends amongst these lands were hard to find and Kef was among the few she could trust, so his hospitality would be allowed and welcomed.

"As always, Holy One. I think I have a little of the seeded bread that you like." Kef replied with half a smile.

"Then lead on, man! Lead on!" The Mistress, now on her feet, ushered him forward.

The pack were allowed to hunt in the dump site that lay behind Kef's cabin. After all, a kingdom as big as Meridien had huge amounts of waste and a small community of pickers had set up camp on top of the piles and made their living from the junk others dumped there.

After a cup of tea and bread spread thick with jam, The Mistress was ready to proceed.

"Shall we begin, Kef, the suns are up and my journey's not yet half done."

"Yes. Please allow me to present my finest work." Kef stood and shuffled over to a golden box by the fire. With loving hands he withdrew an egg from the folds of many soft blankets within the box.

"Kef, you have out-done yourself this time. What a thing of beauty!" The Mistress was not easily impressed, but Kef's egg-nurturing skills were too good to deny.

An egg the size of a child's head lay gently in Kef's hands, its shell a dazzling sheen of purples and pinks. The glow was almost mesmerizing. Hiccup, who had been lying in The Mistress's lap sat up, eyes wide and mouth open.

"Now, little one, it is time to work your magic," The Mistress informed her whilst reaching into her robe for the pack of fire-dust. Hiccup stood and shook herself from head to toe. The little bit of hair on her head stood out at all angles, fuzzy and soft. The Mistress scooped her up and placed her on the table. "The egg, if you will, Kef." The Mistress lowered her voice as she gestured to the table. Kef gently lowered the egg carefully so that it did not roll. He gave a long sigh for he knew this would be his last Royal Dragon and his last chance to witness the power of Mother Nature as The Mistress worked her craft on the egg and turned it into a thing of great force. "Now step back a little, Kef, you know what happened last time." The Mistress advised, remembering Kef's singed hair.

"Oh yes, yes," Kef replied, a little miffed at not being able to be right beside his egg.

The Mistress held the tiny leather packet at arm's length and slowly tipped the shiny crystal fragments over the egg. She closed her eyes and began to chant.

"Red and gold, your fire will be. Eyes of the deepest blue. Scales like armour. Talons like blades. I, MISTRESS OF ALL THINGS THAT BREATHE, COMMAND YOU TO BE!" The Mistress's voice had risen to almost a shout, as the crystals swirled around the egg dancing to an unseen breeze. "NOW, HICCUP!" The Mistress turned to the tiny firefly.

Hiccup had been steadying herself ever since they had entered the cabin. Now was her time to shine. With one huge breath Hiccup let go a long, thin train of fire from her mouth. The heat from it made The Mistress and Kef recoil and cover their faces. As the fire engulfed the crystals each one popped and melted onto the egg, until a molten crystal case surrounded it. Hiccup collapsed onto the table and Kef rushed to her aid.

"My dear, Hiccup. Are you okay?" Kef's large, rough hands raised the tiny firefly to his face.

"I...I...I am well." On hearing the squeaky voice of his most treasured one, Kef smiled with relief and hugged her close.

"Now, Kef, you know what I must do and where I travel next."

"Yes, Holy One."

"My comings and goings are a secret to be kept. We are clear. Yes?" The Mistress had turned a stern eye upon them both.

"Mistress you can trust us. We serve, only you."

"Good. We have dallied too long, let us go to the Picking Sands and bury the egg. There is much work to do." With that The Mistress gathered her cane and travelling bag and headed for the door. Kef came to his senses, placed Hiccup in his pocket, wrapped the egg in a plain blanket and followed the ever-shadowy footsteps of The Mistress.

Chapter 10
The Grey

The Grey sniffed the air. Four long months he had roamed the Dry-lands. Feeding where he could, feeling the hot winds in his fur. Running free and wild, this was his life and he loved it. He was his own master. As the scrawny, black crow landed beside him he knew he was his own master, bar one.

"Rough Wing, what an unwelcome surprise!" The Grey raised only his eyes.

"Grey, I bring a message from The Mistress." Rough wing was always nervous around The Grey. It was the way he licked his lips.

"Speak then."

"She says the time is now. The Sworn are ready. You are to patrol the Marshlands and the Black Road."

"Does she indeed?"

Rough Wing's eyes went wide for such a casual response to The Mistress, would surely mean punishment. On seeing Rough Wing's discomfort, The Grey continued his game.

"Could she not come to deliver the message herself? Am I not a worthy servant?"

"Yes. But please, Grey, we have all been summoned and have a task to complete. If you don't come she will have my tail feathers, please!"

The Grey chuckled under his breath.

"Very well, Rough Wing we wouldn't want your tail feathers plucked out now, would we?"

"No, oh no! You will come then?"

"I will come. Tell the Holy One I will travel the Black Road and head to the Marshlands. I shall give Jengo my full report."

"Thank you, Grey. Thank you." With that Rough Wing took to the sky, grateful to be away from the sly, old wolf.

"Stupid, flea-ridden bird! Does he not realise, that we all are at her beck and call? And it is an honour to be so." The Grey roused himself from his dusty den and shook the dry sand from his coat. He took a long, hard sniff of the dry air, turned and padded towards the Black Road.

And so, it begins was his last thought as he disappeared over the horizon.

Chapter 11
The Mistress

Kef, The Mistress and Hiccup rounded the rocky plains at the outskirts of Meridien. The hot, dry sand was fine and difficult to walk in.

"He will pick tonight, Kef. If the magic burns strong he will need to harness it, or it could take his life." Kef did not look up, he knew it was true. He had felt the boy's temperature rise even as he put him to bed, exhausted and filthy but with a smile on his face.

"I will wake him before sunset, feed him and explain," Kef answered, a little sadness in his voice.

"We are here." The Mistress crouched down and swept up a handful of sand, sniffed it and poked out her wizened tongue to taste a little. "This spot is as good as any other." She knelt and began scooping handfuls of sand to make a small well.

"Kef! The egg." The Mistress reached out greedy hands.

"Are you sure, Holy One, that this is the place? It seems a little…" The sharp eye of The Mistress sent his next few words off into silence. "Yes. As you wish." Kef unfolded the blanket to reveal the crystal-covered egg. The suns' flashing rays danced upon its surface. It was hard to look away. Kef leant over and handed the egg to The Mistress, savouring the last brush of his fingertips upon his wondrous creation.

"Kef, your work is the very best in this whole kingdom. Otherwise I would have gone elsewhere. Now, don't spoil my opinion of you with sentiment uncalled for. The work we do here is for the good of all and none know the sacrifices better than I." The firm tone of The Mistress's voice brought Kef up sharply for he knew none had suffered more than The Holy One.

"Yes. Sorry. Please continue."

The Mistress placed the egg in the hole and scooped the sand over the top until no trace remained. If word were to reach the wrong ear that anyone had hidden an object here that was so precious, well, its loss, would see the world change forever.

"You know what to tell the boy and of the importance of time, Kef?"

"I do, Holy One, I do." Kef was feeling like his whole life was at a standstill. This would be his last Sworn charge. His last days as Master Hatcher. Retirement to the olive gardens was a long sought-after dream, but now it loomed large and lonely.

"And the firefly, she will remain safe with you?"

"She will."

"Good. Then my work here is done. Take care, old friend." She clasped Kef's hand in a rare show of affection.

"Until we meet again," Kef whispered.

The Mistress blew the bone whistle that hung from her neck and headed out into the Drylands.

Chapter 12
Dax

Kef gently sat on the edge of Dax's bed and stared down at his dirt-smudged face.

"My boy, you will see wonders which have never been seen. You will travel to places which can only be dreamt of and you will feel pain which no one can imagine." Kef sighed, the events of the last few days taking their toll. He gently shook Dax awake and smiled as the boy's sleepy eyes focused on him. "Time to wake up, Dax! There is work to be done."

"What time is it?"

"Time to eat and bathe. Then I have a telling for you."

Dax had dragged himself from his bed and was now stuffing his face with bread and jam. Kef waited patiently, amused by his charge's gusto.

"If you have quite finished, young sir, shall I begin?" Kef smiled as Dax swallowed and wiped his mouth with his hand.

"Yes, of course, Master Kef, please. A telling you say? Is it to do with my dragon?" Dax was keen to get to his father's chambers and receive his reward.

"In a way, yes, but not just your dragon, Dax. It is the story of all the dragons, and how it came about that we are the keepers of the eggs and the deal your great-grandfather had to make, to keep us all safe. This, my boy, is the telling of Meridien itself." Kef paused and let his words sink in. Dax sat back, swallowed again and nodded for Kef to start.

Kef brought his cup to his lips and took a long gulp of the hot coffee he had brewed.

"Are you sure you're quite finished, your majesty?" Kef almost laughed. This young boy in front of him held the future of the whole kingdom in his hands and judging by the jam around his mouth the kingdom was already lost.

"Yes, yes, please start."

"It's not just a telling, young Dax, but 'THE' telling. This is the telling of how Meridien came to be. How our arrangement with the dragons was struck and how the kingdoms were formed." Kef took another draw on his coffee and waited for Dax to settle.

"You see, Dax, this land was once covered in swamp. Oh yes, there were dry patches, even rocky places, but essentially it was all one kingdom, all one people. As time went on tribes formed, land was claimed and as you know that is the start of wars." Dax relaxed back in his chair.

"The volcano was a great source of heat and life back then and the tribes that lived there defended it fiercely. Barricades were built, weapons fashioned, and the fighting began. Sand dwellers, from the south and clansman, from the forests, joined together to take our land from us. They were dark days. Spies and assassins were at every turn and the families of old had to stick together, a plan had to be made." Kef paused to swig his coffee again and realising it was turning cold, grimaced and placed his cup back on the table. Dax hadn't moved a muscle and was staring at Kef, with unbelieving eyes.

"Your great-grandfather was head of the families and decided something needed to be done, something to secure the volcano for good. A gathering was called, and a plan was made. There had been talk for many years of an island far to the east, an island that had a volcano also. It was believed that there were dragons there, but no one had seen any, and it was decided that if their help could be acquired to win the war, then it was worth the risk of trying to find it." Kef shuffled in his seat, old age never sat right for long, in a hard chair.

"It was decided that your great-grandfather would take a small boat, well supplied, and head east searching for the infamous dragon isle. So, my boy, that is exactly what he did. It is recorded that he travelled for eighteen long days and nights before he spotted a great, savage island rising from the sea. With trepidation and a courageous heart, he beached his boat and set off to explore." Kef stopped talking and looked up at Dax. "Are you listening child." Dax had taken on a glazed look.

"So, there is an island." Dax's mind was reeling.

"Yes, Dax, there is. Where did you think the dragon eggs came from and where did you think they went? Did you not pay attention in lessons?"

"Yes, but I thought it was a story. A legend even. I just thought the eggs were traded." Dax swallowed hard.

"No, Dax. The island is real."

"But, but…" Dax had no words, all that he had been taught in class was now coming back to him. He hadn't given the story much credit. Dragon eggs had been part of Meridien all his life. As a prince he had other things to think about, other mischief to be getting into. He had no concern for the whys and where's of life.

"Shall I continue?" Kef asked a little amused at Dax's lack of knowledge of their kingdom's past.

"Yes. Please."

"Well, after a few days of trekking through jungle-like terrain he came to the centre of the island. It was the base of the volcano. There he found three dragons. Not the huge flying things from story books. Three small, horse-sized dragons. And if the writings are to be believed they were close to extinction. There were two females and a male. It is said that their volcano had died. It's heart finally going cold, extinguished by the seeping in of the ocean." Kef grabbed for his cup. Remembered the coffee was cold and rose to brew another pot.

"But why don't I know this, Kef? Why did I think it was all a story?" Dax was fidgeting now, trying hard to make head or tail of what he was hearing.

"You do, young man, you do. You just heard it as a story not as a telling, that's all. Try and remember your lessons, try and recall." Dax just slumped back in his chair. The realisation that the world stretched out further than what he thought was quite a shock to his spoilt self.

Kef poured another cup of hot coffee and snatched up a cushion from his bed. His bony backside couldn't take another hour of this telling, without support.

"Now your great-grandfather, even though a brave man, was terrified that his life was about to end and threw himself at the dragons' mercy, only to find them searching for mercy themselves. Only the male spoke and they treated for hours until an agreement was struck and a deal that was unbreakable was made."

"Hang on, Kef, you must be missing parts. That sounds a little too easy." Dax was starting to question Kef's telling abilities.

"Young sir, I am only telling what has been written! What happened in that treaty has died with your great-grandfather and we will have to take it as truth and believe it was so!" Kef was starting to get irritated by Dax's lack of knowledge and his interruptions.

"Yes, yes, of course. Sorry. Please continue." Dax would keep his doubts to himself if he wanted to get to the end of the telling.

"Any way, it would appear that the dragons were dying out, unable to heat their eggs now the volcano's heart had died. They couldn't see a way forward. Your great-grandfather offered to take the eggs and heat them for the dragons and return them when they were ready to hatch. In return they would help us win the war." Kef drained his cup and savoured the black, bitter liquid.

"On his return he found things worse than ever. Many of his friends and kin had been killed. He gathered those who were left and told his tale. All were in awe of the eggs but swore to protect them until they were ready to be returned to the island. For three months they huddled in the dark tunnels of Monmoo, turning the eggs, protecting them from invaders, until one day they were ready to hatch. Under the cover of darkness your great-grandfather loaded them onto his boat and once more, set sail. He was gone a long time and the tribesmen of the volcano had given up hope. Food was scarce, war was closing in on all sides. A surrender was imminent, when at last he returned and this time he was not alone. The male dragon had journeyed with him and was ready to fight." Dax sprang forward engulfed in the telling. Eager to hear of bloodshed and victory. Kef raised a calming hand. "Well, within a week the war was over. Lines had been drawn. Deals had been made. For what the dragon brought with him was fire, Dax. A fire unlike any other and he had bestowed the gift of using that fire upon your great-grandfather. A gift that shall now be yours."

Chapter 13
The Mistress

The Mistress and pack hurried their way across the sand. She squinted, one eye on the suns. They had lingered too long here. She had to make up some time.

"My lovelies, we will have to take a horse." The rats skidded to a halt, the implications clear. "Come now, you are the feared pack of The Mistress, the ever-present mob, ready to strike." The Mistress almost laughed aloud seeing the rats all stare at her, with their reluctance showing. "We shall be taking a horse whether you like it or not. I'm sure this will not be the last time we shall make such a judgement before the day is through." The rats eased themselves into an orderly squad, silent and watchful. "That's better. With a horse beneath us we shall make good time. Onwards now!"

Mistress and pack scurried away from the city. Horse traders could be found here. It was the only way to cross the Drylands with any hope of survival and cross them, she must. She sought The Black Road. It could be found at the point, a thin strip of land that curved out into the ocean. It was where the Drylands, the Forest and the Marshlands all met, and the Black Road began.

Sand horses are the swiftest in the land. Their hooves flat and webbed. Their eyes meshed against the grainy wind. They were horses bred for the desert. The horse traders were a nomadic clan. Their tents were dotted around a small watering-hole. The head trader's tent had strings of tiny, gold bells dangling from its doorway. The Mistress approached the entrance and waited.

"Who seeks my father?" A tall, thin girl rounded the tent and stepped up to face The Mistress.

"Greetings! Please tell your father that I have business to discuss."

"You must state your business to me first, old lady. My father is a very busy man." The girl stood her ground.

"I have no time for the arrogance of children. If you don't announce me, girl, I will announce myself." The Mistress spat, growing impatient. She bore her gaze into the girl, a faint, blue haze started to swirl in her eyes. The girl narrowed her own eyes, unsure whether this was trickery or glamour. The Mistress shot out a bony hand and clasped the child by the front of her dress. "You will enter that tent and tell your father that I am here. Do you understand?" The Mistress let her eyes fill with the power of the craft. Deep blues, like pools of midnight, filled the child with terror.

"Yes, oh please forgive me! I meant no harm. I shall go now. Please!" The girl squirmed and wriggled under The Mistress's grip, desperate to be free from those cold, blue eyes.

The Mistress released her grip and straightened her back. "Now, if you will, your father." She prompted the girl, who had now frozen in fear. The girl jumped and spun on her heels and hurried through the tent's entrance. "Always some delay! We may have to spend the night at the point. Not ideal, but the suns are too high and even if we take the Black Road we will never reach the Marshlands in time." The Mistress spoke to the rats but they were too busy chasing small sand spiders in and out of their holes to be paying attention. "Go then, my lovelies, have fun while you can. The journey across the Drylands will be one you will want to forget."

The tent entrance was swept aside and a huge, fat trader waddled out, his face red with anger, huffing and puffing. Leather purses of all colours hung from his belt and wet patches of sweat clung to his tunic.

"Who dares frighten my daughter?" The trader bellowed.

"I" was all The Mistress stated.

"And who might you be?" The trader had lost some of his rage on seeing The Mistress standing alone, small and humble.

"I am just a tinker seeking passage across the Drylands. The purchase of a horse would be most pleasing."

"Purchase. Well, if your coin is good I'm sure we could come to an agreement." On hearing the word purchase all thoughts of confrontation were soon washed away and the words profit and easy coin entered his greedy head.

"My coin is as good as any other," The Mistress replied, producing a small pouch of her own and jangling it in front of herself.

"Well then, to business." The fat trader held back his tent flap and gestured her in. "Wine, girl and fruit!" He snapped his fingers at his daughter and followed The Mistress inside.

After refusing any refreshment The Mistress got down to business.

"I require one good horse and two carrying baskets for my pack." She stated.

The trader stopped stuffing his face with grapes and lowered his hand.

"Pack? Pack of what?" he asked suspiciously.

"None of your concern, man." The Mistress needed to be away and this rotund, little man was becoming an irritation.

"Horse is three gold coins. That's only on a borrowing basis. Are you going to the point or the mines?"

"The point."

"Well, still, three gold coins which ever. I have men at both places and they will return the horse to me."

"Very well. Those are acceptable terms."

"And the carrying baskets? What size is required?" The trader had stopped eating and was wiping his sticky fingers on his trousers.

"Big enough to carry, let's say, twenty cats."

"Cats! Well, a gold coin should do it."

"Agreed." The Mistress had her pouch open before the trader had closed his mouth. She placed four coins on the table in front of herself then sat back and waited.

The greedy trader snatched up his payment popping each coin into his mouth and biting down.

"Good, hard gold," the trader waffled on. He then felt their weight in his hand. "Good weight." He was just about to squirrel them away when he noticed the writing on the coins. "Mer be blessed!" he threw the four coins back onto the table. "Them's old house money, where did you get them?"

"They are mine. They belonged to my family. Is there a problem?" The Mistress asked, a little amused.

"Yes, yes, a big problem! Only those gifted with the craft come from old house money. Brings trouble. Brings war." The fat trader had shrunk back into his seat and had turned to the colour of milk.

"Well, if you won't take my coin then I shall have my horse for free. Agreed?" The Mistress made to rise.

"Yes! Yes! For free, go, be gone!" The trader was gawking at The Mistress like a child that had seen a ghost. "Take whichever horse you want. Please go!"

"Why, thank you for your kindness. I shall be away." The Mistress left the tent in almost a good mood. There's nothing like a bit of old legend to scare greedy, fat trader's half to death. She blew her whistle and headed for the horse stalls. As The Mistress ran her hands over the many horses, the pack remained crouched behind the fences. She selected a horse and demanded the carrying baskets. Each one she dragged behind the fence and offered the transport up to her pack.

"In now. There's no time for hesitation. In! Okay, by the toe of my boot then." The rats clawed their way up into the baskets and huddled together eyeing their beloved Mistress with the sullen faces of scolded children. "Look, I don't like this as much as you don't, but we must get to the Black Road and you cannot make it across the sand in good time." The rats just stared and curled themselves tighter. "Very well, sulk then." And with that she slammed the lids shut and bound them. The workers hauled the baskets onto the horse's back and strapped them tight.

"For the love of Merfolk, what's in these baskets?" One well-muscled worker enquired.

"Cats" was all The Mistress replied. The large confused eyes and furrowed brows of all those around brought a smile to her lips. "Help me up." She demanded of those closest to her and help they did, for the head trader had informed them this old lady was to be furnished and got rid of as quickly and quietly as possible, with no questions asked.

The Mistress kicked in her heels and they were away, a long, dry ride ahead of them. If there were no irritations along the way they should reach the point by the afternoon. She hoped that a night spent at the point would not interrupt her task.

Chapter 14

The Mistress flew across the sand like a ragged tornado, robes flapping behind her. Her horse was a blur of rich yellows, its coat and mane whipping in the wind like streams of gold. After an hour of travelling she pulled her horse to a stop and slid herself from its saddle. She untied the basket lids and the rats streamed out from their crude carriages.

"Run and stretch, my loves. We still have a way to go." The Mistress reached inside her pouch and pulled out a flask of water and drank deeply. She scanned the horizon and instantly froze. A small figure, that of a child, walked slowly and with a limp towards them. She blew on her whistle and the pack came running, eager for water. "Not yet, my loves. You see that small crop of rocks? Take yourselves off and sleep awhile in the shade. We have trouble afoot and it's not the sort you can help me with."

The pack hissed and scanned all around looking for a foe.

"No! You cannot defend me here. Go! Return only when I call. And do not try and help me, no matter what you hear or see. Do I make myself clear?" The Mistress removed her cane from the horse's saddle and swiped at her pack to get them moving. The rats bounded away confused and alert. "Now, what in the name of Mer have we got here?"

The small figure was close enough for her to see, it was a girl of about five or six years limping heavily, bedraggled and filthy.

"Stop! Approach no closer!" The Mistress called. The girl kept coming. "I know what you are, ghoul! You cannot hope to win here." The girl came closer still. "So, a show of force is what you have chosen." The Mistress whispered to herself. The child stopped just short of swiping distance. "Show your true face, ghoul! Do not hide behind that of a child."

"Mistress, how I have searched for you!" The tiny mouth of the girl twisted and stretched in a sickening manner.

"Seek me no more. What is it you want?"

"Come now, we were friends, me and thee. Do you not remember?" The small girl opened her hand and blew sand into the air. It swirled and from its cloud formed the body of another small girl. "This is you. No?"

"Your shams and trickery are of no interest to me, beast."

"So, you do remember. Look closely, Arieanna!" The Mistress took a floundering step back.

"Speak not my name, foul creature. You have no power here."

"AH BUT I DO!" the girl screamed. "THIS IS MY HOME-LAND, WITCH, AND YOU BURNED IT. BURNED IT TO THE BARREN LIFELESS HELL IT IS TODAY!" The girl was screaming so much her neck had stretched and her head swayed like a thing possessed.

"So, we come to this?" The Mistress spoke in soft and gentle tones. "You will not get satisfaction from me, ghoul."

The girl, so enraged by The Mistress's lack of concern, raised her arms to the sky.

"You will pay, witch, for what you did!" The earth started to shake and the girl writhed and screamed in pain. From the body of the child grew a twisted thing, not human or beast but a joining of the two. Flesh split, bones cracked, and a thick, black ooze began to spill from the creature's eyes.

"I know you now, beast. So now we dance." The Mistress clasped her cane and thrust it into the sand. "Shall we begin?" She beckoned the ghoul. And the ghoul began to advance.

The Mistress raised her chin. Her eyes were swirling pools of every blue imaginable. She clapped her hands together and summoned the power of all creation. A keen breeze rose around her and swept her robes around her feet.

"Come, wind! Come, sand! Come at my call!" Her voice took on an edge of command.

The ghoul likewise was gathering its power and struck first. Shooting its hands in front of itself it released a surge of grit and sand. The Mistress grabbed her cane from in front of her and thrust it, crystal first, at the barrage. A light as pure as snow emanated from the crystal, engulfing The Mistress. The ghoul's barrage battered and pounded but was repelled by the shield and blew away to nothing. The Mistress smiled.

"My turn," she whispered. She opened her arms and screamed, "UP!"

The Mistress's robes began to flutter and to fold. She doubled over and caved in on herself. Bones cracked. Skin stretched and from the pile of cloth that was The Mistress and her robe, rose an eagle. Its talons sharp, its beak like a razor. It rose and rose. Its immense wings swept the air like giant sails. Finally tilting its head back, it swooped over into a dive, straight for the ghoul. Not to be out-done, the festering lump spewed up a sticky, thick, black tar and began forming it into a ball. But the eagle was upon it before it could release its dripping weapon. It tore at flesh. Ripped at sinew and bone. The Ghoul let out a wailing cry of pain, as the eagle and demon flailed and grappled for the upper hand. The Ghoul managed to grab the eagle's neck and flung it to the ground. As the eagle skidded across the sand, wings turned to robes, beak into face and The Mistress lay gasping in the sand. The demon chuckled deeply.

"So! The great Mistress, in the dirt where she belongs!"

The Mistress rose and stumbled forward.

"Your strength has grown, little Rebecca. You were such a sweet girl. What a foul creature you have become." The Mistress spat at her feet.

"You did this to me.! You did this to all of us!" The ghoul shrieked, dripping thick, black blood from the wounds the eagle had made. She was weak. But not finished yet.

"I had no choice, Rebecca. No choice." The Mistress had gathered her senses and was ready to fight again.

"It will be my greatest hour finally killing you and tasting the revenge I have planned for many years, witch!"

"By all means, foul thing, you can try."

The Mistress snatched up a handful of sand and brought it to her lips. "I call you now, essence of the earth! Grant me this, elements of stone! Bind yourself. Be as one." The small handful of sand began to move. Each grain melting into the next. It became solid and hard, growing in size. Taking on the shape of a stone. The Mistress raised it above her head and calling on the power of the wind, hurled it at the demon.

"Bind yourselves. Be as one!" The Mistress screamed to the surrounding sand. Grain by grain the sand obeyed, sweeping into the air and raining down upon the beast. The stone grew to a boulder bearing down on the demon. "Crush it!" She howled like a wild banshee, robes in tatters, hair streaming behind her in the chaos and raging wind. The boulder grew, engulfing the ghoul, bearing down its hard edges and incredible weight. It hit the sand with an almighty thud and embedded itself deep in the tiny grains that it had once been. The ghoul completely crushed beneath it.

The wind dropped and only The Mistress remained.

Chapter 15
Click

The massive supply ship had been docked at the harbour for some weeks now. The crew were seen only at night scurrying over its deck like ants. Deep within its bowls an evil stirred, waiting for her minions to do her bidding. Each with a task to complete. Each with a threat of torturous pain if any were to fail.

The Queen flexed her spindly fingers and selected a crystal from an assortment on the table.

"Shall we see how our dearest Kef is doing today?" Her voice was as light and as soft as feathers as she spoke to herself. She caressed the amber crystal and placed it in a silver holder, shaped like the outreaching branches of a tree. The crystal began to glow and the amber colours within evaporated, until the blurry image of Kef filled its void. "There you are. Now, let's see if the little firefly is still within your pocket, shall we?" The Queen continued to spy as the ship rocked gently in the harbour innocuously.

Once given his orders, Click had slunk his way from the ship, while the moons were high. He hated the heat of Meridien and was thankful it was first on his list. He rounded the junk heaps and made a small den for himself amongst the waste. *Now, The Mistress, has left, that little bug shall be my first catch of the day,* Click thought. He was a little wary of how he was going to catch a firefly. If the legends were true, he could be burnt to a crisp, but The Queen must be obeyed, so a plan, he would make.

Chapter 16
Dax

Kef sighed deeply. The telling had exhausted him and Dax's reaction was troubling. Dax slumped back in the chair and ran his fingers through his thick hair.

"But how? When?" Dax didn't know where to start. Questions were buzzing around in his brain like flies. Kef stood.

"Now don't get yourself upset, young man. Take a breath."

"Take a breath? I can't even think straight." Dax rose and started pacing Kef's tiny kitchen. Kef rounded the table and stepped in front of his royal charge.

"Calm yourself, Dax."

"But it's all true. How can this be?" Kef reached out and took Dax by the shoulders. "How could I have been so stupid? I didn't listen. It all seemed so unimportant." Dax hung his head.

"Come now, we can figure this out together. The legend is true yes, but the only person who can give you your answers is your father." Dax snapped his head up. Eyes wide. His father barely spoke to him, only of things important to his role as prince, his duties to the royal line. How was he going to speak to him of dragons? Dax thought miserably.

"Sit yourself back down, boy. Come now." Kef manhandled Dax back into his seat and shuffled round to his own. "There is more, Dax, much more, that I cannot tell you. All I can say is that this will be our last meeting, boy. Your journey is just beginning. Great things are planned for you."

"What things?" Dax whispered.

"You have passed your test, Yes?"

"Yes."

"Well, did you think we would just hand you a Fire Dragon and send you on your merry way?" Kef almost laughed.

"No. But. Well, yes." Dax didn't like where this was going.

"A Fire Dragon has to be bonded to you, Dax. You will both be bound together until death. I know that sounds a bit dramatic, but still, it is the way."

"Bonded. What do you mean?"

"Your Fire Dragon has to feel that you are worthy. That you have got what it takes to be its bonded partner."

"How do I do that?" Dax felt sick. He had only just passed one test and the idea of another was daunting.

"You shall return to the palace and find your father. He is waiting, I'm sure. This is a big day for him too you know." Kef had taken a firm tone, he knew it would not get any easier for Dax.

"Okay, then what?"

"Then, my young scoundrel, you shall start on your path as Dragon-Master." Kef sat back and let the whole afternoon's events sink in.

"But can't you help me? Teach me yourself? Just like you have been these past years?" Dax was becoming nervous. He felt so overwhelmed by these last few days and the idea of his father trying to teach him something, something important, set his nerves on edge.

"No. I have served my purpose, boy. Today will be the last time we meet." Kef swallowed hard. Tears prickled behind his eyes. Saying the words out loud had made them true and the loss hit him hard.

"But you will still be here? Here in your shack? Here at the Hatching Grounds or at the volcano?" Dax rose again, his chin almost quivering.

"No, my boy, I won't. You were my last student. Tomorrow I retire to the Olive Gardens, to see out my days." Kef also rose and tried to clutch Dax's hand.

"No! I won't have it. I need you, Kef. Please!"

Kef drew Dax in and wrapped his thin, frail arms around him. "I can't, boy. It is written. You path is your own now. Be brave and remember all I have taught you." Dax sagged into Kef's arms and returned the hug.

"What will happen to me?" Dax whispered.

"You will become a comrade of the Sworn. You are Fire Sworn. There are others. Blade Sworn. Serpent Sworn and Water Sworn. Together you will become a team." Dax drew back.

"A team, for what?"

"I have said too much. Come now, your father awaits you. Do not embarrass me with your tardiness." Kef gently pushed Dax away and rubbed his face to hide his grief.

"Thank you, Kef. For all that you have tried to teach me. I know I haven't been the best student but thank you anyway." Dax had a hollow feeling in his gut. He had never felt as alone as he did right now.

"You are most welcome, Your Highness." Kef winked at the young lad in front of him, the young lad he had trained since he was a child. Oh, how he would miss him! "Come now, off with you! I have packing to do. The Olive Gardens call." And with that Kef turned and busied himself with pots and pans. Dax slowly turned and made his way to the door. This was not his life, he thought. There must be some mistake.

"Bye, Kef. I shall miss you."

"Yes, yes, bye." Kef could not bear to turn and face him. Tears flowed freely down his wrinkled cheeks. Dax closed the door softly behind him and Kef was alone.

"Mistress protect him. For the love of the Merfolk, please." Kef lowered himself back into his chair and wrapped his arms around himself. *How I shall miss this!* he thought, glancing round his tiny home. He had been offered large quarters at the palace but he liked to be in the hub of the noise and bustle, he had refused, it kept him grounded.

Kef shifted and shook himself. He felt cold. *How long have I sat here?* he thought. He rose from the chair and turned to the window. It faced the open plains of the Drylands. He was just about to turn for his travelling sacks when he heard a scratching at the door.

"Whoever you are, go away! I have no time for visitors today." Kef stared at the door hoping whoever it was would leave when the door slowly swung open and a long shadow slunk its way into the room.

"Well, well, well. What have we here? All alone are we, Kef? What a shame." Click's slow, spiteful voice whispered from the doorway.

"YOU!" Kef exclaimed. "But how? Why?" Kef had backed up against the wall. Heart thumping.

"We won't bother with the how's and why's. I have come for two things, old friend. One is the Firefly in your pocket and the other is your life." Click lunged and Kef fell.

Chapter 17
The Mistress

The Mistress fell to her knees. Sand filled her mouth and nose. She scrabbled at her neck for her whistle then remembered the order she had given for the pack not to interfere. She scrambled around for her cane and hauled herself to her feet. All was still. All was quiet. She brushed at her eyes with the edge of her sleeve and squinted to get her bearings. The heat of battle had taken her a fair distance from her horse and pack, a hot trek was needed, so The Mistress stepped to it.

"You may come out now, my loves." The Mistress's dry voice was barely a whisper. The pack came running, bounding to their leader. They pawed her and sniffed her, searching for wounds, checking for damage.

"Enough now. I'm fine. A little battered and bruised but still alive." The Mistress smiled. She could almost call them friends. Rats and Mistress made their way to her horse. It had hidden itself in the shade of some rocks and whinnied at The Mistress's gentle hand. "Come now, my beauty. All is well. No need to fear me." The horse nuzzled into The Mistress and the gesture was returned.

"Now let us drink and be away. That creature has cost me time." The Mistress handed out water and drank deeply herself. The rats were again harassed into their baskets and the unsightly job of getting on her horse was done. "We will not see the point until nightfall now." She spoke to herself. "But idling around here will not aid us." She dug her heals in and they were away, a golden streak across the horizon.

Chapter 18
Click

Click licked the rich, red blood from his jaws and stretched his neck high.

"Come out, little thing. Click wants to see you." Click sniffed the pocket Hiccup was in. "I won't hurt you. Unless you make me." Click pawed gently at the fabric. "Come now, don't be shy. I have someone who wants to meet you, tiny one." Click knew this creature could hurt him, burn him, if it chose.

Hiccup uncurled herself and clawed her way out of the pocket. She stood on shaky legs. The man that protected her was dead. All she had trusted was gone and now this beast loomed over her, smelling of blood.

"Well, there you are. What a fine Firefly you are!" Click was cautious and he stepped back a few paces. "Shall we take a little trip, me and thee?" The Queen had warned him the only way to capture the creature was through persuasion not violence. Click only knew the latter but he had to serve, so flattering words it would be. "You truly are a fine beauty. Are you hurt?" The tiny Firefly shook her wings and ventured a nervous smile at the huge wolf that stared down at her.

"All will be well, little one. You are safe with me. You can see what I can do." Click gestured towards Kef's throat, or what was left of it. "He could not protect you. Or keep you safe. But I can." Click lowered himself to the ground.

Hiccup looked away from Kef's wounds. She felt deserted and afraid. *The wolf looks strong and he says he will protect me*, she thought.

"Come now, small thing, climb onto my back and I will take you away from this horrible place. I have a nice warm nest for you. And no one will bother you again. How does that sound?" Click was losing patience and the urge to snap the little bug in half was rising every second. Hiccup tiptoed forward and slid herself down Kef's chest.

"That's it, pretty thing, just a little further."

Hiccup made her way to Click's side. She left behind her tiny footprints in Kef's blood like drops of red rain.

"On you climb. Don't be scared. I'm here now. We are friends, yes?" Hiccup nodded her head and climbed upon Click's murderous back.

Chapter 19

Dax

Dax slouched his way along the corridors of the great palace, his home. It felt alien to him now. He dragged his feet as he headed for his father's chambers. He couldn't get his head around all that Kef had told him. And having a long heart-to-heart with his father, the great and mighty King was not something Dax was looking forward to. Before he knew it he was facing his father's door, fist raised to knock.

"Come in!" His father answered before Dax had even knocked. Dax pushed open the large, metal door and stepped inside. "Ah, Dax, I have been waiting for you." His father gestured to a seat by the fire as he took the one facing Dax. "Have you spoken to Master Kef?" Dax just nodded. "I see. Did you listen to his telling?" Again, Dax just nodded his head, his eyes cast down.

King Max knew the boy's head was in turmoil and moved to crouch by his side.

"It's okay, Dax. I felt the same when my time came." Max gently lifted Dax's chin with his long, scaly fingers. "I know you're overwhelmed, and I know I'm the last person you feel like talking to, but talk we must."

Dax ran his fingers through his hair and turned his head to face his father.

"Kef said you had a gift for me?"

"Yes, yes, but we need to take a little walk first, my boy." Max rose and made for the door. "Please, Dax, there is a lot for you to do and time is not our friend." Dax rose and followed his father to the door.

"Where are we going?"

"We are going into the Drylands. Not far, just outside the city. There is something there you must find. Something that I cannot help you with." Dax's face took on a miserable scowl. "Don't worry. You can do this."

Father and son made their way to the city gates and passed through unchallenged. *I really have spoilt that boy*, Max thought as he glanced at his son's sulking face. After a little time crossing the sand Max stopped and sat down. Dax looked at him with disbelief, The King sitting in the sand was not a sight he was used to.

"Come, sit." Max chuckled. "There's no need for royal protocol tonight." Dax sat.

"What are we doing all the way out here?"

"My father brought me out here when I was your age, Dax. It seems like so long ago now." Max scooped up a handful of sand and let the grains drain through his fingers. "The dragon magic that runs through your veins has to be used, Dax. It has to be used soon or it will burn you from the inside." Dax rubbed his arms. He could feel the magic pulsing through his veins. It was making him itch.

"Each Fire Sworn youngster has to harness their magic and use it to bond with their dragon. If you listen to your inner voice, Dax, you can hear your dragon calling to you. It's not easy, believe me. I was out here all night with my father and I don't want that for you." The King turned to his son and grabbed his hands.

Dax jumped at the gesture and pulled his hands away.

"This is all too much! Just a few days ago I was playing tricks on Lex and running rings around Master Kef. Now, well, now I feel like it's all gone, everything I know just gone." Max shuffled up to his son and placed a long arm around his shoulders.

"Everything will be alright. I promise. You just need to look ahead, to the future. You knew being Sworn would mean your life would change. And I know it all has happened so quickly. That's just the way it is, I'm afraid." Max rose and offered Dax his hand. "We need to start, son."

Dax scrabbled to his feet, rejecting his father's hand and looked up at the three moons high in the sky.

"Where do I start?"

"Right here, son. Right here." Max swept his hand across the barren landscape. "What you seek is buried somewhere out there. The only way to find it is with the dragon magic." Dax swallowed hard. "I know it sounds alien to you but with a little patience the magic will speak to you at will." Max took a few steps forward and nodded for Dax to follow. "Bind your eyes, boy. I found it helped." The King handed his son a long, black piece of cloth and helped him tie a blindfold around his head.

"What if I can't get the magic to...you know, talk to me?"

"Dax, it doesn't actually speak words. It's more of a feeling, like a nagging in your gut."

"Oh." Dax calmed himself and took a deep breath.

"That's it. Just relax and breathe. Soon you will feel which way is right, and when you do, just follow that feeling."

Dax tried to clear his mind, to think only of his prize, but his mind kept wandering back to Kef's telling and what would happen after all this strange nighttime adventure with his father.

"Dax, I know this is hard, especially for a boy of your nature, but you really need to concentrate."

Dax lifted the blindfold. "I'm sorry, father, I don't think I can do this."

"Listen, Dax, I felt the same way as you. I did it and so can you. I believe in you, son. Now cover your eyes and breathe."

Dax once more covered his eyes. He relaxed his shoulders and slowed his breathing. Then he felt it. A small tickle in his veins, like a spider's footsteps. Then he felt himself being pulled sideways. Just a few steps. He couldn't explain why. Max gave a small smile to himself, for he knew Dax would learn quickly once he got going. Dax felt dizzy, he knew where he should be going, like an old memory, but he couldn't explain where that memory had come from. Before he could think he was marching across the sand blind, no heed for potholes or rocks, with Max trailing behind.

"That's it, my boy, follow the magic! It will not fail you!" Max shouted, now many paces behind.

Dax could feel the dragon magic in his blood surge. He felt giddy with its tingle. He felt alive, but more than that, he felt the life force of another, his dragon.

Chapter 20
Click

Click slunk his way through Meridien, careful to avoid man or beast, the little firefly buried deep within his neck fur. The journey across the Unclaimed Lands would take him the best part of the night and he knew The Queen would be waiting. Click rested at the city's outskirts and checked the sky, the moons were nearly full height, no time for sleep. The Unclaimed Lands were a vast stretch of rocky, flat pastures, between Meridien and the Ocean Harbour. Home only to shepherds and large flocks of goats and sheep. Click headed off, nimble of foot, for the shepherds carried spears and travelled with packs of hunting dogs strong enough to take down a lone wolf. But The Queen had given her orders and Click would obey. The little firefly nestled herself deeper, memories of Kef's warm pocket long forgotten.

Click was thirsty, so thirsty. The harbour was in sight but with sagging spirit he knew he would get no rest. He padded cautiously to the edge of the harbour village and lay down in the shadow of a large merchant house.

"Little one, look! See where I bring you." Hiccup released her grip on Click's fur and raised her head. The three moons shone onto the gentle ocean and gave the harbour an ethereal look, almost magical. "See, is this not a wonderful place?" Click stood. He knew the moons would give way to sunrise soon. Time was running out. "Just a little further and you will meet my Queen. Oh, she is very excited to meet you, my love, very excited indeed." Click sniffed the air for humans and made his way to the dock.

After a little detour to avoid a few drunk stragglers from the inns and taverns he felt the cold wood of the jetty under his paws.

"Stop right there!" Click froze. "State your business."

"My business is with The Queen, you filthy imbecile! Let me pass!" Click drew himself to full height, his chest puffed, his neck

73

stretched long, a slight show of his many sharp teeth for good measure.

"Forgive me, Click! I did not recognise you in the shadows." The watchman quickly stepped aside, a cold sweat prickled his neck. Click's reputation for cruelty was well known.

Click padded up the gangway and boarded the ship. It's gentle swaying making his stomach instantly queasy. He hated the ship. He made his way to The Queen's cabin, relishing the fearful looks from the watchman aboard. The guard at The Queen's door swiftly knocked on seeing his approach and made himself as small as possible as Click swaggered passed him and entered the cabin.

"You return then? And with little time to spare." The Queen sat at a table, potions, jars and tools at hand.

Click bowed low.

"Yes, Your Majesty. And with the task complete."

"Well?" The Queen tapped her long fingernails on the wooden bench.

"You can come out now, little one," Click coaxed. Little movements ruffled Click's fur and one by one the tiny limbs of the Firefly appeared. Click crossed to his Queen and lowered himself to the floor.

"Greetings, tiny creature. I trust Click has treated you well?" Hiccup stared up at the beauty before her. The Queen's long, black hair almost touched the floor and her eyes, ablaze with fires of blue flame were mesmerizing. "Speak, small thing!" She lent down and offered her palm to Hiccup. Hiccup reached out the smallest hand the Queen had ever seen and grasped her finger. Click stood stock still, holding his breath. "That's it. Come now, a little further," the Queen encouraged. Hiccup climbed onto The Queens hand and sat curled up in a ball. "Now, don't be shy. What is your name, sweet thing?"

"My name is Hiccup, your majesty." The tiny voice of the firefly was as soft as a feather.

"Hiccup! What an enchanting name." The Queen threw a stern glance at Click and he retreated to the other side of the room. "Click, you will leave us now. Follow the Black Road to the Marshlands." Click's shoulders sank, tiredness racked his bones. "I have already sent a Blood Wing to keep watch. You should meet him on his return journey to me. The information he gives you should lead you to your next task." Click opened his mouth to beg for rest then thought better of it.

"Yes, my Queen." And with another low bow he left the cabin, cursing the day he'd rescued the wretched baby that he now served.

"Where were we, my sweet?" The Queen lowered her hand and tipped Hiccup gently onto the table. Hiccup stood and stretched out her wings and shook her small round head. She straightened her minuscule dress and gave The Queen her best smile.

"Do you know who I am?" Hiccup shook her head. "Do you know why I have brought you here?" Again, Hiccup shook her head, a tiny trickle of fear ran down the Firefly's back. "You are going to help me. Yes?" Hiccup nodded yes, but she was starting to feel nervous. "Good. You can start by telling me about Kef and any visitors he has had." Hiccup thought of The Mistress and of Kef's promise not to tell; of the soft, comfy pocket in which she had slept; Kef's kind, gentle voice and the love they had shared. Suddenly she didn't feel so special, she didn't feel so safe and she didn't like this Queen at all. "Come now, Hiccup." The Queen whispered. "You don't want me to lose my patience. Do you?" The Queen picked up a small blade as thin as a hair. "It would be an awful shame to lose your wings!" Hiccup ran, she ran with all the speed her tiny legs could muster. The Queen snatched out her hand and grabbed Hiccup in her tight fist, pressing her thumb into Hiccup's throat so she could not breathe out her fire. "You will tell me want I need to know, creature, by your own will or by mine!" A microscopic tear ran down Hiccup's cheek as she realised what she had lost and what she was expected to tell. The Queen steadied the blade and went to work.

Chapter 21
Dax

Dax lurched forward, stumbling clumsily through the sand, The King scrambling behind him.

"Yes, my boy, yes, follow the magic!" King Max was dry of mouth making his words a high-pitched screech.

Dax halted suddenly and dropped to his knees. He could feel the vibrations of his dragon, hear its calling. He ripped the blindfold from his eyes and started digging, both hands scooping. The King dropped next to him sweating and gasping.

"Dig, boy, dig!" The King had waited for this day ever since Dax had been found to be Sworn and he would relish every moment.

After one final, desperate dig the egg was revealed, the exquisite colours glowing softly in the moonlight. Dax sat back and swallowed loudly. "You did it, son, the egg is yours." Max mopped his brow with his sleeve and clasped Dax by the shoulders. "Take it, boy, quickly now!" The King pressed Dax forward, the boy's shock evident.

"It's so beautiful, father, where has it come from?"

"That is of no concern now. We must be away." He scanned the surrounding area for dangers. "Dax, the egg, seize it!"

Dax snapped out of his trance and bent down to clasp his prize. Its shell felt smooth. His hands trembled as he held the egg. He stood on shaking legs.

"Here, wrap it in this." Max offered his son a length of cloth. "We must not dally here, Dax. The egg will need to be bathed in the river of fire!" Dax gently engulfed the egg in the cloth and held it close as if it were a child. He raised his face to his father. Tears trickled down his cheeks. "I know, Dax, I know. I too have felt what you feel now. There is no need to explain. But, come we must be away."

Father and son made their way across the Drylands and headed for a small, side gate into the city, not often used. The guard had been told of their arrival.

"Your Majesty." The guard bowed low, keeping his eyes to the ground.

"Thank you for your service this night. You may secure the gate after we have passed and take up duties else-where." Max's voice was a low whisper. The guard gave a small nod but kept his head bowed.

After they had swept through the gate The King drew Dax to a halt.

"Let us rest a while, Dax, there is still much to do and I fear an old man is in need of water." He drew a flask from his cloak and drank deeply.

"Father, what is to happen now?" Dax's eyes were wide with fear and wonder.

"Now we go to hatch your dragon, boy, now the fun begins." Max offered the flask to Dax, but he could see nothing could divert the boy's attention from the egg. "Come then, let us proceed." Max shook out his cloak and smothered down his beard. "Lead on, my son, as I presume you know the way."

"Father, will I have to leave?" The question bit into The King's heart.

"Yes, Dax, you will." And together with heavy hearts they headed to the caves, the entrance to the heart of Monmoo.

Dax and his father sat on the hot, stone floor in the heart of Monmoo. The air was dry and hot and the night had nearly given way to the dawn. Dax sat cross-legged, cradling his egg in his lap.

"Dax, before we begin, I have a gift for you." The King reached deep into his robes and pulled out a soft package. Dax remained focused on his egg. "Dax," the King spoke softly. Max chuckled to himself for he had once been consumed with wonder for his own egg. "Dax!" he spoke a little louder. Dax raised his face, his eyes like saucers. "I know you don't want to let it out of your sight, but I have a gift for you." Dax glanced down at his father's hand. A small package wrapped in red silk and tied with ribbon lay there. "For you." Max whispered and placed the gift in front of his son. Dax gently pulled the ribbon and unfolded the silk. A soft glow emanated from what now lay on the stone floor. "It's Shanzzy, my boy. A glove made of Shanzzy." Max pronounced proudly.

"A glove!" Dax declared a little confused.

"Yes, Dax, a glove. For with this you can wield the power of fire. Oh, you cannot create fire but you can bend it to your will. You can conjure up attacks and defences like no other." Max was flour-ishing his hands about, getting caught up in drama.

"A glove" was all Dax replied. A little taken aback, the King went on to explain.

"Dax, this glove gives you immense power. Between you and your dragon you have a great responsibility. Fire Sworn are the most feared and honoured of all the Sworn chosen." He gestured for Dax to put on the glove. "Place your hand inside the glove, Dax, then you will understand." Dax picked up the glove, it was beautiful and it had been sewn together in such a way the surface looked like tiny, silver scales. He slithered his hand into the seemingly delicate fabric. "No need for such caution boy, that's a Shanzzy glove, it can endure almost anything." Max smiled at Dax's delicate handling of the precious glove. He too had treated it like a babe in arms when his father had presented it to him.

The instant Dax's hand and forearm where inside the glove it started to move, it shrank to his exact size. Dax gave a small gasp of surprise at the encasement of his limb until he realised he could no longer feel the glove as a separate thing. Glove and hand were now one. Dax could feel the dragon magic in his blood surging towards his hand like tiny fire ants under his skin, a weird sensation, painful and pleasant at the same time. Dax wiggled his fingers and raised his hand up to his father in amazement.

"I know, son! I know the feeling like it was yesterday." The King started to rise to his feet.

"Now what?" Dax exclaimed, torn between looking at his egg and waving his arm around.

"Now we have to hatch your dragon. The glove will protect you from the heat and damage of any flame. It will allow you to lower your egg into the heart of the volcano." Dax eyed the river of fire fearfully. From his previous visit down here he knew just how hot that river was. Max saw the doubt in his son's eyes. "Not here, boy. This is not the heart of Monmoo." Max laughed out loud. "This is just a fake, a rouse, if you will. Intruders and spies are plentiful these days and our secret is well kept, son."

Dax stood and stared at his father. *I don't think I know this man at all*, he thought, looking at the sweating, excited King before him.

"This way, my boy!" The King exclaimed, striding it seemed towards a wall. "What I'm about to show you only a few have seen. Not even your brother knows of this, not yet anyway." Max, followed by a bewildered Dax, turned to face the wall. Dax frowned and went to speak then thought better of it. The King reached out his hand and gently glided it over the rough surface. To Dax's surprise tiny symbols appeared before him. They swirled and twisted together to form a circle. Each symbol interlocking with the next, each symbol had flames of orange and red dancing inside them. "Your hand, Dax, it requires your hand." Dax reached out a shaky, Shanzzy-covered hand and placed it on the wall in the middle of the now brightly glowing circle. With his breath held he looked to his father. "Take courage, boy. Hold fast." At that the wall began to shake, the ground began to tremor, and Dax nearly pulled his hand away. "Steady now, boy!" Max clasped his son by the shoulder, giving him the strength he needed. The vibrations that were flowing through Dax's hand were becoming unbearable, sweat ran down the boy's face and his knees began to buckle. Then as quickly as it had started, it stopped. Dax staggered backwards, his egg clutched for dear life.

"Father, what was that?"

"That, my boy was one of the wonders of this world. You have just opened the Deep Gate, the entrance to the heart of Monmoo. Look!" Dax turned his now itchy, dry eyes towards where his father pointed. A small hole had appeared in the ground, nothing more. Dax looked at his father quizzically. "Come now, let us be away. The guards will be here soon for their morning duties and this will be difficult to explain away." Son followed father towards the hole and both peered down. A small stone staircase led downwards and from what Dax could see, downwards and downwards and downwards.

Chapter 22
The Queen

"Oh dear. Look what you made me do!" The Queen laid down her wafer-thin, sharp knife. "You were such a pretty little thing. If you had just spoken up a few moment ago I wouldn't have had to resort to this unsavoury business." The Queen reached out and with thumb and forefinger picked up Hiccup by her wing-tip. "Still, I have never been one to shy away from what needs to be done." With that she tossed the battered and broken Firefly into a small, brown bag. She rose from the table and swept her long hair behind her shoulders. "Guard!" The heavy door to her cabin creaked open and a tanned, toothless face peered in. "Come in, fool. Take this bag and place it with our supplies." The Queen held up the bag as if it were empty. "Click has one more visitor to bring me today and then we shall make our way to Boar Keep. Make sure everything is ready for our departure."

"Yes, my lady." Smoky shuffled towards his Queen, head bowed and eyes low.

"Take it, you fool and remove yourself from my presence. Your odour is offensive."

"Yes, my Queen." Smoky took hold of the bag and clutched it to his chest all the while shuffling backwards.

"Oh, and Smoky. If word comes to me that you have spoken of my business to that tavern wench you have been seeing… Well." The Queen reached for her knife. "Just remember lose lips peel away as easily as soft fruit."

"Never, my Queen." Smoky swallowed into a dry throat.

Once outside the door he blew out a long breath and looked down at the bag. He knew there was something alive inside but the price of peeking was too high. *How did I end up like this?* he thought to himself, *I had only become a sea dog to build my coffers and buy a piece of land. Raise my sheep. Live a quiet life. Shepherding is in my blood, not this.* He glanced down again at the bag. "And now

80

I'm serving a wolf in sheep's clothing." Smoky hacked up a cough and spat over the side of the boat. "Oh well, orders are orders." And with that he tossed the little, brown bag onto a pile of crates and whistled his favourite tune as he carried on his chores.

Chapter 23
The Mistress

The Mistress arrived at The Point just as the suns were setting. The point was a mishmash of taverns, trading posts and fishing huts, all noisy and smelly. It made the rats restless in their baskets. She reined the horse to a trot and made her way to the tavern that looked the least trouble. The dirty brick exterior of the last building on the track looked sturdy. *At least it's far away from the fishing huts, so the smell is minimal*, she thought. She rounded the tavern and proceeded to look for any sort of stable-hand to relieve her of her horse. She found none. A small wood shed and a lean-to made do for stables, filled with water buts and straw bales that looked past their best. Two tired old nags chewed the pathetic offerings as they raised their eyes to The Mistress.

"What a sorry sight you two are." The Mistress spoke as she slid from her horse's back and led him to the lean-to. Neither horse paused from eating and lowered their eyes. "Now where shall we put you lot for the night?" The Mistress whispered to the baskets. She was answered by desperate scratching from inside. She released the lids and the pack spewed out like a black waterfall, stretching and scrabbling around her feet. "To the wood shed with you all. Go on. I'm sure there are mice and spiders aplenty. You will not go hungry." The pack shot her a look of thanks and darted towards the dark, cobweb-covered shack. The Mistress followed and bolted the door behind them, making sure they were not being spied upon.

After securing her horse in the lean-to and resting a while to catch her breath, she made her way into the tavern. A growling stomach and an unbearable thirst must be answered first. The door to the tavern was heavy and had a thick layer of dirt and grease for decoration. She heaved into it and with much protest it opened inwards. The smell and noise that met The Mistress made her regret not hunkering down with the horse. Bitter ale and pipe tobacco hung in the air like a rancid fog. Most of the tables were occupied and two small serving girls were running food and drinks from the back out to the customers.

"Welcome, friend." A large, sweaty inn-keeper waddled over to The Mistress. "What brings you to the point then, my lovely?" A single brown tooth showed itself every time the woman spoke.

"Just passing through. One night only." Was all The Mistress replied?

"Well, you come to the right place. Old Jeannie will sort you out good." The innkeeper pressed herself closer with every word. She smelt of sweat and fire smoke. And the apron she wore struggled under the weight of her huge belly.

"I require one room for one night. And I have deposited my pack of…cats in your woodshed. Five coins will be your price, and I am expecting dinner as well. Do I make myself clear?" The Mistress turned her eyes to the inn-keeper who was now so mesmerized a large chain of drool ran down her chin and dripped onto her overly large bosom.

"Yes. Please come and sit. The girls will prepare your room."

The Mistress swept her eyes around the room to find the warmest spot and on feeling herself dismissed, old Jeannie sucked up her dribble and flustered over to the bar to rally her children to do The Mistress's bidding.

"Clean sheets in the front room, Floss and give the floor a sweep. Maudie, fetch that old girl over there a plate, the good stuff mind, no gristle." Both girls looked at their mother as if she were a stranger. "Now! You two little fleas, before I give you both a thick ear." The girls flew off in opposite directions wondering if their mother's kind gestures were a sign that she had finally gone mad and they would be rid of her vicious tongue and quick fists.

The Mistress made her way to a chair by the fire. The current occupier stopped mid-smoke and raised a snarling face to her. "What are you looking at, old crone? Get out the way, you're blocking the fire!" His gruff tone and callused hands revealed him as a fisherman.

"I am just an old tinker seeking a little warmth for my bones," The Mistress offered, her tone light and fragile.

"Well find it elsewhere! This here's my place. Now move!" The tavern was starting to notice the stand-off.

"Shall you not give up your seat to one less fortunate than yourself, kind sir?" *One last try,* she thought.

"I'll say it one more time, old witch. MOVE!"

"Very well." As quick as a flash The Mistress whipped up her cane, hooked it under the man's armpit and twisted him out of the seat and into a crumpled heap on the floor. Gasps and wide eyes swept round the crowded tavern. The Mistress stepped over the fisherman and lowered herself into the warm seat. "Thank you, kind sir." She smiled down at the shocked face still lying on the floor. The tavern waited with baited breath for his reply.

"N-no problem. I was just teasing, that's all. Everyone knows old Billy here likes a laugh or two." The fisherman clumsily rose from the greasy floor and shambled his way to the bar. Nervous whispers and pointing fingers soon gave way to drunken singing and raucous laughter. Ale was the medicine to all crossed words in a tavern.

After filling her belly and quenching her thirst The Mistress made her way to her room. Floss had even put a handful of buttercups in a small glass next to her bed. The Mistress chuckled. That woman's death will be at the hands of her children if she's not careful. Sleep came easily. Not for the pack. For not an insect was safe from their claws and teeth. They had not had such full bellies in days. Every corner of the dark shed held a mouthful and soon the shack was quiet, except for the sound of a sleeping pile of rats.

Chapter 24

Dax

Dax had never felt so hot and uncomfortable in his life. The narrow stairway went on forever and his father held a fast pace. At last the stairway opened out into a small chamber.

"Rest, boy, take some water," his father encouraged him, offering the flask. Dax almost snatched it from Max's hand and glugged the cool water down without stopping for breath. "Easy, son, that has to last."

"Sorry," Dax gasped as he wiped at his soaked chin and handed the flask back to his father. "Where now?" Even though Dax was tired, excitement urged him on.

"Just a little farther, this way." And The King was off again. Max groaned and made to follow.

The small chamber was lit with shafts of light that shone down from many holes in the ceiling. Dax suspected these holes were carved down by hand from the volcano's surface. At the far side of the chamber was a low arch leading to yet another stairway, Dax rolled his eyes but followed down. At the bottom of the stairway Max halted and turned, his face inches from Dax.

"Now, my boy, what you see here is not to be spoken about, not turned into a tale of adventure or gossip." Dax just blinked, the heat making him feel faint. "Dax, I need us to be clear on this matter. Do I have your word?" Max stuck out his hand. "A royal handshake is as good as a bond, son, come now." Dax grasped his father's hand limply, not quite sure what was going on and feeling waves of dizziness clouding his brain. "Done. Now feast your eyes on the heart of Monmoo." Max stepped to the side to reveal a circular room, its walls smooth. A stone structure, carved with dragons and flames rose from the floor. A small crucible at its centre. "Get closer, boy. What has to be done needs to be done quickly." Dax edged closer. Something moved in the centre of the stone crucible. He closed the

85

gap, one slow foot at a time. There, curled up like a small kitten was a dragon, not a live dragon but one made up entirely of fire.

"Father!" Dax panicked. "Is it alive?" The little dragon stirred. "Father, Please." Dax started to backtrack.

"Hold, boy, you are in no danger." Max kept his distance. This was for Dax alone to face. The little dragon raised his head and spoke.

"Welcome, Dax. I have been waiting a long time for you."

"Err. Hello." Dax was thrown by the dragon's soft voice. It belied its deadly appearance.

"Have you brought the egg?"

Dax had forgotten all about his precious egg.

"Oh yes." Dax thrust the egg in front of him like a bad smell, wanting whatever this was to be over.

"Bring it close." The dragon's voice was mesmerizing, and Dax could not divert his eyes from the flickering and dancing flames that made up its body. Dax was almost in touching distance. "Closer." Dax was face to face with the little flame dragon. The heat had sweat dripping from his chin and brow. "You have the dragon magic in your blood, I can feel it. Good, good. All is well. Now pass me your prize, young prince." The dragon held out a flaming claw and Dax obeyed, switching the egg to his gloved hand he offered it up. Once the egg was in the clutches of the flame dragon, Dax stepped back a pace and turned to his father.

"Steady now, Dax. Wait."

The dragon began to chant.

"All that is holy, hear my plea! Invoke this dragon with my flame. Invoke this dragon with my heart. Invoke this dragon with my power. Mother Nature, hear me now! By The Mistress's command I serve!"

Dax's egg started to glow, clutched in the claws of the flame dragon. The crystal shell began to shimmer and shine. Colours bounced off the walls and ceiling.

The little dragon continued, "Come forth, beautiful one, you are the embodiment of my heart, my flame, my power! Serve only she who knows, she who commands. The Mistress has work to be done!"

The shell began to crack and shake and the flame dragon glowed a ferocious red. Dax fell to his knees. Sweat blurred his vision. He could feel the dragon magic pulling at his very soul. A great whoosh of scalding air filled the room knocking both him and his father to the ground. Followed by a silence that almost deafened father and son.

"Come my prince. Look! Your dragon awaits you." The flame dragon's voice was barely a whisper.

Dax opened his eyes and stumbled to his feet. There, in front of him stood a dragon. Its scales as red as blood, each one shining with the flames of Monmoo. It stood two heads taller than Dax. Its tail curled around its legs. Dax stared straight into its eyes and felt his blood rush, his heart pound.

"Master," the dragon spoke as she lowered her head.

"Claim it, boy! Quick. Claim it!" Max was frantically scrabbling to his feet.

"Now, Dax!" the flame dragon spoke as it curled up again in the crucible. "If you don't claim your dragon, Dax, all will be lost!"

Dax slowly stepped forward and reached out a shaky hand.

"Father! I'm scared!"

"Now, Dax! For the love of the Merfolk, now!"

Dax placed his hand on top of the dragon's bowed head. Its scales were smooth and hot. "I claim you," Dax whispered. The dragon reared up and opened its jaws wide.

"AND I CLAIM YOU!" the dragon roared.

"FATHER!" Dax screamed. The dragon sprang upon Dax, mouth wide, tail whipping. He engulfed Dax completely and dragon and boy were gone.

Chapter 25
The Oracle

Deep within the forest, within the cold realm, a beautiful snow-fox snuffled through the undergrowth.

"An evil is stirring, my love." The little snow-fox lifted her tiny, perfect face as the Oracle spoke. "I fear that what was written will soon come to pass." The oracle's delicate, bare feet trod softly in the forest and left behind barely a footprint. "I'm sure my sister will soon come calling."

The snow-fox lowered her head and returned to her foraging. The warm realm was of no concern to her.

Chapter 26
The Mistress

The Mistress opened her crusted eyes and tried to swallow. The dusty air she had breathed on her journey across the Drylands had her reaching for water.

"Thistle! Oh." Realising where she was, she sat up and rubbed her face.

She fumbled her way out of the bedsheets and reached for the water jug and bowl. Three long and welcome splashes of water had her face clean and her eyes clear. She sat on the edge of her bed and allowed herself a moment to ponder.

"The day will be long. I must show no weakness." She stretched out her aching legs and feet and chuckled to herself. "If my enemies could see the wizened thing I have become under my robes and arrogance they would laugh at their fear. But still, a fierce glance and a sharp word do go a long way." With that she rose and gathered her robes and boots. Once dressed and her many packages and hidden pouches checked, she bent to the task of donning her boots. "Thistle, if I was ever in need of your service it would be now." The Mistress complained to herself.

After wrestling with her footwear and re-binding her hair she turned for the door and froze. Small shadows danced underneath the doorway and small sniggers rose and fell. The Mistress took two quick steps and wrenched the door open. Floss and Maudie flew inwards and landed in a pile of bony limbs and tangled hair.

"Spies!" The Mistress accused. And slammed the door shut trapping the two children in her room.

"No, Mrs! Please! We ain't no spies!" Floss had clambered to her feet and was holding her hands out, pleading her innocence.

"Stop your whining, Floss," Maudie snapped, brushing off her skirt but staying on the floor.

"But she's a witch, Maudie. Mother says so. Oh, please don't eat us, Mrs!"

"Eat you! Why on earth would I eat two little, bony fleas like you?" The Mistress reached for her cane and poked Maudie in the back.

"Leave off! You ain't no witch. Just an old hag, who smells bad." Maudie rose from the floor and stuck a dry tongue out at The Mistress.

"Well, old hag I may be, but still, I know a few tricks." The Mistress enjoyed the company of children. Their ability to find the plain truth in things, she respected. It was a pleasure she had been denied.

"Show us then, prove it!" Maudie goaded.

"No, Maudie, please! Mother will plain beat us if she found us in here." Floss gripped her sister's sleeve and tried to drag her towards the door. Maudie shook her off like a naughty puppy.

"Go on then, witch, show us a trick."

The Mistress lent her cane on the bed. "Are you sure? Once you have seen what is possible, you will never believe things are impossible again." Both girls stood still blinking with anticipation mixed with a little fear. "Come close." The Mistress beckoned. Both girls shuffled forward.

The Mistress began to rub her small, wrinkly hands together. "The world is not ours for the ruling. Another sets the board. She brings beauty and balance. But! Defy her will and chaos she will bring." Both girls held their breath. The Mistress cupped her hands and blew a long, slow breath into them. "Everything starts small." As she uncupped her hands a tiny seed lay in her palm. "Are you sure you want to see?" She asked with a small wink of her eye.

"Yes! Mrs, Yes!" Floss was now as eager as her sister.

"Very well." The Mistress focused her eyes, blues and silvers swirled in them until no whites remained. Maudie gasped and clung to Floss. "Grow, little life giver, grow!" Upon the last word leaving her lips the seed started to split. A tiny slither of green rose from the seed-case and wriggled its way free. The Mistress resumed blowing onto it, small, gentle breaths. "Grow now, my lovely. Show us your face." The little seedling reached up and up and a small bud fattened at its tip. The sisters bent their faces closer. "I have two friends here that wish to say hello." The Mistress whispered. The little bud started to break apart and one small petal at a time emerged. The girls peered closer still. The small, white daisy turned its flower head to face the sisters

"Hello!" The words fell from the flower's tiny lips upon its tiny face.

"WITCH!" Both girls screamed and scrabbled backwards. Shrieking and crying they both flapped for the door-handle, pushing each other out of the way and shouting insults and cusses aplenty.

"I did ask if you were sure." The Mistress chuckled smirking at the girl's attempts to open the door. "BOO!" The Mistress shouted. And the girls near wet themselves as they threw open the door and ran hollering for their Mother that a witch was upon them.

"What a fun way to start my day! Come now, Arieanna, scaring babes with parlour tricks is beneath you." The Mistress berated herself. "But what fun, this journey is far from over and danger lies at every turn. There's no harm in a little trickery to lighten the mood." The Mistress frowned to herself. Was that her voice in her head or Anya's? These days she could not be sure.

After a well-cooked breakfast served by a shaky and pale Floss and supplies purchased at the price suggested by The Mistress and agreed to by the ever-hypnotized Jeannie, she set off to collect her pack. The horse would be collected by the traders, one less thing to worry about. The suns were up and the air fresh and ripe with the smell of the Marshlands.

On opening the wood shack door she was greeted with many sets of eyes peering from all manner of holes and cracks.

"Come now, my lovelies, the day is upon us. A perfect day for travelling to the Marshlands." With that she turned and strode towards the Black Road with the scurrying pack behind her, and a slight spring to her step.

The Black Road sneaks up on a person. A chunk here, a lump there and before you know it your feet are treading the bewitching path. The Mistress found herself plodding along said path and made a decision

"Halt, my dears! This will never do. As much as I need the speed my thoughts are becoming clouded and my mind wanders from my task. Now is the time to enter the Marshlands." The Mistress took out her water flask and sipped, eyeing the surrounding land.

The Marshlands were not an easy place to enter. Tightly packed trees and vines ran straight up against the Black Road, as if to touch it they would surely perish.

"There! Up ahead a small gap." The rats scampered ahead and clawed and chewed at the undergrowth around the small opening.

By the time The Mistress had caught up with them the hole was wide enough for her to shuffle through, all be it nearly bent double. Mistress and pack emerged onto the soft soil like a horde of unsavoury beasts. Twigs and leaves stuck in their hair and fur.

The Mistress checked the suns and scanned the land. "This way. Our friend Grumble will be taking his morning dip and I don't want to miss him. Rooting around under a tree for him will take up too much of my time. Forward!"

Chapter 27
Grumble

Grumble poked his tiny face through the leaves that covered the miniature entrance to his home and smiled. The suns were warm on his green, gnarly face and he felt joy. Joy that he lived. Joy that his task was coming to an end and he could finally sleep the long sleep. Grumble, you see was a tree elf. Tiny and green covered in rooty tendrils and gnarly bumps. His one and only job was to tend the Yok Yok tree. Once there had been an elf for every tree but now only a few elves remained. Grumble had received word that The Mistress was coming this morning and he had to be ready. He pushed his miniature body through the entrance hole and shook himself. Stretched his little arms and legs and padded down to the river. He left his tree once a day to wash and gather water. He blended in so well with the bushes and grasses, few animals were even aware he was there. Grumble lowered himself into the cold, fresh river and shivered. A tiny smile on his lips.

"I will miss you, my icy friend." He whispered to the mute tide. He dunked his head under and ran his tiny fingers through his wavy hair, dislodging twigs and feathers aplenty. After his bath he filled his small carrying cup with water and headed back to his tree. His mind wandered as he dried his skin in the warm spring breeze. As he approached his tree he heard the soft scratch of claws in the marshy soil. He stopped and sniffed the breeze. *Rats,* he thought alarmingly to himself. Grumble slunk down low and crawled through the last remaining grass before the trees roots turned the soil bare.

"You can stand now, Grumble, I know you are there." The Mistress's voice snip and harsh swept over the grass patch.

Grumble froze, blinked and stood. He was afraid to run, afraid to venture closer. Who had spoken? Who knew his name? From around the back of his Yok Yok tree scrambled a black torrent of vermin. They swarmed twice as high as Grumble and he trembled in fear. Behind the rats swept a cloaked and hooded being. Woman or child, Grumble couldn't tell, but he could feel the power radiating from the cane they carried.

"Come now, little one, we are not here to hurt you, just to end your wait."

"Oh, err; pleased I am that my time is ended, but afraid I am of your rats." Grumble managed to stutter.

"They will not hurt you." The Mistress reassured, "Not unless you displease me." Grumble gulped and with knocking knees walked forward. "That's better! Let me see you." The Mistress bent down on one knee with the help of the Cane and beckoned Grumble forward, "You were told of my coming, yes?" The Mistress asked.

"I was told my task was complete and today I would be able to sleep the long sleep." Grumble kept his eyes on the hooded figure. Only a shadow of a face could be seen but the rats terrified him and he could not bear to look into their hungry eyes.

"Well, I am here to end your task and allow you the long sleep." The Mistress stood and gestured towards Grumble's tree. "Is it safe, is it unbroken?"

"Yes, oh yes, Great One." Grumble cheered on realising that this was The Mistress. "Good care, I have taken. Much love, I have given." Grumble became excited; he had tended the egg like it was his own offspring. Turning and cleaning it, even humming to it the odd tune here and there.

"Good. I shall have it now, and then your service is done." The Mistress held out a small, pale hand.

"It is deep inside the tree it is. I need a few moments to retrieve it." Grumble started towards his leafy entrance as he spoke.

"Make haste, tiny one. My time here is running out. Do not delay."

Grumble nodded and crawled into his home. He made his way through the roots and down and down he crawled through his little tunnel, through the stony soil that lay deep below the tree. At last he came to a small cavern lined with feathers and leaves. It was snug and warm. A small shaft of light filtered in through a hole in the roots, barely enough to see a hand in front of you. Grumble lowered his water cup and knelt. He gently swept aside soft, white feathers and small, dark, green leaves from the cavern floor; he gently dug into the stony floor and eased out a small, wooden box with the care of a loving father.

"Come now, my little one. Do not fear. This is your time now. Your time to grow and become big and fearless." Grumble snuggled the box to his weathered face and purred a soft, low purr. The box gently moved to the sound of Grumble's voice bringing a smile to his dry, thin lips. He turned again for the tunnel, an empty pain in his heart and stomach for he had grown to love his pearl-like egg and its loss was almost too much to bear. As Grumble emerged from his entrance hole the rats chattered and hissed making him jump almost dropping the box.

"Careful now, Grumble! That is the only one left in the world and we wouldn't want its breaking to be your cross to bear now, would we?" The Mistress slid to Grumble's side.

"Give it here, little man; you knew it was not yours to keep." Grumble gently kissed the box, whispered a tiny goodbye and as small jewel-like tears trickled down his lumpy cheeks he offered up his precious box. "Thank you, Grumble, your reward shall come tonight. Now we must be away." She turned to the rats, which had gathered at her feet, and motioned for them to leave. Grumble could only stare and tremble. Giving back the box was the hardest thing he had ever had to do. He turned and started to crawl back into his woody home.

He did not notice the keen eyes of the small, brown Blood Wing watching from afar and as his tiny foot slithered into the leaves the bat turned and headed for its home.

Click will be pleased with me, the bat thought smugly to himself.

Chapter 28
The Mistress

The Mistress and her pack had made it to the marsh docks; fur and robe wet with sweat and covered in grass seeds. The dock was small in the Marshlands, merely three moorings and a wooden shack that housed the boat-master. The mistress glanced at the suns.

"We are good for time, the suns are high still. Now, to get this little precious one to its nest." The mistress mused, as she shook debris from her robe.

The boat-master had seen the old hag scurry up the marsh road. He had seen her muttering to herself. *Easy coin.* He wrongly thought.

"Gather, my lovelies! This is no journey for you." The rats huddled and chattered their teeth.

"I will be gone a while. Use your time here to hunt and drink. We still have work to do this day, long work." The Mistress made to leave but the pack crouched low, as one, and stared at her with begging eyes. "Go! Now! Before I use my cane to send you on your way!" The Mistress raised the cane a few inches from the ground and the pack was gone. She felt beneath her robe for the small, wooden box. "Not long, precious one. Not long." She started for the boatman's shack. "Slowly now, for I am just an old beggar looking for passage." The Mistress counselled herself. *This is my favourite role,* she thought.

The Mistress walked tentatively onto the rickety docks that led to the shack. She knew he was watching. A good performance was needed. She lent more heavily on the cane and wheezed and puffed for breath. The boatman watched, stroking his greasy beard.

"Easy coin, indeed." The Boatman rose from his chair and swung open the shack door. A smile of friendship and trust, mastered over time, beaming on his face.

"Hello there, old timer. What assistance may I offer?" His words as sweet as a peach.

"Greetings, Boatman! I seek passage to Vine Island." The Mistress hunched low.

"Vine Island? That's no place for a lady. What be your business there?"

The Mistress reached into her pocket and pulled a full purse from its folds.

"Well, then! No explanation needed. Coin speaks for itself." The Boatman's mind was on murderous things. He closed the shack door behind him and fetched oars from a rack. "This way, if you please." He swept his hand towards a small riverboat tied to the first mooring.

"Your kindness will be rewarded." The Mistress gave the Boatman her ugliest smile and wiped her nose with her hand.

"Your death will be a kindness, rotten, old witch." The Boatman whispered to himself. Repulsed by the snot trail left on the old woman's hand.

Mistress and Boatman made their way down the mooring and both climbed into the small boat. The Mistress struggling, clambering, clumsily. She settled herself on the hard plank and drew her cloak around her shoulders.

"One gold coin there and one for the journey back." The Boatman demanded from the rear of the boat. The Mistress fumbled in her cloth purse and pulled out a single coin. The Boatman snatched it from her hand before the purse was closed. "The current is rough here. Best you hold on. Wouldn't want you to take a tumble now, would we?" He laughed at himself and spat into the river.

The little river boat bobbed and struggled down the river. The Mistress sat silent. The Boatman rowed, planning and plotting with every stroke. Vine Island was the last in a row of three small islands. Solitary. Deserted. Or maybe not. The Boatman turned the boat against the current and threw a rope ashore, its metal hook snagging a low branch. Hand over hand he pulled the boat ashore.

"End of the road." He stated flatly.

"A little help?" The Mistress pleaded, stretching out a withered hand.

"Extra coin for help."

"Of course." The Mistress again retrieved her purse and once more drew out a coin. The Boatman placed one booted foot ashore and straddled the boat. He roughly grabbed at The Mistress and hauled her out. Dumping her onto the rough edge of the swampy shore.

"One hour. Then I leave. With or without you!" He spat again and sat down heavily in the boat.

"One hour then." The Mistress turned to leave.

Chapter 29
Malya

Malya stirred and rolled over. She was wrapped in her huge, woven blanket, the one her mother had made. She peered around the hut through sleepy eyes. Her mother was busy feeding the fire with moss and small twigs. The sunshine streamed through the small doorway.

"Mother!" Malya suddenly yelped, realising she had over-slept. "Why haven't you woken me? My chores, they are not done." Malya started to struggle to her feet, the blanket now becoming a hindrance.

"Stop, child, you have no chores today!" Koiya's face was soft, there was no anger in her eyes and Malya couldn't work out what was different about today.

"But I have chores every day; I don't want the little ones burdened with mine." Malya rose from the wooden cot and joined her mother crouching at the fire.

"Today is a special day for you, Malya. Today you will face a challenge, one you have been preparing for these past years." Koiya sat back on the earth floor and turned to Malya.

"You will need to ask mother earth's guidance and wisdom, my beautiful one. I have faith that you will do well."

Malya was silent, taking in everything her mother had said. *So, this is what the old man meant when he said I am ready,* Malya thought to herself.

"What sort of challenge, mother?" Malya asked softly.

"I cannot say, child."

"Can you tell me where it will be?" Malya was becoming concerned at her mother's lack of information and coldness crept over her.

"We will eat a simple breakfast, and then I will take you to the place." Koiya could see the fear starting to rise in Malya and gently held her hand. "Please do not worry. You are ready. This is what you were born for, my daughter, my precious child."

Malya swallowed her doubts. *If mother has faith that I am ready, then ready I will be,* Malya thought.

"Thank you, mother." Malya whispered through soft tears. "Thank you for filling my journey with love and patience. I would not be the woman I am today, without your guidance and care. I love you."

Koiya joined her daughter in her sorrow. Both knowing they were soon to part ways. Neither wanting to say goodbye. Koiya wiped her cheeks and moved away from the fire.

"Would you like to gather some water for our tea, Malya, it will give you a chance to check the little ones before we go." Koiya needed Malya to leave the hut, her sorrow was too overwhelming to bear and she needed Malya to be strong for what was to come.

"Shall I say goodbye?" Malya asked.

"No, child, I don't want a fuss. We shall slip away unnoticed. Let me do the explaining after you have gone." Koiya turned and busied herself with the fire.

Malya headed out into the warming sun and sighed, "What a strange day this will be!"

Chapter 30
Grumble

Grumble dreamed of floating things. Of clouds and soft petals. He had completed his task. He had pleased The Mistress, now he would sleep the long sleep. His bumpy, little body was engulfed in its feather nest, curled into a tiny ball.

Grumble dreamed of raindrops against his skin, big round drops, the kind that stung and bruised.

Small clumps of earth plopped onto the feather nest.

Grumble dreamed of small, round acorns scattering around his feet.

Large stones and rocks fell into Grumbles little cave.

Grumble dreamed of a darkening sky, rumbles of thunder in the distance.

The tunnel under the Yok Yok tree gave way.

Grumble dreamed of threatening voices, whispering violence and horror.

"Well, well, what do we have here?" Click peered down onto Grumble's sleeping form. "Sleeping the long sleep, are we?"

Click reached down and snatched up the limp Grumble.

"Not for long." With that Click tossed poor Grumble into his mouth and was away through the marshes.

Chapter 31
The Mistress

"She is here. She comes." The soft, hissing tones whispered through the swamp. Long slithering bodies made their way to the Island's centre. All knew what must happen. All knew it was time. The great Manuk must be born. The great Manuk must be chosen.

The Mistress made her way over vine and through mud. Over boulder and swamp. At last she reached the small, wooden bridge that crossed to the henge circle. She felt their presence. *Lots have come. This is good,* she thought.

"Come! All!" She spoke as if to herself. "Tomorrow she will come. All must be in place. Remember your vows, serpent kind. Remember, he must be chosen."

Snakes of all colours, all sizes, made their way to the henge. Slipping and writhing. Hissing and snapping. A mass of scales, surging together as one. The Mistress reached the centre of the henge and struck a stone talisman, which was embedded into the earth, with her cane. The talisman shuddered and screeched as it slid to the side, revealing a small, stone stairway.

"Forward, friends! There is no time to waste!" The Boatman had taken his time and the suns were starting their journey towards dusk. Snakes rushed forward and flowed down the stairway, a river of scales and fangs. Not until the last serpent had entered did The Mistress take the first step. The narrow stairway opened into a cave. Its walls coated with vines all twisted and ugly. "Everyone must find their place!" The Mistress demanded, her patience thin. "Do not squabble or challenge!" She moved to a low, thick vine as the snakes hid and camouflaged themselves. She removed the wooden box from her robes and gently lifted the lid. A wave of hissing erupted from the vines.

"Holy One, we worship you!" Came the faithful words. Every snake humbled. Every snake coiled in certitude. She eased her small fingers around the egg that was Manuk and lifted it from the box.

"Behold, friends! The egg of Manuk! The last of his kind." All was silent as The Mistress nested the egg into the thick, soft vine. "Sleep now, precious one. For tomorrow she comes. Tomorrow your work begins." The Mistress replaced the box within her robes and turned to leave. "If I hear of any dishonour, any act against the Sworn child, the pit will be waiting." The snakes hissed and writhed in the vines. "Do I make myself clear, serpents?"

"Yes, Holy One. We will please you. We will honour you. She will be treated as one of our own." The snakes all spoke in unison.

"You will, my friends. I have no doubt about that!" With that The Mistress was away.

The mistress returned to the boat, over rock and stream, through mud and muck. She knew the Boatman would be waiting, waiting to steal her purse, waiting to see her to a watery grave.

"Thank you for waiting, kind sir." The Mistress said returning to her role as helpless old hag.

"No trouble. Your coin is as good as any other." The Boatman had a plan.

"A little help?" She extended a filthy hand.

The Boatman spat into the river and roughly hauled The Mistress into the boat. She settled herself on the plank seat and huddled her robes around her, waiting for the Boatman to make his move.

"What business did you have on that Island, old timer?" The Boatman asked, feigning interest. The Mistress said nothing.

"There's no trade there, no bartering to be done." Still The Mistress said nothing.

"Fine, have it your own way!" The Boatman growled.

They were half way across the river when The Mistress decided to speak.

"You know, stealing my coin will only be bad for you, Boatman." She smiled as she spoke.

The Boatman stopped rowing and turned a nasty, snarling face towards the huddled figure.

The Mistress kept her smile, "Best you just take me to shore and go about your day."

"Is that so?" He lowered his oars and felt inside his pocket.

"And if you think I'm going to be easy to kill, think again." The Boatman sprang forward. A small pocket knife in his hand, but The Mistress was ready. As quick as a whip she flicked her cane up and caught the Boatman square between the eyes. The Boatman shot backwards stunned and blinded.

"Now." The Mistress spoke with calm words. "That's enough of that."

But the Boatman kept coming. He regained his footing and was upon her again. The Mistress blew the bone whistle that was around her neck and again struck the Boatman with her cane.

"Don't make me deal out pain for you, man. Know when you have been beaten!" The Mistress was tiring of the game and needed to be away to the White City.

"Give me the purse and I'll spare your life, old fool! There is no one to help you here." The Boatman had had enough. She had broken his nose and he didn't want another beating with that cane of hers.

"Row me ashore at once and I will spare YOUR life!" The Mistress had seen the pack enter the water on the far shore.

"Last chance! The purse or your life." The Boatman, his eyes ablaze with fury, lunged at The Mistress and wrenched her from her seat. Then the rats were upon him. Teeth tearing and ripping his flesh. Claws scratching and slashing. The boatman screamed and swatted at the rats, tipping and swaying the boat.

"Be done with him now, my lovelies. We lose time." The Mistress clung to the boat's edge, the idea of a swim not appealing. The rats swamped the boatman and brought him down. A squealing mass of blood, man and rats hurled into the water.

"Now, that's better." The Mistress reassured herself and settled her robes about her. The rats surfaced and swam ashore. The Boatman did not. She grabbed the oars and started for the shore all the while tutting at the Boatman's arrogance in trying to kill her. The sweat was beading on her brow, souring her mood even more. She moored the boat and clambered onto the dock.

"For the love of Merfolk, that has set us back; we must be away now, my beauties. Away to the White City! We will have to take the Black Road, to make up the time." The Boatman's shack stood empty as his chewed and slashed body was carried away by the river.

Chapter 32
Malya

Malya and her mother finished their breakfast, cleared the hut of dishes and pots and gathered their things.

"Mother, what shall I pack for this journey?" Malya asked softly.

"Not much, child, just a little food and your blanket."

"Oh." Was all Malya could muster.

"Come now. The suns are high and we must leave without being seen." Malya looked at her mother and was about to ask why but thought better of it. Koiya had given nothing away as to the place she was going and how long she would be away so Malya thought an answer unlikely.

Koiya and her daughter crept from their hut and slipped through the village unseen. The children were at the river swimming and most of the adults were busy in the marshes collecting eggs and herbs. Before they could make the last turn the old man stepped out in front of them

"Oh! Hello." Koiya stuttered, caught off guard.

"She leaves then?" The old man stated, turning to Malya. "She will do well. I have faith."

"Yes. She leaves." Koiya whispered.

"Many blessings upon you, child." With that the old man turned and left.

"Does he know what is to come?" Malya asked.

"Yes, child. He has trained many Sworn. But he loves you more than any other. You are his last. His time is soon over. Mother Nature will claim him soon." Koiya made to lead them on. Malya followed, sadness in her heart. She had grown to love the old man and knowing he may not be here on her return was hard to bear.

The two slowly made their way through the Marshlands. Koiya taking Malya's arm. Giving blessings to every Yok Yok tree they passed. Until they came to Grumble's tree. The side of the tree had been demolished. Rocks and stones flung far and wide. Roots had been ripped up and a large hole had been dug under the tree.

"For the love of Merfolk! What has happened here?" Malya cried.

Koiya ventured closer and peered into the whole. She could make out a small cave below, but nothing stirred.

"I don't know, my love. But nothing good. This kind of dishonour to a Yok Yok tree is unheard of. We must be away. Something bad has happened here."

The two women fled the scene. Malya's senses alert for danger. Koiya led them towards the river. She stopped sharply and led Malya to a patch of bushes and bundled her in.

"We will rest here awhile. Let us eat and drink and say our goodbyes." Koiya was breathing heavily her legs cramping from the forced retreat. Age was not her friend.

Malya was becoming alarmed. The Yok Yok tree's violation had shaken her and hiding in the bushes with her mother was only causing her more concern. Koiya took out the food they had packed and shared it. Malya took hers and nibbled at it. She had no appetite for food, but she could see her mother's relief as she ate.

"What now?" Malya asked, praying for an answer.

"Malya, listen to what I tell you, child. You are to go to the Vine Island. There you will have to pick."

"Pick what, mother. The vine island, but there is nothing there." Malya stared at her mother.

"You are to pick a serpent to bond with." Before Malya could speak Koiya continued.

"You are Serpent Sworn Malya. You will become one with the natural world, tracking and hunting, beasts will be drawn to you." Koiya became silent, letting Malya take it all in.

"Serpent!" Malya whispered. "I knew being Serpent Sworn meant I was at one with animals and plants. Allowing my senses to become heightened. But to bond with a snake! How am I meant to do that mother?" Malya's eyes where wide with fear.

"Calm yourself, my love. You were born for this. I cannot help you in this matter. You will know what to do. You have been trained by the best."

Malya closed her eyes. She knew her training was complete. There was nothing left for the old man to teach her. She was Serpent Sworn. She could do this.

"Now, we rest until the suns are a little lower, then I will take you to the Boatman. He knows what to do." Koiya handed her child the water skin and encouraged her to drink. Locking away her own fears. *Darkness comes*, she thought. *Mistress please protect my daughter.*

After a while Koiya packed away the little food that was left and gently clasped Malya's hands.

"We go now, my beauty. There is no more time."

She led Malya from the bushes and they walked towards the docks. Malya looked around nervously. She could tell something odd had happened here, and not that long ago. The air smelt of vermin and the docks had no sounds of anything living, no creature stirred. They stepped onto the wooden walkway and approached the boat house.

"Hello!" Koiya called tentatively. There was no response.

Malya could feel danger. All her training was telling her to flee. They crept closer to the Boathouse door, Malya's hand gripping her mother's arm. "Hello!" Koiya called out again. There was no answer. "We cannot delay. You must reach the Island by nightfall. You must row yourself." Koiya whispered. *Whatever happened here was not good*, she thought, feeling panicked.

"What! But I don't want to go to the Vine Islands alone. There are rumours, tales of people never returning, you know that, mother, please!" Malya started to edge backwards.

"Take the river downstream. Pass the Rock Isle, then the Woodland Isle. The last is Vine Island. It will be shrouded in mist by nightfall, and you don't have much time." Koiya was coaxing her daughter to the small boat, bobbing on the river.

"But, mother, this is all too soon, I'm scared!"

"I know, child, but the sooner you are away from here, the safer you will be."

Koiya ushered the shaking Malya into the little boat and passed her the oars.

"You will be fine rowing, my love, you are strong and the current will make the journey swift."

"Mother!" Malya almost screamed. Koiya stopped and grasped her daughter's hand.

"I know you are scared and confused, but all will be well. Row to the Vine Island, make you way to the centre and find the giant stone's. Now, go. And remember I love you. I will be waiting for your return every day." And with that Koiya turned away and hobbled into the marshes. Malya stared after her mother and fought back tears as she picked up the oars.

"I am Serpent Sworn. The land and I are one. I can do this," she whispered as she heaved on the oars and picked up the river's current.

Chapter 33
The Grey

The Grey had seen the Blood Wing, had followed it for as long as he could. He now searched the forest for Jengo. He must make his report.

The Grey was the largest of all forest wolves. A tracker like no other. He took no mate and fathered no litter. The hunt was his life. He was first born, healthy, strong, a son to be proud of. But The Grey had other ideas. Jengo had been born second. His sense of pack was ferocious and the brothers where soon at odds. The Grey was the rightful leader, but he knew Jengo would do a better job than he. The elders wanted no part of The Grey's comings and goings. Sometimes for months he would travel the lands following his quarry. He loved the freedom, the feeling of him against the world. He had no time for the whining of others, the bickering over dens and territories. He was free, and he was alive.

Jengo had allowed him to remain a part of the pack, against the better judgement of most. He was his brother and in times of need he was valuable. When The Mistress had told Jengo that the Sworn were to bond he had sent word to The Grey, that his help was needed, and, on his word, he had returned.

The Grey approached his brother's den with stealth and grace.

"Jengo. Brother. I have news." Jengo startled at the voice of his brother.

"Grey, please come close. You are welcome here. What news?" Jengo knew his brother would not fail him.

"A Blood Wing. Over the marshes."

"What! In the daylight? This is grave news, grave news indeed. It would appear someone or something has minions in place." Jengo knew he must investigate for The Mistress. The Mistress must complete her tasks. He must deal with this alone.

"What would you have me do, brother?" The Grey replied, staying a good distance from Shenka. Her dislike obvious.

109

"We must travel the Black Road; it's the only way to reach the Marshlands quickly. We must search out any trouble there. Whatever that Blood Wing was looking for he must have found it."

"As you wish." The Grey turned and made his way to the forest brush, there he rested while Jengo said his goodbyes.

"Shenka, gather the others. See them safe. Then go to the elder's den. Inform them of what has been seen and where we head. I shall meet The Mistress at the edge of the White City as planned and inform her of this news. Be safe, my love." Jengo nuzzled Shenka's face with his then turned to his brother.

"Lead on, Grey. We have not time to spare." With that the two majestic wolves, one dark and one light, rushed into the forest.

Jengo let The Grey take the lead through the forest. Brown wolf following grey as they streaked through the trees. At last the brush thinned and they came to the edge of the Black Road.

"Are you sure you want to do this, brother?" The Grey asked sniffing the air.

"Yes, we must. I must meet The Mistress at the edge of the White City just after nightfall. This is the only way we will make it to the Marshlands and back to her in time. If there is danger afoot she needs to know." Jengo placed a determined paw on the rough, black surface of the formidable road and turned to The Grey.

"Which way, brother?"

"The Blood Wing flew from the west. From the heart of the Marshlands."

"Lead the way." Jengo allowed The Grey to set off first. His knowledge of the Black Road was vast.

The two wolves sped down the road, ever alert for danger. The Black Road had been torn up in places, even built on by some. But all now had deserted the idea of taming it. Bridges had been slung across it. Tunnels dug underneath. But still the Black Road prevailed, driving back its enemies with its unforgiving feeling of doom.

The Grey suddenly halted, bringing Jengo to a skid beside him.

"Quiet now, Jengo! Look! Humans!" The Grey had caught the scent of Malya and her mother scampering for the bushes. "Something has unnerved them. I can smell their fear." The Grey stated, sniffing the breeze. "Careful now. Let us track where they have come from. Whatever has them hiding in bushes may be what we seek." Jengo and The Grey crept off the Black Road and into the Marshlands.

They stalked over boggy rivulets and through stubby grasses, retracing the human's tracks. They came across the destroyed Yok

Yok tree and both came to a sudden stop. The scene before them unfathomable.

"This cannot be!" The Grey snorted with anger at the desecration.

"Brother, who would dare such an act?" Jengo scanned the area, his hackles rising.

"Let us be on our highest guard. I smell wolf!" The Grey had picked up the scent of humans, of The Mistress and her pack but the overwhelming smell of wolf had him fearful.

"Are there any from your pack that hunt this far out?" The Grey questioned his brother.

"No. No pack comes here, it is not our land."

"Then who? Maybe a loner?"

"I know of no such wolf." They both stared into each other's eyes both thinking the same thing but neither daring to speak his name. "This must be what the Blood Wing was looking for. I must retake the Black Road if I am to meet The Mistress in time. Brother, would you join me? I know she will value your skills in this matter." The Grey took a moment to consider.

"For you, brother, I will come. But I will stay only as long as my help is needed."

The two brothers headed once more for the Black Road, ever present, never welcoming, but a tool of speed for the brave.

Chapter 34
Manuk

Deep within the Island, within the cave, within the vines, an egg stirred. It gently tipped from side to side. The snakes swayed and hissed encouragingly. A tiny crack winked its way from top to bottom, reaching out around the egg. Manuk coiled and writhed inside. Small flakes of shell began to peel away revealing a soft sack. Manuk nuzzled against the walls of his confinement, bristling his scales. At last the sack tore open and the tiny, green and brown snake slithered from within.

"We are here to serve you, great one." The snakes all hissed as one. "She will come, and we will be ready."

Manuk uncoiled his body and raised his tiny, hooded head. His eyes of piercing blue scanned the cave.

"Hear me now!" Manuk hissed. "My name is Manuk. I am now head of this nest! You will serve only me!" He let the demand sink in, for he knew he had little time before they turned against him and they all must serve.

"We serve only The Mistress." Came back the answer.

"The Mistress and I are one. The girl comes. Do you need to be reminded what happens to traitors?" Manuk could feel himself growing; soon he would be full size. *I must install fear. I must take control,* he thought.

The snakes had started to edge from their concealment, Manuk's small form was no threat to them. The brave amongst them started to lean in close. Manuk's scales where breaking away with the speed at which he grew. He whipped and flicked his body to free it from its old skin.

"Why should we serve you, new comer? You are small and weak!" A fat python had drawn close to Manuk. Its head held high.

"You think me helpless and weak because I have yet to grow, python?" Manuk had doubled in size but the python still towered over him.

"As you know in our world only the strong survive." The python flicked his forked tongue at Manuk, smelling for fear. Manuk turned his face to the python, all the time his body growing, expanding. Fresh scales and skin stretching.

"I shall forgive this insolence only once. Bow to me and I shall spare your life."

"Bow to you? NEVER!" As quick as lightening the python lunged for Manuk, its many coils ready to squeeze and crush. Manuk had the python in his jaw before the first coil sprang. He released the limp, dead body and rose high above the cave floor.

"Does anyone else challenge my place?" Manuk swept his blue eyes around the hissing vines.

"No Manuk, we serve only you."

"Very well. Let us prepare." Manuk's large head was covered in perfect scales of greens and browns. His body was sleek with muscle. The king of the cobras had returned.

Chapter 35
Malya

Malya had been rowing for some time and had passed two islands when a third came into view. Her hands were blistered and the sweat that had drenched her tunic and skirt was now uncomfortably dry, itchy and sore. The little rowboat skipped and skidded on the river as Vine Island loomed ahead. Her mother had been right; as the light faded the mist had wafted up from the water and hung around the island's edge like a soft sheet. With the mist came a cold breeze which chilled her and her teeth started to chatter. She pulled on the oars and the boat headed out of the current and towards the shore. The little boat bumped and bounced against the long-twisted vines that wove their way out into the river. Malya struggled to keep control of the little craft. Eventually she wedged it between two tree branches and secured it with a piece of rope from inside the boat.

"Now what?" Malya asked herself trying to see through the thick fog. Malya pulled out the woven blanket from her travelling sack and huddled it around her shoulders.

"There is no way I'm going in there at night, in this fog." She sulked.

"I'll wait for sunrise, right here in this boat. Thank you very much." Malya felt angry. Angry she was here instead of asleep in her mother's hut amongst her family. Angry the Boatman had let them down. Angry her mother had left her, clueless and alone. She nursed her bad mood and drifted off to sleep, alone in the small boat rocking at the island's edge.

Malya woke a few hours later with a stiff neck and cramped legs, another reason to feel angry. She stood and shook out her blanket and drank deeply from her water skin. The fog had started to clear. *I might as well get this over with,* she thought sulkily to herself. She checked to make sure the rope was secure then she headed out.

The ground was harsh on her bare feet. The vines were tough and sharp. She studied the trees and mud around her, smelling the air and listening for animals of any kind. The air smelt of dampness. The trees were wild and unforgiving. As for animal life, she could sense none. Malya clambered over thick vines and came to a mud track. She bent down to study the little prints left in the wet mud.

"Well, someone's been here recently." Malya pondered standing and studying the vegetation around her. "A single person, heavy on their feet, a cane or walking stick to aid them." Malya spoke to herself noticing the small, deep holes left by The Mistress's cane.

"One set of prints onto the island and one leading out." Malya started along the track slowly, quietly, observing as she went. After a short time she could hear water. Not the rushing of a river, more the quick surge of a brook or stream. The vines began to thin and she came to a small, wooden bridge, Muddy footprints crusted onto the bridge told Malya that a person had crossed here. She chose to follow.

The serpents stirred in the cave.

"She comes. She is near."

Malya crossed the bridge and stared in awe at the huge, stone henge that stood on top of a clearing ahead. She faltered and sank to the floor.

"I can't do this. I'm not strong enough for this." She whispered to herself as fat tear drops splashed from her chin onto the mud. As she rubbed her face and stared glumly around, she caught a whisper on the breeze. Malya sat up right and turned her ear towards the echoing sound.

"Come to us child. We are whom you seek." The serpents were drawing her in with their chant.

She stood and listened hard. The voices seemed to be coming from the great stone monument. She was scared. The thought of being alone amongst the stones was making her nervous, but the voices were too much to resist. She started up the slope to the henge. Her toes sinking into the wet mud. She reached the stones and stood still to listen. "You are safe here, little one, do not fear us." The serpent's voices rich and smooth flowed from the ground beneath Malya's feet.

She made her way to the centre of the henge. A stone tablet on the ground looked out of place. She crouched down to examine it.

"Is this where I'm supposed to be?" Malya questioned the mammoth stones. No answer came from the giants of time. She looked around, lost and scared she prayed for answers.

"Down here our, sweet child. We are waiting." The voices swam their way from the stone tablet.

Malya ran her hand over the smooth stone. The disc started to tremor, to move. Malya jumped back and crouched low, ready to run. The disc slid to one side revealing a stone stairway, then all was still. Her breath was coming in short, sharp gasps. Her hands had gripped the earth so hard she came away with handfuls of mud as she stood.

"Do not fear. Come join us. Pick." The soft voices had become so mesmerizing Malya felt herself tip toe towards the stairway and peer down. The stairs were narrow and damp and they curled round and round. She carefully placed a foot onto the top step and took a breath.

"Mother. I trust you. If you think I can do this, then I can." Malya wiped her hot brow with her hand, stuck out her chin and descended the stairway.

Malya tip-toed carefully down each step, her bare feet making no sound. She smelt the air. Damp, but not unpleasant. She felt no breeze, heard no water. She reached the bottom and paused, allowing her eyes to adjust to the mottled light. The cave was encrusted with vines. They hung from the ceiling. They flowed down the walls and across the floor. A small, clear path, free from vines, lead to the centre of the cave. Malya tentatively made her way along it. She made a conscious decision not to touch the vines. Some looked poisonous, their leaves thick with red spines. When she reached the centre she looked up. Long shafts of light leaked into the cave where the large stones outside were embedded down into the cave. It gave the place a twilight feel. Malya crouched down and scooped a handful of earth from the floor and smelt it. She smelt serpent and a small hint of herbs. She examined the floor closer and found tiny footprints the same as those she had found on her journey here from the shore.

"Well, I'm here." Malya whispered to herself.

As soon as she had uttered the words the vines began to move. They seemed to sway and writhe. One by one the serpents wound their way from their hiding places. Malya caught her breath. She had never seen so many snakes in all her life. Their colours and glistening scales where mesmerizing. She started to stumble backwards towards the stairway, then remembered why she was here.

"You must choose, child. One of us is for you and you are for one of us." The rhythmic voices of the snakes rose from the vines.

"Choose! But how? You are all, well…snakes!" Malya almost screamed.

"Look at us, child. Look into our eyes! Choose! Choose!" The snakes chanted back.

Malya swallowed and calmed her shaking hands. She took a small step to her right and found herself face to face with a bright, blue snake.

"Is it I you seek?" The snake hissed.

Malya looked deep into its eyes and found only a vicious creature, skinny and vengeful.

"I think not." Malya squeaked, starting to feel a little claustrophobic. She turned to her left. A big, fat red snake with black strips weaved its head back and forth before her.

"What about me? I will serve you well."

Again Malya looked into its red, nasty eyes. She saw greed and gluttony

"No! You are not the one for me." Malya started to feel a little braver. She swept her eyes around the bobbing serpent's heads all eager and needy. She noticed one wasn't bobbing. Its body and head were relaxed, set back from the wall of vines.

"You!" Malya pointed as she spoke. All snake heads turned and hissed together. The quiet snake uncurled itself and sank to the floor.

"Why me, small one? There are snakes here that can kill with a single bite. They would protect you well." Manuk slithered his way to Malaya's feet.

"I can protect myself." Malya said, chin high, feeling mocked.

"Very well. Why me?" Manuk asked again, testing the girl.

Malya looked into Manuk's eyes. She knew instantly he was the one. "You hold no anger. You want for nothing. You kill to sustain life, not for pleasure. We are one, you and I." Malya shook her head as if the words she had just spoken came from another's mouth. A wise and knowing mouth.

Manuk let out a deep, rich laugh.

"Yes, Malya we are one. I will teach you mother earth's secrets. Together we will walk her lands and all creatures will bend to our will."

Malya reached out her small delicate hand and ran her fingers down Manuk's back. His scales were soft and smooth. His body cool and comforting. She extended her arm and Manuk curled his way along it. He wrapped himself around her waist. Malya felt a wave of knowledge and power flow through her body. They were one.

Malya threw her head back and shouted. "I Malya, daughter of Koiya, tribal witch of the Marshlands choose. I choose this serpent as my own." Malya found she was screaming, screaming at the top of her lungs for all to hear. The other snakes bowed and humbled themselves onto the floor. Malya stood knee deep in writhing, twisting serpents and let the power of Manuk take her.

Chapter 36
Koiya

Koiya poked the white ashes of the cooking fire. Her children were sleeping. She threw the little stick onto the ground and went to rise.

"Koiya, may I speak with you?" Lana, a caregiver from the outer huts, stood at the edge of the clearing.

"Yes, sister, please come. Sit." Koiya lowered herself back down. Lana crossed to the burnt-out cooking fire and paused.

"I bring sad news." Lana offered no more.

Koiya knew it was the old man. She had felt his spirit slip away earlier that evening and had been waiting for this moment.

"It's okay, Lana, I felt him leave us. We must prepare his pyre. Wake the men and have them build now. We cannot delay. Come help me stand, I must gather my things for the ritual." Lana reached down and gently helped her to her feet. "He must be replaced, and quickly. Are there any in the village who show promise?"

"Just one. His name is Rubear. He built a friendship with the old man this summer. They fished and hunted together. The old man took him under his wing after his mother died."

"Good. I shall test him to see if he is worthy of the knowledge."

"Yes, wise one." Lana bowed her head respectfully.

"Go now. There is much to prepare." Koiya headed towards her hut, wishing Malya was here to help her.

In the bushes, Rubear, covered his mouth as he sniggered. The little red scorpion scuttled onto his shoulder.

"Quiet now, small one! Our queen has put a lot of time and effort into you. We don't want our plans ruined because of your sniggering." The scorpion stretched his head towards Rubear's ear, "A little more respect. You must pass the witch's test if you are to receive the knowledge, child. You will cry on hearing of the old man's death and you will cry well. Do I make myself clear, stupid boy?" The scorpion was glowing a dark red with frustration. Why his queen had picked a little boy for this task, he would never know.

"When the knowledge is mine you will not speak to me like that. You will fear me!" The boy's hateful whisper had caught the little scorpion off guard.

"Just do as she bids, and no one will suffer." The scorpion hissed, calling the boy's bluff.

Rubear reached up and flicked the scorpion from his shoulder. He hid his little bottle of poison in his cloth bag and turned to walk back to the village.

"Boy!" The scorpion had found his way back to Rubear's feet. Rubear stopped and peered down at The Queen's little servant. "You know what will happen if you fail."

Rubear squashed the scorpion into the earth with the sole of his sandal. Making sure he heard his skeleton crunch.

"I will not fail, pathetic creature. The knowledge will be mine." Rubear walked from the marshes and into the village. A small, lost-looking boy of six. Alone now, his mother and the old man had passed. A small, empty poison bottle at the bottom of his bag.

Koiya slowly gathered the things she needed for the passing ceremony. The old man's death would be a great loss to the village and Koiya knew he would be hard to replace. She had laid out the little bottles of oils and herbs she needed to purify his body for burning and sat down heavily on Malya's empty sleeping-cot. Her mind drifted to her own life and her own mother.

Koiya's father had been the head shaman and had had many strong sons to follow him. The last child his wife had given birth to was a girl. Tiny and perfect, she was his pride and joy. Many thought her weak and stupid. But her father knew she was watchful and careful with her words. Two of her brothers had been killed in a hunting accident and she remembered being carried, tied to her mother's back, as her mother wept tears into every fire she made. It was supposed to cleanse the souls of her dead sons.

Koiya's love for her father knew no bounds and she would climb on to his shoulders and insist on being carried around the Marshlands, high in the sky. He would teach her all the names of the beasts and plants that the Marshes had to offer. Her mother would tut and scorn at the twigs and leaves caught in her hair after such a trip but a little wink from her father deafened her ears to her mother's words.

Her brothers had grown to men and her mother was sure her husband would pick the eldest to follow in his footsteps as shaman. She would fuss over him and boost his ego. So when her father had picked her, her mother withdrew from her and eyed her suspiciously wherever she went. The blow to her brother's pride was too much for him to bear so he had taken a wife from a far village and never returned. This only deepened her mother's dislike for her.

The years passed and Koiya's knowledge of herbal lore and animal care grew vast. Her father had been a gentle and patient teacher. Between them they knew only each other. Koiya's mother grew bitter and jealous and soon refused to leave their family hut and would brood and curse in the confines of her bed.

Koiya grew into a beautiful, confident woman thanks to her father's guidance and love. She tended her mother's needs, choosing to ignore the hateful spite that came from her mouth. Her remaining brothers all married and when her mother passed away it was she who performed her passing ceremony. She put every drop of love she had into the words and was rewarded when her mother's spirit came to her in a dream and begged forgiveness for her hateful ways.

Koiya had married a young hunter from another village but they remained living in her family hut as her father's health was failing and she was to become the village witch upon his death. When his time had come, Koiya had wept for weeks. Every fire she had made was drenched in her tears and her new role as witch was a burden.

Her spirits were lifted only when she found out she was with child. She swore to herself if it was a girl she would love her every second of every day. Her child would not endure the torment her own mother had seen fit to punish her with. And in the dead of night little Malya had slipped into the world. That night her father came to her also in a dream and had shown her the child's future. The path Malya was to take was like no other but her courage would save the world from a great evil and Koiya must see her fit to follow her destiny.

Koiya rose from the cot and wiped small, salty tears from her chin. She gathered her jars and headed out into the sun. The old man's body deserved the best care and Koiya was determined he should have it.

Chapter 37
Selena

Selena looked out across the city, the city she loved, the city she had known all her life. She couldn't get her thoughts in order. Her grandmother had been acting weirdly all during dinner, placing a key in her hand and practically throwing her out of the dining room.

"What am I supposed to do with this?" Selena turned to Minn and held out the silver key.

"It's not for me to say, miss; we serving folk know nothing of royal affairs."

"Minn, please, you know I think of you more like a mother." Selena turned back towards the window.

"Did your grandmother not tell you what it is for?" Minn's voice was soft and gentle.

"No. Just that she will send for me in the morning, I am to dress plainly and speak to no one about the key."

"Then why are you speaking of it, my lady?"

Selena blew out a long breath, "I don't know. You're about the only person I trust these days, and Jug, but he gets enough ribbing just being friends with me. I can't drag him into all this." Selena glanced down at the giant oak where she had arranged to meet him earlier that evening. She closed her eyes and wished she had gone to play Rick Rack, instead of going to dinner with her grandmother.

"Come now miss, to bed with you, you look plain tired out." Minn gently pulled Selena's arm towards the giant ancestral bed, its drapes and covers all woven in rich silks of blues and silvers. Selena really was very tired and the bed looked so warm and cosy that she was happy to be led by the arm and bundled into the sheets.

"Now sleep, my lady, tomorrow things may seem a little simpler."

"Thank you, Minn, Please leave the lamp on a little longer." Minn smiled and lowered her hand from the lamp.

"Okay, little bird, a while longer." Minn slipped from the room as quietly as a whisper.

Selena lay back against the soft pillows and sighed, "The Mistress. Now who, for the love of Merfolk was she?"

Jug gently closed the Rick-Rack board and lent back heavily in his seat. The evening was hot and the shade of the oak tree had the flies swarming for the coolness that the trees canopy offered. He wasn't angry that Selena hadn't shown up for the game, just disappointed. Having a princess for a friend, a good friend was bad enough but a Sworn Princess, well, that's another kind of hard. Jug rubbed his prickly chin with his giant hands and rose out of his seat. "Nothing for it," he whispered to himself, "but a few ales down the Clashing Swords with Sweet Lillie." Jug smiled, then he thought of Selena, "I may just swing by later, just to check she wasn't delayed and turned up late." The flies swarmed his face as if they berated his foolish musings.

Chapter 38
The Mistress

The Mistress shook her robes and rubbed her face. "That nasty little boatman has cost me daylight hours. Now I will be delayed. Whatever possessed me to trust him I'll never know. Never mind, we are all in one piece and the White City is not too far." The Mistress addressed the river-soaked rats, all huddled together and shaking. "Come, my loves, the Black Road calls again." The pack stared up at their Mistress looking as miserable as sin. "Oh, come now, a little water and you are defeated. It cannot be." The Mistress reached into her robe and pulled out a small packet. On hearing its rustle the pack pricked up its ears and scurried to her feet. "Oh! How quickly you perk for a little snack." The Mistress emptied the packet onto the ground and the rats pounced on the pile of mealworms, a juicy treat indeed. "Shall we be away now?" The Mistress inquired with a small chuckle. The rats chattered their reply. "Good. Because Balboar is becoming restless in my pocket and I fear the next part of our journey will be the most taxing."

The Mistress and her pack travelled the Black Road. Only the brave journeyed by the Black Road. Thieves and those of the Black Craft ventured here, looking for naive victims. The Mistress's only tool here was speed. They whisked along the bumpy, black surface like the rolling current of a river after a storm.

"Forward now, my loves! This is no place to be at night!" The Mistress knew the dangers here and a battle of crafts felt like an effort when she still had work to complete in the White City.

The Black Road had large potholes in it that had allowed thorns and nightshades to prosper. The story of its creation had been told time and time again, turning fact into legend and legend into myth. But The Mistress knew the truth. It had been built by a race of greedy people, people that had eventually annihilated themselves and the entire natural world around them. The energy here was bad; it banished all hope, that's why it attracted only bad things.

They finally reached the fringe of the White City, its farming lands opening out like a welcoming hand. The Mistress sighed with relief. Her pack was all alive with not a flash of craft used.

"To the castle! Come now. Time for rest later!" The Mistress stepped off the Black Road and the pack followed.

As The Mistress and her ever-faithful rats reached the edge of the White City, darkness was falling.

"Be watchful, my loves, darkness brings extra patrols. We will enter through the front gate. The guards will think me just a tinker with her wares."

As they approached the gate, three guards barred the way. "You know what to do." She whispered. She blew onto the crystal at the end of her cane until it began to glow. She waved it across the top of the rats and chanted.

"Claw to paw. Fur to fluff. Mother allow me this little bluff. Rats they will be, but puppies they will see."

The rats fur started to soften, their flesh started to plump. Their long snake like tails started to curl. Their faces bubbled and swelled, whiskers started to protrude from their cheeks. The Mistress smiled as she looked down on an excitable pack of puppies, all bright-eyed and ready to play.

"Now remember this is only temporary. Don't go getting yourselves attached to humans. Their hands will be eager to stroke and tickle." The Mistress strode towards the gate. A horde of playful puppies at her feet.

"Halt! Who goes there?"

"My name is Trader Hen Peck. I'm here to trade my pups in the morn." She swept a hand across the now uncontrollable pack. With that the pups bounded for the guards.

"Hello there, little fellows." All three guards bent to pet the pups. The Mistress smiled at the foolishness of men.

She strode on through the gate, she took the whistle from around her neck and blew. All at once the pups stuck their heads in the air and barked.

"That's a clever trick, old trader. How much you selling these little terrors for then?" The largest of the guards bent to pick up a pup. As soon as the puppy's legs were off the ground it snapped and snarled in the guard's face, baring his little sharp teeth. The guard gasped in surprise and tossed him back down, quick smart. "Forget it!" He shouted. "Don't want no flea-ridden mutt anyway."

The Mistress smiled and beckoned her pack.

"You sure I can't tempt you, kind sir?" She teased. The guard made an unkindly gesture and went back to his post. "Shame. His back side could do with a nip." She almost giggled like a girl then caught herself. "Come, pups. To the castle."

Mistress and pups made their way through the City, with each step the pups shed their large, loving eyes and their wagging tails. Sleeker and sleeker they became until a pack of rats followed a robed stranger again.

"Hey! You there! What business have you so near the Palace?" The Mistress froze. A drunk and swaying Jug stood behind her. Angry that he had been abandoned by the Princess that night, and full of cheap ale, he had made his way back to the old oak, just to check Selena hadn't turned up. "Hey, old wench, I'm talking to you." Jug's hand ventured towards his sword.

"Come now. There's no need for violence." She slowly turned, eyes ablaze. "You have seen nothing here tonight, young man." Jug's hand fell loose by his side as The Mistress stared her mesmerizing stare. "Oh! But wait. You are in love." Jug continued to sway. "Yes, I can see. The Princess holds your heart. I may have a use for you." She stepped closer raising her cane. "You will carry a token for me, boy, and when you hear its calling, you will come." The Mistress tapped the end of her cane against Jug's chest and a soft blue light melted into his heart. Jug staggered sideways into the castle wall and tumbled backwards, tripping over his own feet until he landed in the gutter, swiftly falling into a deep and drunken slumber. "Your head will be sore in the morn, boy, but your heart shall carry my token and at my calling you shall answer." The Mistress turned to her pack. "This way. If I'm not mistaken the fat fool Illiwig lives in that hovel over there. Steel yourselves, my pretties, this will be our biggest challenge yet."

Chapter 39
Grumble

Grumble was woken by the cold, sharp shock of freezing sea water being thrown over his tiny body. His eyes snapped open. As his vision cleared he thought himself still deep in his dreams. For this could not be. He was chained and shackled and aboard a ship. Grumble's little body shook with cold. His tiny feet and hands were numb from their tight chains. His back was sore and cramped. He could not fathom his predicament.

"Let me fill you in, small one. You look so confused." A woman's voice drifted over his shoulder. Grumble heard small footsteps next to him and curled himself into a small ball.

"Look at me, Grumble, for I have a deal to offer you."

Grumble, petrified with fear, opened one slit of an eye. Being away from his tree and the Marshlands was so alien to him he thought he had truly died and was in some kind of hell.

"Look at me, Grumble. I won't ask nicely again."

Grumble slowly opened both eyes and gasped in horror. For before him stood the most beautiful human he had ever seen, she was holding a long, thin blade in one hand and in the other one of Grumble's own root tentacles. Blood dripped from it to pit-a-pat onto the wooden deck. It was freshly severed. Grumble fainted.

Grumble could take no more. The cold and noise had driven him half mad and the longing for his warm tree cave had him sobbing. He had woken cold and alone on the harsh floor of the ship. "Please, anyone, help me!" His small, almost silent voice was heard by no one. Eventually they came. Loud, thumping footsteps, deep nasty voices. Grumble had screwed his eyes tight shut and trembled with fear.

"This one's done. You can't cut anything off without him fainting. She got two words out of him. Got her proper mad. Throw him in a sack and make sure he's packed up with the supplies. We leave for Boar Keep, immediately." Grumble felt rough, large hands pick him up by his roots and felt the scratchy sack being tied around him. He prayed for death to take him but his prayer was not answered. Grumble was thrown, bashed and banged for what seemed like a lifetime until he passed out again.

Chapter 40
Koiya

Rubear sat amongst the other mourners around the old man's pyre. It had been a passing to remember. All the families had brought food and wine. The pyre was high and built with care. Koiya had chanted the words with love and respect. Now many had left and the air was chill. The pyre just smouldering ash. Rubear noticed Koiya approach him but chose to stay seated, his head hung low.

"Rubear. I am Koiya tribal witch here in this village. Would you mind if we spoke awhile?"

Rubear just shrugged his shoulders, pretended to sniff back tears and waited. Koiya lowered herself down next to him and took a small flower from her hair.

"Do you know what flower this is, Rubear."

So, Rubear thought, *the test would start now. She's not even going to let the old man's ashes get cold before she tries to test me. Well, witch, let's see how good I am at falsehood.*

Rubear wiped his eyes and looked at the flower. Again he shrugged his shoulders.

"Take another look, child. What's its name, this little flower?" Koiya knew she had to be gentle as his loss was plain for all to see. But the time had to be now.

"Sunfire." Rubear mumbled.

"Good, Rubear. Do you know where it grows?" Koiya asked softly.

"The old man loved to pick those. He said they helped him keep warm when his bones hurt." Rubear hung his head again.

"Where did he pick them, Rubear?" Koiya asked, still cautious not to make him cry again.

"By the river. We used to fish there me and him. He was kind to me." Rubear started to sob. Little, small sobs.

"I know you feel much pain, child, but it will pass with time. Would you like to come to my hut for the night? I have a spare cot and a fire is warming the place as we speak." Koiya really needed to test the boy and she couldn't do it here.

Rubear had his foot in the door, he knew. "Yes please, lady. I am really tired."

Koiya rose and offered the small, tired, little boy her hand. "I even have a large, soft blanket. You can keep it if you like it."

Rubear's mind was plotting and scheming but his face was sullen and scared. Dirty smudge marks ran down his face from crying and he took small faltering steps as he let Koiya lead him to her hut.

The small, red scorpion watched from the overhanging branches of a nearby tree. For no matter how many times the boy had killed him The Queen's magic always brought him back. Rubear had pulled his tail off and his legs and had even thrown him in a fire and watched till he had popped. The pain was real and the little, red scorpion was tired of dying over and over again but he must serve.

"You have done well, boy. The Queen will be told of your loyalty." And with that it scurried down the trunk and disappeared into the Marshes, leaving Rubear to take his test.

Chapter 41
Illiwig

Illiwig leant back in his chair and looked around his small hovel. Five years Illiwig had been living in his little home, a small lean-to made of wood and sticks snuggled up against the great White Palace. Most folk would walk straight by without a glance. It seemed like it didn't exist, but that was the idea. Illiwig burped and stared at the remains of his meal, a feast for Illiwig. Since he had been sent word that it was time for his service to end he had spoilt himself. A bag of snails, a bottle of mead and a loaf of fresh bread. *A feast indeed,* Illiwig thought, swinging his muddy boots from the table and brushing the crumbs from his tattered jacket. He felt the breast pocket and caressed the outline of the key. It had been in the same pocket for so long that the keys edges had worn away the fabric.

"This night, Illiwig, will turn the key. A good job I will do and be rewarded, rewarded in gold." Illiwig spoke to himself and smiled a huge, dirty smile. The day he had crossed paths with the wolf and been offered this service by The Mistress was a memory which had started to fade now.

TAP, TAP, TAP!

Illiwig sat up sharply.

"Illiwig, I know you are in there! Open up, now, fool!" Illiwig scrambled to his feet and knocked his scrappy plate to the floor. He stumbled to the door and quickly drew the bolt. In the doorway stood The Mistress, surrounded by a pack of rats. Pack is an understatement, the rats were the size of alley cats, groomed sleek and black, eyes narrow and spiteful, teeth sharp and bared. They bowed and grovelled at The Mistress's feet. Illiwig stared open-mouthed. "Move Illiwig, let me through!" Illiwig stepped aside as she entered his small home. The rats followed, a liquid blanket of vermin,

"I, I, I wasn't given a time. I am not prepared." Illiwig stuttered and garbled.

"It is of no concern to me that you are not prepared. The hour is now! Proceed man, quick!" Illiwig stepped aside and the rats swept in and surrounded The Mistress's feet. He fumbled in his pocket for the key. "Not here man! For the love of the Merfolk, take me to the wall." The Mistress's voice was sharp and forceful. Illiwig stumbled to the wall by the fire pit and reached out his shaky hand. He paused.

This is my moment, he thought. *I must be brave.*

The rats started to prickle and hiss. The Mistress stepped closer and Illiwig could smell earth and herbs and an overpowering smell of rat urine. She poked Illiwig in the shoulder several times with her cane.

"Are you unwell? What is the delay?" She asked. Illiwig startled. "I am fresh from the Marshlands, Illiwig, and time is precious."

"No Great One, it's just this moment, I have waited five years to see what is beyond this wall. No peek or glance has Illiwig taken. Good job I have done."

"Well then, let us not delay, man." Illiwig placed his hand on one of the faded bricks. The Mistress placed the tip of her cane next to his hand. The bricks started to rattle and shake. Dust dribbled and puffed from every edge, slowly, and with a great scrape, the bricks started to move backwards, one by one. They moved and clunked until the wall had concertinaed back on itself. An opening appeared in the centre of the wall. The rat pack swept forward almost knocking Illiwig to the floor, they piled up and surged forward. "Aside! I must enter first." The rats jerked to a halt and Illiwig moved to the edges of the opening. The Mistress stepped into the black space beyond the wall: The rats scrabbled after, followed by a dumbfounded Illiwig.

Illiwig let go the deep breath he hadn't realised he had been holding and scanned the room. Nothing, absolutely nothing. Just a small slitted window letting in gloomy light and one small wooden door. The Mistress tapped her cane against the stone floor and its crystal tip illuminated blue. The light flooded the corners of the room. Illiwig's eyes swept upwards. A small stairway could be seen in the corner, it twisted its way up and up. The tails of The Mistress's cloak swept up the first step. Illiwig hurried towards the stairs not wanting to be alone in the gloomy room, Illiwig could hear the rat's claws scrabble and scratch as they climbed the steps. Up, up and up Illiwig trudged, following the blue glow and the scratch, scratch of rat claws. He clutched the wall and swallowed, his throat dry and itchy.

"Illiwig, must I remind you of the duties you have sworn to perform." Her voice echoed down the stair well.

"No, no, I'm here, a moment please." Illiwig puffed.

"Fetch him!" She commanded. Illiwig could see a black shadow surging around the bend in the stairwell. Before he knew it, the rats had him; Illiwig was carried upon a stream of rats to the top of the stairs and dumped at The Mistress's feet. He felt giddy from his rat ambush and couldn't get his bearings; his feet became wobbly under him as he tried to stand.

"The key, Illiwig!"

Illiwig fumbled with fat fingers at his shirt pocket. "You do have it Illiwig, don't you?" She leaned in close, the herby smell of breath hit Illiwig's face.

"Yes, yes, it's in here!" Illiwig felt the cool touch of the key and wrenched it from his pocket in such haste he left it hanging from its bottom stitches. The Mistress stepped back and the rats cowered at her feet.

"Don't wave it around, Illiwig! You know I cannot touch it. The lock man! The lock!" She spat with anger. She was so, so tired it had been a long few days and this bumbling fool was testing the last of her patience.

Illiwig turned to his left. There, set into the stone wall was a door unlike anything he had ever seen. Solid silver carved and bejewelled, the door stood at least two men high. "Oh!" was all he could manage to say.

"Now! Illiwig!" The Mistress bristled with anger and the rats hissed and mobbed. Illiwig stepped forward and gently slid the key into the keyhole, he closed his eyes for this was his pay out, his big finale, his duty finished. The key made a small click as the lock turned, Illiwig let his hand fall to his side and waited. "Forward!" At her command the rats surged forward like molten fur and pressed their whole force against the door. With a hiss the door began to open. The smell of oil and metal flooded through the opening. Illiwig covered his mouth with his clammy hand. The rats and The Mistress hurried through the doorway, Illiwig made to follow. "Not for the likes of you, your duty is over, return to your hovel, I will be back within the hour. You will get your reward as promised." And with that the pack heaved the door shut leaving Illiwig alone on the landing.

Chapter 42
The Mistress

"Behave now Balboar. You know this is your last chance. If you fail this time you will go to the pit," The Mistress spoke as if to a child.

Her wizened hand felt into the pocket of her robe and pulled out a ball of silken cloth. The rats started forward. "Back now my beauties, back!" The rats shuffled back but hissed their displeasure. "Now! Where to start?" She looked around the room and spat with disappointment. "Well, so much for preparations, this place looks the same as it did fifteen years ago. Still, that's humans for you. Weak and forgetful of their duties."

The cloth ball in her hand started to heat and glow. "Patience, Balboar." She leant over and placed the ball in a silver holder on a table, in the centre of the room. The cloth slipped and spilled over the edge and was immediately swallowed up by the rats and placed back into The Mistress's pocket. There on the table in the silver holder was a crystal the size of a large egg. Its clear shine began to cloud with blues and whites, so vivid and swirling it was mesmerizing. A blue light, like the one from The Mistress's cane, began to glow from the crystal egg. The rat pack began to panic, they edged back as one and crouched low behind The Mistress.

"Come now, Balboar, I've never known you to be shy." A small chuckle escaped her lips.

"DO NOT BELITTLE ME FOR I AM THE GREAT BALBOAR. WHO HAS SUMMONED ME?" The swirling mass of colour in the crystal softened and formed the face of the great Balboar. It shone with power and glory and filled the crystal. The Mistress swung the cane up and smacked it down hard onto the crystal.

"You dare to raise your voice to me? Balboar!" The face in the crystal swung round to face who had summoned him.

"Merfolk be blessed! Mistress forgive me." Balboar grovelled.

The Mistress gave a tight smile and turned to her pack, "I wish to be seated." The pack sprang forward and engulfed a nearby stool, lurched forward and placed it behind her. She sat without any grace, "Now Balboar, what to do with you?"

"Mistress, please, the chance to serve again, please." The crystal egg glowed blue and bright as the bearded face of Balboar pleaded from within.

"I will choose Balboar. Last time you failed to bond, you failed your Sworn."

"But mistress, it was not my fault. The Merfolk they have ways. They can summon things you cannot imagine."

"Do you not think I can summon just as much pain for you, fool?"

"Yes, Mistress, but another chance, please. I will not fail this time. The great Balboar is at your service. Choose as you will, I will not raise objection."

The Mistress swept her blue, piercing eyes around the circular room. It was filled with weaponry the likes your eyes have never seen, swords, axes, blades and daggers. Shields and spears all silver and all dusty. The Mistress rested her eyes on a shield. "There, bring it to me." The pack swept the room and gathered up a large, silver shield. They struggled under its weight. "No! Way too heavy, this is a girl after all. There! That one." The rats circled the room as one and swept up a sword. "Bring it." The rats flowed up the table and placed the sword in front of The Mistress. "Yes, this will be a fine Sworn weapon don't you think, Balboar?"

But Balboar had his eye on an axe. "Balboar, you will not get another try with an axe." Balboar turned a disappointed face to The Mistress. *The axe! Oh, how I want the axe. That feeling of power as it sweeps through the air, the ease with which it can cleft a man in two*, Balboar thought.

The Mistress ran her finger along the dusty blade. "This will do." She lifted it up for Balboar to see.

"Yes Mistress, a fine sword." Balboar could not hide his disappointment.

"Come now Balboar, a weapon to make your own again. Let's not forget this is your last chance." Balboar knew he would do as The Mistress bade. He couldn't afford any more mistakes. He had already lost the life of one Blade Sworn child. He could not lose another. The pit was his only other option and nothing came back from there, ever.

"Yes Mistress, it is a fine weapon. I will bond with courage, strength and heart."

"You will, Balboar, you will." The Mistress rose and the pack instantly removed the stool and gathered ready at her feet. "Are you ready Balboar? We can't delay any longer."

"Yes Mistress, I am ready to serve."

The Mistress lent forward and grasped Balboar's crystal and with the other hand she swept up the sword. The rats broke away and fanned out each and every one bowing close to the ground and silent. Balboar closed his eyes, he knew what was to come. The sharp pain; the whirling confusion: the blast of memory from the sword. The Mistress raised both sword and crystal above her head and spoke with power and might. A sudden breeze whisked her robes around her feet.

"Hear me now, all that is Sworn! By the power of the Merfolk, the Fire Dragon and Serpent! By the grace of the high craft, I, Mistress of the forest, bind the Sworn Balboar to this blade only to be broken by God himself!" The Mistress slammed the sword's hilt onto the crystal and an almighty light of pure blue filled the room. The Mistress was thrown backwards, stumbled, but held onto the sword. She steadied herself and with both hands brought forward the mighty sword of White City.

Balboar tried to open his eyes, his face whirled and turned inside his crystal home, he focused his mind; he could feel the power and history of the sword rushing through him.

"Concentrate! Come on man, you've done this a thousand times!" Balboar counselled himself.

"Rise my beauties, behold the great sword! Behold the sword of Balboar!" The Mistress's voice was sharp and powerful; the rats squalled and chattered their teeth.

Balboar opened his eyes, he felt powerful, he felt alive. The sword in The Mistress's hand was gleaming with silver, the edge as sharp as glass. The silver hilt was decorated with images of warriors and battles and in the centre clasped and bound was a crystal the size of an egg. Blue and pure was the light that shone from it, for it contained Balboar the Sworn. Balboar opened his mouth and roared, "KNEEL, ALL THOSE WHO OPPOSE ME, FOR I AM BALBOAR, BALBOAR THE GREAT!"

Suddenly the room turned cold. The pack had their hackles raised. A shiver ran over The Mistress. "Quick my lovelies, return the sword to the rack. Balboar, you know what must be done. We must be away, for someone has spoken my name inside the castle wall. A penance must now be paid. The vows have been broken."

Chapter 43

"Forward! My beauties I can't get caught within the city walls. You know what price I will have to pay." The fleeing party of rats and Mistress flowed through the city streets at the speed and colour of rushing sewer water, winding and whispering round corners, over hovels and homes towards the city wall. The Mistress came to a sudden halt, the rats piling up behind her. The gates were guarded. *A little craft will see to this,* she thought. "Stay low, my beauties, quickly, against the wall, wait for my command." The Mistress instructed, she calmed herself and strode with ease towards the guard.

"Stop right there, wench!" the guard spoke with arrogance and authority,

The Mistress raised her cane, its blue light softly glowing as she approached the guard. She gently waved it back and forth in a slow, soothing motion. "Come now, man, there is no danger here. Be still. You saw no one tonight."

The guard was mesmerized by the blue light coming from the cane. "Yes miss, I saw no one tonight."

"You will let us pass unharmed then you will resume your duties, do you understand?" The guard nodded his head, completely under The Mistress's spell.

"Come now, my friends, quickly." The pack surged forward in a silent wave through the gate, The Mistress following with more stealth than her age allowed. Over fields and through orchards they fled until they reached the Kingdom's edge. The Black Road waited, as it waited for everyone. The Mistress crossed the bridge that spanned it and didn't look back.

"There! I see him! Quickly now." The Mistress gasped struggling for breath. At the forest's edge crouched a large wolf, hunched low to the ground, his sleek fur of brown and black blending with the forest's hues, four giant paws dug deep into the rich soil, his blue eyes leading The Mistress's way in the dark. Mistress and rats stumbled forward.

"Jengo, we must not delay, my name was spoken inside the city walls by a royal, tonight of all nights." The Mistress gasped. The giant wolf pricked his ears in alarm.

"Were you hurt, Mistress? Were you followed?" Jengo's voice was gruff and low, the rich sound of a pack leader. He raised his hackles and scanned the surrounding fields.

"No, the ceremony was completed, Balboar has made the blade his. Tomorrow the princess will pick and if he knows what is good for him she will pick wisely." The Mistress paused for breath, she suddenly stopped stone still and sniffed the air. "You can come out now, Grey. I know you are there." The Mistress's voice was flat and quiet.

From the dense brush slunk a low and silent wolf. The largest in the land and some say the most feared.

The Mistress bowed her head in respect and motioned, The Grey, to join them.

"Why are you hiding in bushes? You know I welcome your help whenever it is offered." The Mistress eyed him closely. Something was not right.

"I'm afraid I bring grave news, Holy One."

"Speak, wolf, there is only truth to be had here."

"As you know, Jengo called upon me when he heard the Sworn children were to bond. And I upheld my promise and came as quick as I could from the Drylands." The Grey glanced sideways at Jengo hoping he would pick up the tale. Jengo turned his head; it was The Grey's duty to report what he had seen.

The Mistress grew inpatient. "Yes, Yes!" She almost shouted.

"I was making the sweep of the Black Road as you requested, when I saw a Blood Wing." Before he could finish his sentence The Mistress flew forward and grabbed The Grey's jaw. She drew his face to hers and stared deep into his eyes.

"Don't fight me, Grey, let me see what you saw." The Mistress's eyes began to swirl. Blues of all hues and shades curled together and bore deep into The Grey's memory. The Mistress saw how he had tracked the Blood Wing to the Marshlands and returned to Jengo, how the two of them had taken the Black Road to search out any trouble. She was shaken to the core when they had set eyes upon the ruined Yok Yok tree and had joined him in sniffing the air, the smell of wolf so overpowered her that she released The Grey's jaw and stumbled backwards.

"Mistress!" Jengo was at her side in a second and allowed her to lean on him to catch her breath.

"The tree elf, what of the tree elf that lived there?" The Mistress snapped unable to fathom what she had seen.

"We saw no elf. Nothing was alive there. I would have sensed it." The Grey calmed his words. "I will help as long as it is needed; to my brother I have sworn this. What would you have me do, Holy One?" The Grey had remained where he was. Close contact with The Mistress always unnerved him. That much power in such a small human seemed dangerous to him.

"Go to Meridien. Check the Hatching Grounds. Check the palace. Anything that does not look or feel right report back to me."

"It shall be done, Great One." The Grey turned to leave but Jengo blocked his path.

"Be safe, brother." Jengo lowered his head and The Grey nuzzled his face against him.

"Till we meet again, brother." With that The Grey was off. Not a sound, just an empty spot where the giant of all wolves had stood.

"Shall I carry you from here, Holy One?" Jengo asked lowering himself to take The Mistress's weight.

"No thank you, old friend. With this bad omen I want to check the Holding Grounds. These are important days, Jengo. Nothing must go wrong."

"Then I shall be away. As you say, there is much to do." Jengo turned and slipped into the forest, a slick shadow of the night.

The Mistress started forward followed by the pack, always followed by the pack, for at two hundred years old, a Mistress needs a little help along the way.

Chapter 44
Philamo

Philamo slipped silently through the plain, wooden door at the base of the high tower and into the gloomy, cool chamber. It had been roughly fifteen years since she had entered this room. It was still the same, it felt as if the room had been waiting all these years, just waiting for her. She crossed to the small stairway and slumped down on the bottom step. Her mind drifted back to happier times.

Once the palace had been full of laughter, she had been an only child for so long her parents had given up hope of a Sworn child. She had grown and married a merchant's son, handsome and exciting, full of tales of travel and adventure. She couldn't wait to leave the palace walls. Their daughter had been born not long after their return from a spice finding journey and life felt safe. At age one their daughter was deemed not Sworn. She felt no disappointment for there would be more children for her she was sure, but none came.

Her parents were in their mature years when her mother announced she also was to have another baby. The joy the news brought her parents was unfathomable, and she was over-joyed for her mother.

Time passed and her mother grew ill with child bearing. She became weak and pale but insisted nothing was wrong. Then one summer's evening her mother's labour started and the night was long, painful and filled with worry. The morning brought news a son had been born, but her mother had passed away, weak and old for she could not hold on after her child had been born. Her father was overcome with grief but the tiny baby boy brought him hope and he threw himself into caring for him.

When Jason was one year he was found to be Sworn. The kingdom was in a state of excitement and celebration for weeks. Her father went from strength to strength, the kingdom felt strong, felt united, felt a happy place to live. But nothing lasts forever. A wave of the coughing disease took hold when Jason was five. Her father took every precaution round the clock nurses, witches and potion-makers were called. The worry was unnecessary. Jason was as strong as an ox, unlike her husband who fell ill while she was visiting the palace and was dead before her return journey was complete. She and her daughter grieved together and in time the disease grew weak and vanished from the kingdom just as quickly as it had arrived.

Jason had grown strong and handsome, and a year before his picking, Philamo's daughter married a merchant, as she had. She returned to the palace to care for her father, as age had taken his best years and Jason needed a woman's touch to guide him.

She received the news that she was to be a grandmother with hope and prepared for her daughter to come to the palace for her bearing months. The bond between mother and daughter is special and her memories of this time were her most precious. Her daughter gave birth to a girl and she had a sense of family again. The palace felt full.

Jason's picking day was filled with nerves for her, the age gap was such that she felt more like his mother than his sister most days and the preparations had been left to her. She had walked him into this room and hugged him so tightly he had flinched and gently pushed her aside

"I am a man now, Philamo, time to let me go." Jason had smiled gently as he spoke and had given her a tiny kiss on her cheek. She had watched him climb these very stairs and left the room filled with an empty feeling like she'd lost something very important and she was never to get it back.

Jason had picked a huge axe, a blade to be proud of. After his bonding he was to find the Holding Grounds, and his leaving ceremony was as lavish and loud as any wedding day. He had swaggered out onto the palace steps, axe held high and announced to the world he was Blade Sworn and would lead the White Guards into any battle he saw fit. How she and her father laughed at his prowess! Jason left for the Holding Grounds and all was quiet again. He had been gone not two months when a messenger brought terrible news to the palace. Her daughter and husband had been lost at sea, presumed dead. Their tiny baby girl, not yet one year old was to be sent to the palace forthwith. She was beside herself, her elderly father had not the mental or physical state to help. She must take this child on herself, she had thought, raise her the best she could. There would be no time for tears for her beloved daughter.

Selena had arrived in the dead of night, a ball of screaming red anger, all bundled in blankets and fighting to be free, Minn, her wet nurse had journeyed with her and was cooing and fussing over the child. She would brace herself, she thought. After all this was her granddaughter. After a few weeks of sleepless nights and wrecked nerves Selena started to calm and Minn proved herself a wonderful nursemaid. She spent her days tending baby and elderly father. Palace business was never far from her mind and things had fallen into a routine and life calmed. But fate was to strike one final blow to her life, one she would never fully recover from. For one summer morning a messenger arrived with news that would see her father to his grave and leave her alone and grieving for many years to come. Jason was dead.

Chapter 45
The Mistress

The Mistress had been walking the Holding Grounds till first light. The cages, the cave and pool had all been prepared. Her forest minions had done their work well as she expected.

"Fetch Jengo, my lovelies, for the journey home seems a little too much for me and the morning is upon us." The Mistress spoke quietly to her pack and they obeyed in an instant.

The Mistress spat and lowered herself onto a large moss-covered boulder.

A little rest can't hurt; after all it has been a busy few days, The Mistress thought. She scanned the forest. It had been her home for as long as she could remember and she ruled it with an iron fist. She had her favourites, yes, but if any stepped out of line she showed no mercy. It kept things simple, it allowed forest life to flow and the balance must be maintained. She startled out of her daydream with the noisy approach of the pack and Jengo.

"Mistress, please allow me to take you home." Jengo's voice was soft and humble for he knew what it cost The Mistress to ask for help.

"Please, old friend, I seem to have wandered longer than I intended." The Mistress rose and Jengo lowered himself to the ground. Riding on the back of a wolf was neither easy nor dignified but needs must when the devil drives and he drove pain through her bones this morning.

She dug her fingers into Jengo's fur and bent her head and shoulders low to his back and at a quick pace he was off, flying through leaves, following the forest trails. The forest was vast and dense spanning from the edge of the White City to the borders of the Drylands, but this was Jengo's home, his job as pack leader was to know every twist and turn the forest had to offer. After some time Jengo could smell The Mistress's home.

"Not long now, Holy One, hold on." Jengo knew having The Mistress fall from his back would mean consequences! He had worked too hard to get to the top of his pack and would not allow himself to be disgraced.

Wolf, Mistress and the pack turned a bend in the trail and came to the clearing outside The Mistress's home, half shack and half tree. The cottage rose with the natural twists and turns of the giant oak it had been built round. Wild grass and flowers covered most of the roof and herbs and vegetables covered the ground surrounding the clearing. It truly was a beautiful sight.

"Thank you, Jengo." The Mistress slid herself from the wolf's back and straightened and dusted off her cloak. The rats were tired she knew. "A hot drink and to bed with us all." She ordered wearily.

"Mistress was all in order at the Holding Grounds?" Jengo asked.

"Yes, yes, all was well prepared and in good order. Send my thanks to all who helped, please, old friend, this year we will see the Sworn through to adulthood even if I have to intervene myself." Jengo's eyes flew open, at The Mistress's statement, until he withered under her stare.

"Don't worry Jengo, I will let Balboar take the lead, but if I see him slip, even for a second, I will step in and banish him to the pit. Let there be no mistake."

She lowered her head as she gave a silent prayer, "Do not mistake me for a fool, Balboar, for the love of Merfolk do not fail."

"May I take my leave, Holy One? Shenka is due to birth our litter any time and I need to be close." Jengo's love for Shenka could be seen clearly in his crystal, blue eyes as he spoke.

"Yes, take your leave. Send word of your litter Jengo. Have courage. All will be well." The soft tone in which she spoke was all Jengo needed to feel his place in her regard was set. He turned and bolted into the forest.

"Come, come, let us also take our leave of this day." The mistress smiled at her ever-faithful pack and they all shambled to the cottage door.

Thistle was already bustling at the stove when they came through the door. She raised her head, raised her eyebrows then carried on preparing the tea. The Mistress had taken her voice many years before, all that chitter-chatter had annoyed her and unsettled the rats. She was a much better housemaid now she couldn't talk.

Once inside, the rats gathered and sorted and arranged the chair and footstool for The Mistress, it was their duty and their chore.

They removed her robe and rested her cane against her chair, they ushered her forward and she lowered herself down, each foot was placed with care onto the stool and Thistle poured tea from the kettle and placed it in her hands.

"Truly, what would I do without you?" The Mistress said. But by the time her last word was spoken, the rats had piled up, tails and ears all twisted and tangled together into a large sleeping pile before the fire. The Mistress sipped her tea and chuckled to herself.

"Sleep well, my lovelies, sleep well. "

The pack were sleeping. Thistle was busy fussing as usual but The Mistress couldn't settle.

"Thistle." The Mistress thought she'd test the waters; see what reaction her news about the Yok Yok tree had upon her. Thistle turned and padded over to The Mistress's chair.

"Your people have served in these lands since the beginning of time, have they not?" The Mistress stroked her chin with her free hand, a herby brew steaming in the other. Thistle nodded a big smile on her face.

"Then what say you if a Yok Yok tree had been deliberately harmed, let us say…violated?" The Mistress turned sharp eyes upon Thistle to judge her every expression.

Thistle's eyes flew wide open and her lips flapped up and down, but of course no words emerged. She brought her hands to her face and covered her cheeks she hoped from foot to foot her eyes darting here and there.

"As I thought." The Mistress whispered. "Now how does that tie in with the scent of a lone wolf? All Jengo's pack are accounted for. No wolves from the outer shores would hunt this far in." The Mistress finished her sentence with a small, "No." She made to rise. The pack stirred and wriggled. "It cannot be!" The Mistress made for her book case. Her hands shook as she fumbled through her large spell book. "For the love of the Merfolk do not let it be true!" She found what she was looking for and visibly relaxed with relief.

"There must be another answer to this odd occurrence. The magic is strong; it can be broken by none other than I." The Mistress returned to her chair and Thistle hurried to make another brew for The Mistress as the previous one had been cast across the room on The Mistress's beeline for the book case. The Mistress settled back into her chair to think. She sipped her fresh brew and scanned her memories of the Yok Yok tree and suddenly thought of Grumble and why anyone would want him dead. The egg! It must have been the egg! She knew not of any who had the power to hatch him, none that he wouldn't strike down on first glance. Who knew Grumble was there? Who knew of the egg? With her thoughts whirling she finally slipped into slumber. Dreams of wolves and eggs racing through her mind.

Chapter 46
Illiwig

Illiwig strolled down the street like the cat that got the cream. *A good day this will be for old Illiwig*, he thought to himself as he walked to the bathhouse. *No more scrimping and scraping for a coin. No, sir, not me!* He had spent the night crawling from tavern to ale house drinking himself stupid. No one listened to his tales of coin and wealth for this was Illiwig the filthy street simpleton. There was talk of him coming into coin but most thought he'd turned to theft or trickery to fill his purse.

So filled with thoughts of a good, hot soak to wash away his banging head was Illiwig that he didn't notice the dark shadow following him. It slunk through alley and under hedges never far behind. Illiwig turned down the small lane that led to the bathhouses, but alas, no Illiwig made it to the door

Chapter 47
Selena

Selena woke as soon as the suns first rays slid over her face. She was up, dressed and pacing her bedchamber.

"Try some breakfast, little bird, this day may be long." Minn fussed over the breakfast tray as she spoke, food was always Selena's first thought in the mornings.

"I simply can't eat, Minn. Grandmother should be here by now. Be up and dressed before dawn, Grandmother had said." Minn crossed the room to face Selena.

"Come now, miss, this pacing isn't helping your nerves or mine for that matter." Selena stared into Minn's eyes and saw only love.

"Okay, a little porridge, but then I'm going straight to Grandmother's rooms. Leaving me to send myself half stupid with worry is really not like her." Selena sat at her small table and started shovelling porridge down like it was the first time she'd seen food. Minn smiled to herself, Selena was never too far from food if she could help it. A healthy appetite Selena would call it, greedy, Minn would say, but only to herself.

Selena had just finished gulping down the last trace of porridge when there was a knock at the door. Her eyes flew open and Minn raised a hand to calm her.

"Who is it?" Minn called out, trying to sound unflustered.

"It's me, Minn, please open the door as there is not much time." Philamo's voice was small with the edge of nerves. Minn unlocked the door and quickly heaved it open. Philamo stepped through without her usual grace.

"Grandmother!" Selena gasped. Philamo stood before her in plain leggings, cloth boots and a long smock shirt, not her usual gown and jewels.

"Close your mouth, Selena; it does you no justice in the looks department." Philamo's plain dress could not conceal her regal standing, and her voice was tight and harsh.

"I see you have dressed as I requested." Philamo said as she stared at Selena's plain clothing.

"Yes, Grandmother, but what now, where are we going?" Selena rose from the table and felt inside her pocket. She pulled out the silver key Philamo had given her at dinner and held it out in her hand, eyes pleading for answers.

"Minn, you may leave us now. I wish to be alone with my grand-daughter." Philamo turned a stern eye on the handmaiden, which had her scurrying from the room.

"Selena, my dear, I must help you understand what is going to happen today but my failing last night has made this a difficult task." Philamo took a breath and swallowed. "I should never have mentioned her name, it is forbidden, but what's done is done."

"Grandmother, are you in trouble? Who is this Mistress?" Selena pleaded.

"Hush, child. Do not say her name here, enough damage has been done. Just listen, Selena, and listen well. I haven't much time." Philamo's voice was troubled and Selena's eyes grew wide with fear.

"Today you must pick, child, you must pick a weapon to bond with. That weapon then becomes a part of you. It feels what you feel, it knows your memories, your fears. If you pick badly Selena, if you don't bond completely, things...well, things can go very wrong." Philamo's voice began to fade as her mind conjured up Jason's face as he strolled out onto the palace steps smiling and laughing. Philamo shook her head. *Not now, not here, I must concentrate.* She told herself.

"Pick, from what? From where? I don't understand, Grand-mother. You are frightening me!" Selena had never felt afraid, not really, but now the cold tendrils of danger wrapped themselves around her heart.

"Soon we will walk quietly and as quickly as possible down to the courtyard, we will talk to no one and say nothing. Is that understood?" Selena just nodded, a thousand questions spinning in her mind. "The reason I have had us dress like this is so that no one, and I mean no one, can see us or follow us or question us on where we are going." Philamo tried to explain too much in one go and had to pause for breath.

"Grandmother, where are we going?" Selena tried to speak calmly for she knew the more she pushed her grandmother, the less her questions would be answered.

"We are going to the picking room. Nobody knows it's there, the door is spellbound and only royals can see it." Philamo had gained control and she wasn't going to let this opportunity slip. "We will enter a small chamber and there I must leave you. I see you have the key. Good. You will need that to unlock the door to the picking room." She gently took Selena's hand in hers. "Now, child, all will be well. You have trained hard and you are a clever and kind girl, all I could hope for in a granddaughter. This day will be the making of you. All you have worked for will now come to pass." Tears welled in her eyes, but she would not let them fall, she must be strong.

"How do I pick, Grandmother? What do I look for?" Selena was becoming desperate inside, desperate for any clue as to how she would get through this.

"I cannot tell you, my dear. It is only for the Sworn to enter that room and pick. I cannot give you any help. Just use your heart to guide you and do not be afraid. You were born for this. My love, you are Sworn." And with that Philamo turned for the door.

"Hurry now, child, before the whole castle wakes." Philamo opened the door and ushered Selena out onto the landing.

"Follow me. Remember, no talking, and try to blend in, head down." Philamo and Selena quickly paced along the landing and down the maid's steps, across the hall and out the scullery backdoor. Selena had her head down the whole way, her breathing was becoming fast with fear, her eyes following her grandmother's feet as she tiptoed her way outside.

After some dodging of the horsemen and a little time hiding behind a wagon, Philamo turned to Selena. "The door is under that low roof at the base of the high tower can you see it?" Philamo was out of breath and sweating.

Selena looked up at the high tower and followed it down, there at its base was a small, wooden door, nothing special, you could walk right past it and miss it completely.

"I do." Selena whispered.

"Quickly now, come." Philamo led Selena across the cobbled stones and under the small, low roof. She gently pushed the wooden door and it squeaked open. A cool, damp breeze wafted from within. Philamo stepped inside followed by a pale Selena. Selena scanned the room for reference but there was none. It was cool and bare and empty but for a small staircase.

"Now my love, take courage, you have until sunset to make your choice so please hear my words, pick wisely, use everything you know about weapons to make your choice and most importantly use your heart." Philamo made a desperate grab for Selena and drew her close.

"I love you, Selena, with all that I have and all that I am, I love you." Philamo could feel the tears rolling down her cheeks, she cared not for rules at this moment. Selena stiffened at her grandmother's rough embrace, for such things were not done between them. She could hear her grandmother's stifled sobs and smell the lavender on her hair.

"I love you too." was all she could say. The lump in her throat was painful now and her grandmother's distress had stunned her into silence. Philamo pulled away from the embrace and quickly wiped the tears from her cheeks.

"Now go! Do me proud, Selena, I know you can do this." And with that she turned and whisked out the door, quietly shutting it, leaving Selena alone at the bottom of the stairway.

Chapter 48

Selena stared at the door her grandmother had left through for what felt like an age. She shook her head and lowered her eyes to the silver key in her hand.

"Oh well, let's see what you open then." Selena spoke to herself.

She turned to the staircase and began to climb. Each step she took echoed into the empty room below, "It's all getting a bit creepy in here." Selena whispered to herself. Up and up she went. The wall she brushed her hand on as she ascended the stairway was cool and smooth. The little landing appeared suddenly and Selena stopped and stared. To the left of the landing was a huge, silver door. Her wide eyes looked it up and down. She stood frozen in amazement as Illiwig had the night before.

Selena took a deep breath and stepped across the landing to face the door. She reached out a hand and gently touched the carvings. *Such beauty, and such craftsmanship,* she thought. The key clasped tightly in her other hand.

"Here goes nothing." Selena said, as her shaky hand unclenched to reveal the key. She slipped the key into the lock and turned it. She heard a small click as the lock gave. She lent her shoulder to the door and pushed. The door hissed open and Selena stepped inside.

The room was round and smelled like the blade smithies in town, a smell Selena was used to. Weak sunlight filtered through the widow shutters and gave the room a soothing feel. Selena scanned the room in awe. There were blades and weapons adorning the walls in racks and on hooks; shields and axes; daggers and swords aplenty. She felt at home here.

"Oh." Selena whispered, now becoming aware of what she had to do. She turned to her right and started to walk the room. She dare not touch yet, not yet. She wanted to look, to study all the room had to offer.

"How to pick? Do I close my eyes and just point? Do I hold a few, feel their weight?" Selena shook her head as she spoke. "No, it has to be something more than that." She raised her hand to her chin and pondered.

Balboar had heard the girl approach on the stairs; heard the turn of the key and the small footsteps as she had entered the room. He kept himself hidden, his glow dull and unmoving. *Now's the tricky part*, he thought to himself. *Now I must make her choose me.*

Selena walked over to the axes, for they were the most impressive. She ran her hand down the long, wooden handle of the first axe, it felt too cold. She moved on to the next. This one had an ivory handle with gold decorations swirling round and round. *Too fancy*, she thought. The axes were losing their appeal.

Balboar had focused his mind. *Move on, child these are not for you. Look how they shine with arrogance and pride. You need a weapon to fight with, not boast with,* he let his thoughts drift around the room trying to sway Selena.

Selena came to the shield section. She lifted the first one from its rack and hefted it onto her shoulder, its weight was all wrong. *This shield is built for a man,* she thought. The shield slid down her arm and crashed to the floor. Selena froze as the sound rang round the room, but nothing stirred. Everything was still and silent.

Balboar watched as Selena dropped the shield. "This should be easy," he sniggered to himself and then thought about the pit if he failed. Tiring of being quiet, for that was not his style, Balboar focused his mind again. *A shield is not for you girl, you are a quick and nimble fighter, your blade skills require no shield.*

"I need no shield; it would make me clumsy and slow." Selena said aloud. She turned her attention to the swords.

"Come child, I await you. Take me in your hand, feel my blade weight, and claim me as your own." Balboar's voice was as soft as a raindrop, mesmerizing and beckoning.

She, as if in a dream, reached out her hand and touched the blade of Balboar, she ran her fingers gently up to the hilt. She could have sworn she felt a gentle vibration coming from the blade.

"Yes, child, yes, you are at one with this sword. It feels right, it feels like your own." It took all Balboar's patience not to bellow and shout at her that he was the one, he was her rightful Sworn Blade.

She lifted the sword from its stand and felt its weight; she swung it gently from side to side. It felt right; it felt like she had fought with this sword all her life. It felt alive.

Balboar knew as soon as she said the words she was his and he was hers. He knew the power he would feel, the freedom he would receive and the work that must be done. He prepared himself for the rush. *Just one more little prompt*, he thought.

"Selena, Selena." Balboar kept his voice a bare whispering. "We can be great, we can be powerful. Feel me, and say the words, Selena, speak them aloud." Balboar held his breath.

Selena felt a pulling in her mind a sense of comradeship, a sense of being a part of something, a sense of right and she knew she had picked well. This was her blade. She would claim it as hers. She lowered the blade and shook her head as if waking from a dream, the sword felt safe in her hand and she lowered it so the tip rested on the ground. She closed her eyes and calmed her nerves, not sure of what would happen when she claimed the blade. Fear and excitement mixed in her heart but she was a White City Princess, this was her destiny. As a Sworn she would not let her grandmother down; she would not let the people down. Selena raised the sword once more and took a huge breath.

"I Selena! Blade Sworn! Princess of the great White Palace, claim this sword as my Sworn Blade!" Selena held her breath for fear of missing a single moment but nothing happened, she opened her eyes looked around the room, then at her sword.

Balboar chuckled as he thought to himself, *This is going to be fun, it has been a very long time since I have trained a girl.*

Selena shook the sword. "Well, do something then!" She almost shouted. At that instance the sword started to vibrate, to glow. The large crystal that was bound into the hilt swirled and filled with blue. The face of a man started to appear inside the crystal. Selena's mouth flew open but no words would form, her eyes where wide with terror.

Balboar opened his eyes and looked straight into Selena's as he smiled a sly smile. "Hello, girl, are you ready to begin?"

Chapter 49

Rubear

Rubear was full of knowledge. So much knowledge his head hurt. He had passed the test and the witch had drugged him into an open state and poured all the old man's knowing into him. Rubear had been sick and was hot with fever. But it had passed. The witch had tended him and now he had escaped her and ran the Black Road. Searching out the red scorpion.

Koiya had thought he wasn't ready but the little boy had passed the test and had insisted he was. She mixed the receiving potion and he had drunk it down with great gusto. Then her work had begun. She chanted for the dead man's soul to come forward and release his knowledge and after midnight he came. He smiled at her choice of the boy and she knew she had chosen wisely. The old man stepped forward and let his knowledge pour into the boy, now in a dream state, for the conscious mind cannot handle such information. The boy had been sick and had a fever, which was to be expected. She had nursed him through the night and by morning he was sleeping soundly. Koiya had taken a little sleep for herself and when she had risen, Rubear had gone.

Rubear stumbled along, tripping and wobbling. The power of the knowledge almost too much to bear. His memories were all jumbled up with the old man's and facts about the Black Road kept springing into his mind. It had been built by humans long passed. It could never be lived near or upon. It linked all the kingdoms of this world. Rubear hit himself in the face, hard. Pulled his hair and screamed at the top of his voice.

"Please make it stop. Please!" But no one heard him. No one except Bon.

Bon was a sly, thin thief. He had worked the Black Road all his life now his heart and soul were just as black. He had been camped in a thicket just off to the side. Biding his time for the odd brave trader looking for a quick route to the White City. Bon scrunched up his one good eye and put his little spying glass to it.

"Now, now, what have we here?" Bon whispered to himself, smiling with the idea of fresh prey. He spied the little, cloth sack Rubear wore over his shoulder and lowered his looking glass.

"What's a small boy doing out here all alone? Who cares?" Bon chuckled. "He'll only get a beating from me." Bon laughed a small weasel laugh and prepared to meet the boy a little further up the road.

Rubear's headache was getting worse, and his fever had returned. He rubbed his face with his hands and stumbled forward. "Where are you? You stupid little insect. I'm ready. I'm on the Black Road like you said." Rubear shouted.

Bon stepped from the bushes and swaggered towards Rubear whistling a little tune.

"Good morning, young sir. What brings you down the Black Road?" Bon's face was the picture of friendliness.

Rubear strained his eyes to look the man in the face. "Nothing." Was all Rubear could muster, his own face becoming numb.

"Well now that's not a kindly answer. There's little old me trying to have a polite conversation and you being all sullen and rude." Bon had no time for games. He wanted the sack and to give the boy a beating, just for fun. A little body like that would be easy to bruise.

"Leave me alone, you fool." Rubear mustered. He felt dizzy and wasn't sure how long he could stand.

"Gladly, you little flea. Just give me your sack and I shall spare your tiny life and let you be on your way." All smiles gone from his face, Bon had had enough of this strange boy. He wanted to know what he carried in his bag.

Rubear now understood what was going on. He was being robbed. Robbed by this skinny, vile smelling man. Rubear straightened himself. Sweat ran down his face and cramps tightened his belly, but he would not let this common thief have the better of him.

"Take the sack, mister. Please spare my life. I'm only an orphan on my way to find work in the White City." Rubear turned on his scared, little, lost act and for a moment it seemed to work.

Bon softened his face a moment and reached for the sack. "All right. Stop your whining, flea. Let me see what you got."

Once the thief had the sack Rubear stepped back. He bore his eyes into the man and clapped his hands. The old man's knowledge and the little power The Queen had bestowed on him set to work. Rubear rubbed his hands together over and over and chanted one word. "Rise. Rise. Rise."

"What you doing, stupid, mad boy? Shut your mouth." Bon made to cuff the boy round the head to silence him but as he stepped forward the sack began to wriggle. It bulged and filled with something that made a snipping sound. Bon screamed and dropped the sack. He stared open mouthed as the sack wriggled and writhed on the ground. Rubear continued to chant and Bon stood rooted to the spot, eyes wide at the swollen sack. All of a sudden the seams of the sack split and thousands upon thousands of tiny, red ants spilled out, angry and vicious, looking for Bon.

Rubear clapped his hands again and smiled a dark, evil grin.

"What was that you were saying, good man?" Rubear laughed as the ants swarmed over Bon, filling his mouth and nose and snipping his body into tiny pieces. His muffled screams and pleadings fell on Rubear's deaf ears as blood and flesh lay in small heaps upon the Black Road.

Rubear felt a little better. The release of some knowledge and a little magic had lowered the pressure in his head. He clapped his hands and the ants melted into the road turning to a red dust that blew away on the breeze.

"Now, where are you?" Rubear shouted seemingly to himself.

The red scorpion had been watching from the trees and scurried to Rubear's side. Scared by what he had witnessed he kept his voice humble. "I'm here, your Holiness."

Rubear smiled down on his little red companion. "Now that's a better way to address me don't you think, minion?" Rubear spat at the scorpion and sniggered at its scurry to avoid his spittle.

"Yes, Great One. Shall we set off now for the far shore?" The scorpion knew he would die again at the hands of this distasteful child, but The Queen had given instructions and he knew his duty.

"Lead the way, insect." Rubear, now full of confidence, walked forward, almost treading on his familiar.

The scorpion knew he had to keep his wits about him and scuttled along the Black Road trying to keep one step ahead of this evil boy who had now become his master.

Chapter 50
The Mistress

Thistle sat down clumsily onto her straw bed, her room was a small alcove in the corner of the kitchen. She rubbed her aged hands together and sniffed. She smiled to herself and thought, *to serve when the Sworn are bonding is an exciting time indeed. I have prepared all the liquids for the pool myself, a very important job indeed. The Mistress trusts me.*

Thistle had served The Mistress since she was a child, like all hobgoblins in this world they were born to serve, but to serve a Mistress was the highest honour indeed.

Thistle's thoughts wandered. *Yes, she had taken my voice. Yes, I had sulked for days, but The Mistress knows best. I don't need a voice to serve and serve I will, just like my family before me. But four new Sworn, how exciting!* Thistle couldn't help but rub her cheeks and rock back and forward with anticipation. *The pack will be waking soon and wanting to hunt, I must go and ready The Mistress's food. She will be hungry when she wakes*, Thistle thought. With that she heaved herself from the bed and waddled to the hearth. A good fire makes a good meal. Thistle chanted to herself in her head as she worked.

The pack stirred at the poking and prodding of the hearth, they yawned and stretched and rubbed their whiskers. She jabbed the poker at them and pointed to the door. They untangled themselves as Thistle slowly plodded to the door. She unlatched it with thick fingers and stood aside as the pack slunk out into the afternoon air. She shut the door behind them as quietly as she could for she knew The Mistress hated to be woken before her time. She gathered roots and herbs from the kitchen cold store and a pitcher of water from the stream. She worked The Mistress's garden like it was her own creation. There was always a crop to be had, and Thistle was proud of her work.

A good stew is what The Mistress needs, all that roaming around the Holding Grounds getting herself a chill. These will be long days ahead, indeed they will, Thistle's thoughts started to wander as she prepared the stew.

"Thistle, are you still with us or have the fairies taken your mind?" The Mistress asked, seeing the faraway look in Thistle's eyes.

Thistle jumped nearly knocking the stew pot from its hook: She turned to The Mistress and gave a pleading look.

The Mistress sniffed the air long and deep. "Stew, I take it, my love?"

Thistle nodded her head, smiling with pleasure that she had cooked a favourite of The Mistress and that she had noticed.

The Mistress thought to herself, *she nods like an excitable pup, but her stew is so very good. Maybe one day I shall give her voice back, but then again...* The Mistress glanced at the green, glass jar on the mantel piece that contained Thistle's voice. *Maybe not.*

With the stew eaten and with a fresh robe adorned The Mistress sat by the fire and sipped her herby brew. The pack were hunting and Thistle was cleaning pots in the little stream behind the house. She had checked her spell book again as soon as she had woken from a restless sleep, only to find the same answer. The magic was strong. It could not be reversed. A knock at the door brought her to her senses.

"Not a moment of peace in this entire world. For the love of Merfolk, who's there?" she shouted before she opened the door.

"It is I, Mistress, I bring news." The small, black crow cowered on hearing The Mistress's rage from the other side of the door. The door flew open and nearly sucked Rough Wing in with its draft.

"Well? Speak! I have not all day." The Mistress peered down at Rough Wing.

Rough Wing stuttered "I did as you instructed, Holy One, I stayed nestled into the roof of the tower and listened."

"Yes, yes, what news." The Mistress was getting anxious. Had Balboar failed was he claimed?

"She has picked Mistress, I heard the words myself."

"Yes, Rough Wing, but has she claimed Balboar?" The Mistress had stumbled outside and had backed Rough Wing against the wall.

"Yes, Holy One, she has, but..." Rough Wing tried to make himself as small as possible as he spoke.

"BUT, BUT, BUT! I will have what is left of his miserable life if he has messed this up, believe me, Rough Wing, believe me!" The Mistress hollered and huffed like a mad thing.

"No, no, Mistress, the words were said. The pairing is complete. It's just that…" Rough Wing searched for the words, he didn't want a swift kick for the news he brought.

"SPIT IT OUT, ROUGH WING!" The Mistress shouted.

"It's Click, Holy One, I saw him as I was leaving. He was watching, watching the tower. He knows."

"How can it be so? The Yok Yok tree. The egg. Grumble. Merfolk help us all!" The Mistress pale and shaking leaned against the wall and Rough Wing stared unbelieving in what he saw. If The Mistress was to fail they all would surely perish.

"Mistress!" Rough Wing ventured a little closer. "What now?"

The Mistress had no answers for him. *The magic has been broken. Click's return can mean only one thing,* she thought, *evil has returned to this land and the timing is no coincidence. I must think. The Ancients will need to be summoned.* The Mistress blew her bone whistle to summon the pack and rounded the house to find Thistle. Rough Wing followed.

"Mistress, what will you have me do?"

"Fetch Jengo and tell him nothing. When you return you must fly to Meridien. Seek out The Grey, he has a report for you. Tell him to return, and, Rough Wing, do not tell him why. If you do, he will seek out Click himself and I need him here." Rough Wing made to leave. "If I hear that you have betrayed me in this matter I will cast you to the pit, crow, make no mistake."

After sending Thistle for the Ancients and returning to her chair, she gulped down a red phial of liquid and let the pain relief flood through her body. *I must consult The Oracle on this, my books have no answers,* she thought. *The Oracle will guide me. In her I must trust.*

She rose and picked up her cane. She stumbled to her private room and fumbled with the lock on her small, wooden chest. The pain medicine dulling her senses. At last the lock snapped open and she removed a small, silk purse. "A token will need to be given for knowledge asked." The Mistress bowed to no one, but The Oracle had her respect and the power she held equalled that of The Mistress. She chose a small, green crystal from the purse and hid it deep within her robe. She closed the door to her cottage and headed into the woods all the while thoughts of Click and his return worrying her to the bone.

After a lot of twists and turns, the narrow, lone path led her to a small clearing. No plant or tree grew there. She held her breath and waited for an invitation to enter.

A soft woman's voice drifted up as if from the ground. "Welcome, Holy One, you may enter my realm." The Mistress stepped forward.

Chapter 51
Selena

Selena backed away from the sword that now lay on the floor where she had thrown it. Her thoughts were all jumbled, her hands were shaky, and her throat dry. No words would form.

"Pick me up child! For the love of the Merfolk! Thrown, by a girl! Know your place child, PICK ME UP!" Balboar had never been so insulted. He huffed and bellowed.

"You! You spoke! You're a sword and you spoke." Selena couldn't believe what she had heard, what she was hearing now.

"No, fool, I am not a sword, I am a Sworn sword! Now come here and pick me up." Balboar was losing patience.

Selena crept forward and peered down at the sword she had chosen.

"Now reach down and hold me by the blade, I want to be able to see your face."

She slowly reached out and grabbed the sword by the blade as instructed. It felt warm and familiar. She brought the hilt up to her face and stared at the large, blue crystal bound into it.

"Now, that's much better don't you think?" Balboar's words were soothing. He was happy to be off the floor.

"What are you?" Selena asked a little afraid of the answer.

"I, little bird, am Balboar. This is my sword, well, our sword to be precise. We will be as one together, you, me and the sword. We are now bound by the great craft. We will fight as one."

"How is this possible? What do you mean, great craft?" Selena couldn't make sense of it all. These past two days had been a blur. Her world had changed so much in so little time.

"All will be revealed in time child. Our only task now is to bond and bond properly. I require your dedication, your willingness to learn all I have to offer, your strength and courage. Can you do that for me, Selena, can you be the warrior you have trained to be, that you are destined to be?"

Selena looked into Balboar's eyes she felt the rightness of his words, his soothing tone, his power in all things of war and battles. She knew this was her path, her warrior path, all things had led to this and she felt calm for the first time in days. This was her path and her path alone.

Selena nodded her head. "Yes, Great One, you have my word."

"Good. Now, make your way down the stairwell. We shall begin at once. The evening shall be upon us and there is much to do."

Selena held the sword by the blade and quickly made her way to the door. She heaved it open and stepped out onto the landing.

"Close the door. This room has served its purpose we will not need to come here again."

Selena turned and looked for the silver key she had left in the door.

"No good looking for the key child. Like the room, it has served its purpose. Each key is forged for a Sworn. No one else may use it, it has gone." Balboar stated.

Selena didn't reply. She turned and hurried down the stairs, sword held out at arm's length. She reached the bottom and raised the sword to eye level. "Now what?" she asked. She had no control over this situation and she felt very alone.

"Now, my child, we begin. We can't leave this room until we have fully bonded, so now we fight."

Selena swallowed, her mouth and throat dry. She realised she hadn't eaten or drank since breakfast and that seemed like days ago.

Balboar knew the girl was thirsty, hungry and scared but he knew he must proceed.

"Walk to the centre of the room, Selena."

Selena slowly crossed to the middle of the empty room.

"Now take a breath. Centre yourself."

She closed her eyes, steadied her nerves. *For Grandmother,* she thought. *For the White Palace, for the Kingdom.*

"With your sword-hand grip the hilt, wrap your hand completely round me and let our souls combine." Balboar's voice was steady, strong, for he knew what was to come and the girl would need courage.

Selena opened her eyes, took one last breath and grasped the hilt. The room lit up with a blast of blue light. Selena was no longer in the small chamber at the bottom of the high tower. She was no longer in the White Palace in the great city. She was spinning, searching, scanning for substance, anything to help her get a bearing on where she was. She heard cries and shouts, clashing of weapons and the dying groans of men. She was on a battle field and Balboar was at her side. Not the blue crystal, but the man himself, a great giant of a man covered in blood and in his battle throes.

Balboar turned his fierce, hardened face to hers and spoke, "Now the game begins, my child."

Chapter 52

The Mistress

As soon as The Mistress's foot touched the floor she knew she had made a mistake, she would be lucky to leave with her life. The temperature dropped and all around her the forest had an icy sheen. What once was lush and green, now had long ferns of ice frozen on every leaf.

"Well, well, well. We meet again, ARIEANNA! The Oracle loved to play games." Her thin, cold voice drifted around the clearing.

"Do not speak my name, Witch. It is not yours for the taking." The Mistress knew this would happen. For to speak a person's true name meant you could own a piece of their soul.

"I take what I want here. All here bow to me." The Oracle stepped out from behind a tall, thin tree; every step she took lifted frozen flakes from the floor. Her arms and legs were unnaturally long. Her fingers glistened like icicles.

"I come with news." The Mistress stood still judging the path the game would take.

The Oracle's hair, as white as snow, blew softly around her smooth, tiny face. Her blue, large eyes gleamed a shade lighter than The Mistress's; she was a beauty to behold.

"What news could you bring that I don't already know?" The Oracle stood before The Mistress, a thin haze of blue and white swirling gently around her.

The Mistress knew this had to be over quickly. The Oracle will try and keep her here for as long as she could, draining The Mistress's craft, adding it to her own.

The two powers faced each other, one old and wise, one cold and powerful. The world was silent, waiting and watching. A voice as gentle as rain whispered to the two matriarchs.

"Do you both serve me?"

The Mistress thought it a trick. As did The Oracle.

The voice rose louder, stern and forceful. "You are both my servants. There is work to do. You will join or perish."

The Mistress felt a slow grip around her heart and clutched her chest.

The Oracle likewise gasped in pain.

"For over two hundred years I have kept silent letting you rule for me. The peace has been kept. The lines of war and battle drawn. But now the lines have been broken. Broken by one who seeks to destroy my work and enslave my world."

The immense power of the voice had the two woman paralysed. All they could do was listen.

"I have given you both powers, powers to do my will on earth. These powers have made you both boastful and arrogant. But you forget I can easily take those powers away. Put aside your petty jealousies, there is work to do. My work. If I must return it will not be good for you both. God has decided to send you both an ally. You both know he does not do this lightly. For him to intervene means the balance has been tipped and he has been left with no choice. Look to the North, Mistress, you will find him waiting when you are ready."

The Mistress and The Oracle tried to speak and found they couldn't. They both knew who had spoken to them. Both sets of eyes wide with fear and awe.

"You will join together and share your knowledge, or the worlds you both know will burn and perish and all that will remain will be ash." The voice began to fade and The Mistress and The Oracle felt a great releasing as their mouths and hearts were their own again.

Both dropped to their knees and prayed with tears and fear for forgiveness for their petty games as the immense power of Mother Nature diminished as quickly as it came.

"I bring a token for knowledge, sister." The Mistress gasped speaking quickly, wanting this exchange to be over.

"I accept the exchange." The Oracle whispered, still overcome by what she had just witnessed.

The Mistress withdrew the green jewel from her robes and handed it to The Oracle. The stone turned to an icy chip and disappeared into The Oracle's hand as she absorbed its power.

"What is it you come seeking, sister?" The Oracle now stood as eager for this to be over as her counterpart.

"Click has returned. I need to know how." The Mistress leant heavily on her cane. What had happened here would need thought and time to understand and she could not do that now.

The Oracle gathered her white robes around her and flicked her eyes side to side as if expecting Mother Nature to return.

"I felt that the magic we bonded together to hold him had been broken. I knew you would come. He was summoned. Summoned by one who holds the power of us both. There is a great battle to come sister. Look to the North, you and your Sworn. This is the war that will end all wars." The Mistress and The Oracle stood face to face both knowing it was the truth, both knowing this would be the end of days.

The Mistress turned to leave. Then spoke softly over her shoulder. "Sister, one last request, if I may."

"You may."

"I have left a token in a boy's heart. When he needs calling can I trust you to do the asking?"

"You can, sister, you can."

The Mistress stumbled from the clearing, cold and alone. She knew she must not speak a word of her meeting with The Oracle and the warning from Mother Nature. She drew an elixir of health from her robe and drank it down. She slowly set off towards the clearing of the Ancients

Chapter 53

Thistle had been stumbling around the forest for hours. Each Ancient had their home and she knew she had to proceed with humble respect. The Mistress would hear of any dishonour. All the Ancients had now been summoned and she must now make her way to the Gathering-Site and meet The Mistress. Her feet were sore and her head thumping but she was to serve and serve, she would.

Thistle made her way along the small forest trail and at last came to the clearing. A fire had already been lit in the centre of the circle of stones and she could hear the pack scratching and scrabbling around.

"Thistle! At last! Have they all been summoned? Were they made aware of the importance of this meeting and the danger we all face?" The Mistress didn't even turn for an answer. She knew Thistle would have shown them all the secret talisman that meant they must attend. Sometimes she wished she hadn't taken her voice, but it was a passing thought.

Thistle knelt beside the fire and warmed her hands for a moment, only a moment, for she knew it was her job to keep the fire going, sometimes all through the night, and she would need wood and lots of it. She rose to her feet and started looking for firewood. She clicked her fingers at the pack and pointed to the fire, then to the forest. They hissed their displeasure but scurried out to collect the kindling.

Thistle was hungry and took out the small napkin filled with berries from her pocket. Not her first though, never her first. She waddled over to The Mistress and offered out her sweet horde.

"Thistle you never fail to surprise." The Mistress said, taking a handful of the soft fruit, and cramming them into her mouth, wishing she'd had extra stew earlier. Thistle smiled and nodded, happy she had pleased The Mistress, and returned to her fire building, whilst savouring the rest of her sweet treat.

Jengo had not stopped pacing the clearing since they had arrived and it was starting to grate on The Mistress's nerves.

"Jengo, come. Sit. Let us talk awhile." The Mistress knew he was worried about Shenka and she knew Rough Wing had blabbed. "I'll deal with that little cretin later." She sneered to herself.

Jengo slunk over to the seated Mistress and sat by her feet.

"I am sorry, Holy One, my thoughts are not in order tonight."

"Jengo old friend, all will be well. No doubt which ever evil Click is working for, he will be on his way to make his full report." The Mistress spat with disgust. "I do not feel his presence here, do you?" Jengo let his senses flow out into the forest and sniffed the night air.

"No, Holy One, he is not within the forest."

"Now rest, my friend, this will be a long night." The Mistress leant back against the cold stone and considered what it might mean for them all now that Click was back.

The fire was high and the pack were sleeping when they heard the first sounds of an approach. A small flame-coloured fox slipped quietly out of the forest brush, the pack instantly bristled and clicked their teeth.

"Can you not control your minions?" the voice of the High Vixen was as sweet as treacle.

The Mistress hissed at the pack and they cowered and retreated to the back of her stone chair.

"Forgive them, High Vixen, they are young and eager to please." *They will feel my boot later,* The Mistress thought to herself.

"No harm done, Holy One." The High Vixen found a warm spot by the fire and lowered herself to the floor; she stretched her legs out in front of her, the colour of the flames making her fur seem alive with crimson shadows. She turned towards Thistle. "I see she still has no voice. Do you not find that inconvenient?" The High Vixen's words where soft, betraying the sharp, nasty teeth her mouth held.

"My serving goblin is of no concern to you Mishka."

"Apologies Mistress, I meant nothing by it." Mishka looked sideways at Thistle, her dislike for the goblin obvious.

"As you can see Mishka, you are the first. Hopefully the others will not be far behind." As The Mistress spoke, a huge gust of wind swept the camp as a large, pure white owl swooped down to the ground next to Mishka.

"Nice of you to join us!" Mishka said neither flinching nor bristling.

169

The owl's wings folded like a majestic jigsaw, each feather soft and perfect.

"White Wing, welcome. I hope we will not have to wait long for the others. I do not wish to delay your night hunting." The Mistress knew she would have to go cautiously to keep the gathering from turning into a brawl.

"Mistress. Mishka." White Wing lowered his head to both as he spoke, his voice as cool as the wind. He settled himself for the wait; he was not one for wasted words.

Mishka turned her attention to Jengo. "How is Shenka these days? Last time I saw her, she was looking a little…shall we say fat." Mishka chuckled under her breath.

"My mate has had a litter as you well know, fox." Jengo had no time for the meddling sly temptress, he would love to rip her small, sweet head off and gorge on her guts.

"Stop, beast, you know we are in the presence of The Mistress. No violence, please." Mishka had hit her mark and seeing Jengo bristle with rage delighted her.

"I see you two are at it already." The deep, smooth voice of the High Stag rumbled from the forest. All turned to see Theodore emerge with grace and presence, his large antlers spread wide above his head gave him a foreboding look, although he was greying around the muzzle his body was hard with muscle. The Mistress relaxed. He would keep these two from each other's throats. She wouldn't want to enforce an understanding with pain. Not just yet, anyway.

Behind Theodore came Ludwig all fur and muttering. "Sorry Mistress, I'm so sorry, I'm always the last one. Oh, I see you're here, Mishka. How…nice." Mishka hissed on seeing the elderly badger fumble his way from the forest. She rose slowly to her feet.

"Oh good, then we are all here; the silent, the angry, the handsome and now the stupid."

"Yes, yes, all here." Ludwig agreed until he realised he was the stupid. "Oh."

"Steady, everyone, we have bigger things to discuss. Settle yourselves. I have grave news." The Mistress picked up her cane and laid it across her lap, a sign that she meant business. All five Ancient Ones lowered their heads in respect and settled down around the fire.

"The reason I have gathered you here this evening is because Click has been seen within the walls of the White City." She leant back and let the news sink in.

"What? When? Is he here now?" Theodore raised his mighty antlers and sniffed the air.

"No. Calm yourselves. He is long gone."

"But Mistress, the pact, the binding, how is he able to tread here? The magic was strong. How has he managed to break it?" Ludwig felt unsafe, alert, he itched to get back to his colony. Day watchers would need to be called.

"Mistress, what do you want us to do? What measures would you have us put in place?" White Wing's need only for words of importance stopped the panic of the others.

"We must all be on high alert. Set your sentries and warning guards. Have extra patrols throughout the forest. I want to know immediately if he steps one evil foot on my land. Do I make myself clear?" The Mistress rose and leant on her cane. "White Wing, have the flocks make round trips to the castle and out to the edges of the volcano. Ludwig you will comb the inner forest. Jengo have the pack patrol closer to the Marshlands, keep a close eye on the dock. Mishka, the orchards and fields are your responsibility." Mishka bowed her head and turned to leave. "And Mishka…" Mishka raised her small, beautiful face to The Mistress. "If you ever come to a gathering with the intent of ill words again I shall skin you myself and hang you on my wall, do you understand, fox?"

Mishka knew she had over-stepped and calling her a fox was the worst insult The Mistress could have given. Now was the time for grovelling and she knew it. "Yes, Holy One, many apologies. May the Merfolk forgive me." With that she scurried into the brush.

White Wing rose into the air with nothing but a nod. Ludwig bowed and hurried off into the forest as if his life depended on it, which in truth it did. In times of great trouble the badgers were always the first to suffer.

"Mistress, as my herd lives closest to the river, do you think I should move them to higher grazing land? I must protect them." Theodore's gentle manner belied his deep concern.

"No, Theodore, I need you to patrol the Black Road. It's the quickest way to White City. Any travellers will take that road. I know the danger it brings, my friend and I'm asking a lot, but I will sleep better knowing it is you that holds this task, faithful one." The Mistress held no remorse for his task as she knew Theodore was the most loyal of forest Ancients and would not desert his post. *Unlike others*, she thought, seeing Mishka's beautiful face.

"It shall be so, Holy One." Theodore lowered his huge antlered head and made for the Black Road.

"Jengo, you must return to Shenka. Do not think of hunting Mishka down." The Mistress was tired and the thought of punishing Jengo for killing that insolent creature seemed all too much effort.

Jengo finally lowered his hackles and turned to The Mistress. "Do you think Click is a real danger, Mistress?" His voice was hopeful for a lie.

"Yes, Jengo, I do. He has found a way to break the magic. I don't know how but I know he must have had help, and that kind of power worries me, Jengo. It worries me that I don't know where or who it has come from." With that she turned towards her cottage path. "Safe travelling, Jengo, and save a pup for me. I've decided to give Thistle her own protection. I will train the pup. I won't always be around to protect her and good serving goblins are hard to find, especially ones with no voice." She smiled at Jengo a fake smile but he needed reassuring, for he would not leave her side if he knew she was in danger and she felt danger was just around the corner. "Now come my beauties, let us leave this place. Thistle, see to the fire and don't dilly dally. I'm hungry and thirsty and in need of my chair." Jengo turned to leave but stole a long glance at Thistle. A pup? For her? She shall have my runt! He gave a small, low growl at her and flew into the forest.

Thistle kicked earth and stones onto the fire. Now only smoke wisped into the night. The pack were desperate to leave, they had been still for too long and needed to run and scurry. Thistle followed The Mistress and the pack down the cottage path smiling her biggest smile. *A wolf pup all for myself,* she thought, *what a lucky hobgoblin I am!*

Chapter 54
Illiwig

Deep below Boar Keep Illiwig felt a single tear run down his cheek and drip of off his chin. Illiwig was bound and chained. He had felt enough pain in his life to toughen him up, but what he had endured through the night had him wondering if he really was still alive.

"Come now, Illiwig, let's be friends." The slow, creamy voice of the torturer spilled from the shadows. "I've taken some fingers, an eye and, let me see, yes, one ear! My work is far from complete. All you have to do is tell. A whisper will do. What do you say? Are we friends yet?" Illiwig knew he would never tell, not he, not old Illiwig.

"Well, you can't say I didn't try." With that the sound of metal scraping against stone filled the room. "One last chance, Illiwig. Nod if you feel like chatting." Illiwig stayed still. He would not tell. He knew more pain was to come, but he would not tell.

"Okay, Illiwig. Have it your way. Shall we see what your guts look like?" Illiwig closed his eyes and thought of his little hovel, his desperate screams and howls were heard by no one.

Chapter 55
Dax

Dax opened his eyes. Mottled light filtered down onto his face from the canopy above. He tried to roll over, but his pounding head had him lying back down. Dax swept his eyes over his surroundings. *Where in Mer's name am I?* he thought as he remembered the dragon advancing on him. He lifted his hands to his face certain they would be burnt to a crisp.

"I see you are finally awake." The clear, crisp voice boomed through the trees. Dax sprang to his feet setting his head spinning. "Sit down, you fool, you will only fall."

"Stay away! How did I get here! Where is my father?" Dax shouted, fearful of whatever had spoken.

"Sit down and I will explain all, boy." Dax sat. "Now, that's better. I am Ingrid, your dragon." Dax hugged his knees tight and squinted, scanning the trees to find where the voice had come from. Ever so slowly the large form of a dragon began to appear. It's scales changing from the colour of bark and leaves to the reds and golds of fire. Dax's eyes were as huge as dinner plates when the camouflage was finally revealed. The dragon stalked towards Dax as he dug his fingernails deeper into his legs.

"You, you, can change?"

"No, not change, disguise. We dragons have learnt to blend in over thousands of years. We don't fly well anymore so catching our pray needed another approach."

"Where are we?" Dax felt small and helpless.

"We are deep within the dragon isle that is what humans call it. But to us it is called Babishmoore. Home of dragons. Birth place of fire." Ingrid lay down in front of Dax and fixed him with a stare. Dax shrank back. "Dax, you cannot fear me. We are bonded. We have work to do and not a lot of time to do it."

"Sorry." Dax lowered his eyes, tears threatening to fall.

"You father knows where you are, boy, he knows you are safe." Dax looked doubtful. "You will rise, dress and follow me. There is someone I want you to meet."

Dax looked down at his body. He was naked except for the glove. He flushed red with shame.

Ingrid chuckled, "Come now, you are not the first naked human I have seen. To get here, the way we did, takes a lot of deep magic, dragon magic, and materials burn away on the journey. You will find an assortment of human garments over there behind that well, take your pick and while you are there drink deep, my young charge, long days and nights are ahead." Ingrid rose and made to leave. "When you are finished call my name and I will come." Dax nodded and rose covering himself with large leaves from the ground. Ingrid gave a deep laugh as she blended into the jungle.

Dax stumbled over to the stone well and peered inside. A small bucket hung from a winch, he reached out to lower it, dropping his leaves, he startled and whilst scrabbling to keep his modesty the bucket dropped down deep into the well. "For the love of Mer!" He shouted at no one. Dax slid to the floor and held his head in his hands. *How can my world change so much?* he thought sadly to himself. A small, single tear dropped down his cheek and landed on his foot leaving a silvery trail. He stared at his gloved hand and flexed his fingers. He hadn't realised till now how much it tingled and itched. Dax heard his father's voice in his head. This is what you are born to do, Dax, this is your destiny. He rose, the handful of leaves forgotten and leant into the well. He pulled the little bucket up by the chain and drank deeply. *Well, if I'm going to do this, I would rather do it clothed,* he thought.

Dax stared down at himself and smiled. He was dressed in tight green leggings and a black dress shirt that came to his knees, he had tried to shorten it using a brown woven belt, he had found amongst the pile of odd garments, but had given up when he realised it made him look even more foolish. On his feet was a pair of brown riding boots, a little big but in good condition. He drank again from the well and ran his scaly hand through his hair.

"Ingrid!" He called with a croaky voice.

"I'm right here!" The voice was so close it made Dax leap back with fright.

"For the love of the Merfolk!" Dax shrieked.

"You'll have to learn to spread out your senses, boy, if you intend to keep up." And with a snort, Ingrid emerged from the ground like red larva.

"How long have you been there?" Dax asked, a little miffed.

"Long enough to snigger at you messing around with that belt."

"Oh."

"Come now, boy, this way, I will talk and you will listen." Ingrid cocked her head to Dax, waiting for an answer.

"Okay, okay. You talk, I'll listen. Where are we going?"

"Somewhere very sacred."

"And who are we meeting?"

"That's not listening that's talking."

"Okay. It's just that…"

"Talking," Ingrid sang. Dax snapped his mouth shut around his next question and followed his beautiful dragon through the trees.

"Your father will have explained the glove and what it can do, yes?" Dax just nodded.

"Good. We dragons have the ability to make fire but not control it. Yes?" Dax nodded again his mouth and mind itching to speak.

"Well, while you are here with us you will learn to use and enhance those skills." Ingrid stopped and turned to Dax. "Show me your hand." Dax raised his gloved arm. "It itches, doesn't it?" Again, Dax nodded, biting his lip in case anything slipped out. "Once you start to use the magic, that will stop." Ingrid turned away and continued through the brush. "Now you have claimed me, young Dax, we will be bonded till the end of time. We will fight as one, one cannot fight without the other. Your bonding will begin once the Ancient One has blessed us and you have learnt to hold a single flame in your hand."

"How long will I be here?" Dax blurted out.

"As long as it takes." Ingrid paused and let out a deep sigh. "There have only been two Fire Sworn before you Dax. Many flee, some are not worthy and some… Well some don't make it."

"Don't make it? What does that mean?"

"Some, Dax, get burnt away. They let the power of the fire consume them. They allow themselves to become one with its life force engulfing their souls. But enough of that. You, boy, will not let that happen, will you?"

"Err, not if I can help it. Burning away sounds painful."

"Painful no. Unchangeable, yes." Ingrid whispered.

Ingrid and Dax emerged in to a clearing, both deep in thought. The ground was smooth, scorched stone and in the centre was a round, low crucible like the one deep within Monmoo.

"Now what?" Dax asked.

"Now, we wait." Ingrid made her way to the centre of the clearing and lay down, Dax followed.

"Rest, child, you will need it." And with that Ingrid closed her eyes.

Dax sat crossed-legged and slumped his head into his hands. His mind wandered to home. He wondered what Kef was doing now. Had he journeyed to the Olive Gardens was he relaxing in their shade? Was his father worrying about him? He missed the jokes and carefree life he had had. He felt that was all behind him, as if it had been someone else's life. Just as his eye lids began to droop he thought he heard a noise. Dax sat upright and scanned the surrounding jungle. Nothing looked out of place, he had been fooled by this twice and now he wasn't going to make it a third time. He shaded his eyes with his hands and squinted to look deeper into the trees.

"Wrong direction, boy." The deep whisper bellowed onto Dax's neck making him startle and lunge forward scrapping his elbows on the stone.

"But you are learning, young one."

Dax spun round and from the stone emerged a dark, green dragon. Not as large as Ingrid but wider and more heavily scaled, its eyes a dark, emerald green.

"Hello, Ingrid." The elderly dragon's voice was rich and deep. Ingrid uncurled her tail and rose, taking a deep bow as she stood.

"Great one, this is Prince Daxion."

"I know who he is. I have waited a long time for you, boy."

"He has promise." Ingrid stretched her legs and whipped her tail as she spoke.

"My name is Papa, it is not my birth name, it is the name the dragons have given me. It means father in one of the ancient languages of this world." Dax just stared.

The green dragon seemed a lot older than Ingrid, his tail had a slight kink in the tip, his claws were chipped and one had broken away. His heavy scaling around the mouth and nose gave him an almost turtle appearance.

"We have come for your blessing, Papa, and to start our bonding." Ingrid spoke with deep respect.

"Well then, we had better make a start."

Papa and Ingrid made their way to the stone crucible, Dax, followed. "Dax, are you ready to learn? To train hard and listen to Ingrid's counsel at all time?"

"I am, I mean, I will." Dax was tongue-tied with nerves.

177

"Very well, we shall begin." Papa pulled himself up to his full height and turned a fierce eye on them both. "Dax, take your gloved hand and place it onto Ingrid's scales." Dax did as he was bid. As soon as his hand touched Ingrid's scaly back a warm sensation shot through his arm, alarming but not unpleasant.

"I, oldest of all dragons bless this bonded pair. Allow them to fight as one, to defend as one. This bond can be broken only by The Mistress herself. Dax, you have a responsibility to Ingrid now, as she has to you. We shall begin." Papa stepped back and breathed deeply in through his nose then opened his mouth and blew a slow, soft stream of fire into the stone bowl. It spluttered and faded until a single flame remained.

"Your only job tonight is to take your gloved hand and hold the single flame, keeping it alive. Can you do that for me, Dax?" Dax stared at the tiny flame and shrugged.

"Doesn't seem too hard." His arrogant response had Ingrid and Papa both share a knowing glance.

Dax reached out and cupped his gloved hand. He bent into the crucible and scooped up the flame. It instantly fizzled and died.

"Oh, wait! Again, please. I've got this." Dax was eager to prove himself.

"As you wish." Once again Papa made the fire and Dax failed to keep it alive.

"What's the trick? What's the joke?" Dax was becoming impatient. He was the one who played the jokes at home and he wasn't enjoying being on the receiving end.

"No joke, young one. The flame needs your dragon magic to stay alive. You need to channel the magic that is in your blood. Learn to control it, to feed your flame." The ancient, green dragon turned to leave.

"Hey wait!" On hearing his disrespectful tone Ingrid whipped her head round to face Dax.

"You dare to insult Papa with your childish temper, BOY!" She had puffed to full height with her anger. Her wings out-stretched, almost knocking Dax over. Her eyes were wide and glowing. Dax shrank back raising his hands to fend off any blows.

"Ingrid, it's all right, he is an innocent. He meant no harm." Papa had turned back to face them.

"Yes, yes! He's right I meant no harm. Err, sorry, Papa." Dax offered the old dragon a meek smile.

"Very well, I will let your innocence be your excuse this time, but I expect respect from you when addressing Papa, at all times.

Do I make myself clear, boy?" Ingrid snorted hot breath from her nose and made sure it skimmed Dax, just as a warning of course.

"Yes, sorry." Dax felt foolish, he still had so much to learn.

"Ingrid will provide the flame for you and you will stay here until you have the flame in your hand." Papa turned once more to leave.

Ingrid re-folded her wings and sighed, "Dax, I know this is all so different from your life in Meridien but you have the magic in your blood and the intelligence to understand how to use it. Just calm yourself, relax and look deep within. The magic will call to you and you will answer. Shall we try again?" Ingrid softened her tone fearing a long night ahead. She blew gently into the stone crucible; her flame was even smaller than Papa's.

"Okay, relax, breathe." Dax said reaching out a tentative hand. He tried to scoop the flame again.

Papa woke at first light and made his way to the clearing. He gently pushed through the trees for he knew what would await him. There on the ground was Ingrid, curled tight, her tail covering her eyes, fast asleep. And leaning against her side was Dax, deep in slumber, his hands in his lap. And in his gloved hand a tiny, red flame flickered.

"There is hope yet, child, all we need is hope."

Chapter 56

Dax crouched low behind a small outcrop of rock. His clothes were a dishevelled mess, his hair a greasy mop. He ran his ungloved hand over his face.

"Are you sure he's here?" He whispered to a pile of dead sticks and leaves.

"I am sure. I tracked him for two days." The leaves replied.

"Are you sure we are ready?"

"I am sure. Don't worry so, Dax. Oh, he will try to hurt you. Of that I am sure but still it would be no test if there were not fear. Fear of real danger." The pile of leaves started to solidify, brown turning to red. Ingrid emerged from the gloom.

"How long have we got?" A nervous Dax asked.

"Until sunset. You have trained for this Dax. Six long weeks of getting your skinny little hide whipped, you must be sick of losing by now." Ingrid chuckled.

"Hey! That's not fair. I've done my share! Okay maybe at first I whined a bit but come on!"

"Okay, okay. You listen now but it took a good few thrashings to open your ears." Ingrid looked down at her human and felt a mother's protective love. *Stupid boy,* she thought and shook her head. "It will take everything we have learnt together if we are going to outwit Papa. You know that, yes?" Ingrid had hardened her tone.

"I know. Thank you, Ingrid."

"What for boy?"

"For putting up with me." Dax shrugged, a slight blush on his cheeks.

"You are welcome, my prince." Ingrid faked a low bow and smiled.

"Stop it. We are equals you and I." Dax reached out his gloved hand and ran it across Ingrid's neck, feeling the warmth of her dragon magic tingle its way up his fingers and into his palm.

"I'm ready," he whispered.

"Good," replied Ingrid. "Let the game begin."

For six weeks Dax had learnt to move with stealth. To open his senses to all sounds and smells. He could find Ingrid now without even thinking about it, something she had found irritating. They had learnt to bond their magic and fight as one with the power of fire as their tool. He had taken many a scold or burn trying to catch flames and turn them into weapons but he had never given up and was now a master at moulding flames into arrows or clubs, a fearsome skill indeed. Now the final test was to track Papa and fight him. When he was told of this he argued against such a harsh test but Ingrid had assured him that those that had come before him had had to endure the same test. "How do you think Papa got his battle scars, boy." Was her answer. It had silenced Dax for days but with coaxing from Ingrid he had come to realise that the test was an honour not a punishment. If Papa thought he was ready, then prove himself he would.

Dax rose and slowly scanned the tree line.

"I see him!"

"No, Dax, you don't. Papa is very good at duplicating his shadow. Look a few feet to the left."

Dax turned his head slightly and saw the illusion.

"Sly, old goat." After realising what he said, Dax ducked. He knew a blow was coming for his disrespect. None came.

"Yes, he is." Ingrid chuckled. "So, we will need to be even slyer."

"What approach do we take?"

"You see above him, the way the branches of that tree are staggered."

"Yes."

"As soon as we strike he will climb. It's his favourite tactic. He will have the advantage."

"Sooo…"

"So, we start high. You will make your way through the tree branches. I will make a diversion."

"Okay, but won't he be expecting that?"

"He will. Which is why we will play along. For now." Ingrid had beaten Papa only once. The chances that she and Dax would win were slim, but she liked an outside chance. It gave her drive.

Dax started climbing the nearest tree, then paused.

"What happens next?"

"Wait and see, young prince, battle can never be planned to the last little move. Your instincts and training will lead you." Dax shrugged and continued to climb.

Ingrid waited till he was out of sight and strode towards what she perceived to be Papa.

Two things happened next at the same time, Ingrid fell into a trap in the ground and Dax was set upon by Papa.

"Ingrid!" Dax shouted from the top of his lungs. He had seen the ground open up and his precious dragon fall. He had heard Papa's roar behind him and had fallen. Dax lay on the ground face down in the mud, the world stood still. "Up Dax! Get up!" He had screamed to himself. He sprang up and made for the hole he had seen Ingrid fall into. He heard the crashing and thrashing of Papa making his way from the trees, his heart was pumping so fast he thought it might burst from his chest.

"Ingrid!" He screamed as he launched himself into the hole not knowing its depth, not knowing if Ingrid had survived.

Dax landed with a thud. His knees buckled as the bottom of the trap came quicker than he expected. He stumbled forward scraping his knees, with his lungs winded he gave out a loud gasp.

"Shooosh, boy." Ingrid whispered, right next to his ear. He wanted to hug her but refrained. "He is above us but cannot see this far down into the darkness. Surprise is our only option. Climb onto my back."

"What?" Dax had always wanted to ride Ingrid but she had said it is an insult to dragon kind to carry cargo. Now she was demanding it.

"Just climb on, we have no time."

Dax carefully clawed his way onto Ingrid's back, not an easy task in a dark, cramped hole.

"Now I will climb, and you will prepare. We must come out of this hole like Papa's worst nightmare. He has the high ground, he will be waiting."

"I'm ready. Go!"

Ingrid dug her huge claws into the muddy sides of the pit and hauled herself upwards. Dax and Ingrid flew into the clearing, Dax screaming and Ingrid breathing a long, thick plume of flame, Dax stood upon Ingrid's back and threw himself forward, taking hold of the flame and willing it into a long spike of fire. He landed on his feet and looked up just in time to see Papa charging, jaws open ready to strike. He pulled back his arm and launched his spear rolling to the side just as Papa was upon him.

"Dax! Over here!" Ingrid shouted. She was crouched low ready to spring. Dax ran.

The fire spear had hit Papa square in the face blinding him for a second, nothing more. He turned and charged.

Before Dax had reached his dragon, she spat a huge ball of fire his way. Dax slid to the floor. Raising his hand he caught the ball mid-flight and flipped onto his feet, Papa only inches behind him,

"Now!" he shouted. Ingrid buried her nose under his feet and flung him into the air. Dax dived and launched his fire ball onto Papa's wing where it exploded into a thousand sparks. The mighty green dragon faltered, skidded and stopped. Dax landed behind him and raked in a deep breath. He knew this wasn't over. Ingrid flung herself at Papa, trying to wrap her massive wings around him. Papa roared with pain as his damaged wing bent back in the scuffle. Dax ran around the tangled mass of struggling dragons and crouched low, waiting. Ingrid realised she wasn't strong enough to engulf her beloved Papa and in desperation threw him backwards with her front claws. Papa landed on his back and was writhing and howling to right himself. Dax ran in front of Ingrid and raised his hand. He had to finish this, seeing Papa in pain was unbearable. Ingrid breathed out a quick line of flames and Dax caught it, swung it round his head and transformed it into a long chain of flames. Just as Papa had managed to get to his feet Dax swung the chain wide and unleashed it like a whip. The chain struck Papa around the neck, wound itself around the scaly master and lashed him to Dax's hand. The roar the green dragon gave out that day had never been heard before and never since. No Fire Sworn had ever been able to make a chain of fire and its drain on Papa's magic was absolute. The once proud and noble Papa was reduced to a quivering, huffing pile of scales. Alive but barely.

"Quick, Dax, release him!" Ingrid screamed at a dumbfounded Dax.

He looked down at his gloved hand holding the end of the chain. He slowly relaxed his fingers and let the chain tumble to the ground, its fire dying out as it fell.

"Papa! Papa!" Ingrid was clawing at Papa's body desperate for him to move, desperate for signs of life.

"I'm sorry. Please, Ingrid! What have I done?" Dax fell to his knees. Fear and adrenaline making him shake.

The earth shook, as Ingrid fell to the ground, her head resting on Papa's neck.

"Please, Papa. Don't leave me!" Her voice was a broken whisper. Papa was dead.

Chapter 57
King Max

King Max slumped back in his favourite armchair, Meridien's finest brandy in hand. Dax had been gone nearly six weeks and it had been a fretful six weeks for the king. The nights were turning cold. Max pulled his silk robe tighter around his waist. *The boy will be fine*, he thought to himself, *he has been well trained, well counselled.* Max's thoughts turned to Kef. He'd heard nothing from him since Dax went away. He assumed he was enjoying his retirement at the Olive Gardens. The King rose and dashed the last of his brandy into the fire. *Who am I fooling? Dax is wild, headstrong. He will not last the bonding.* Max let out a deep sigh and returned to his chair. His mind wandered back to his own homecoming and the festivities his father had laid on. His dragon had been called Sasha, she was an orange beauty. But it had all come to a bad end because of Jason. *That arrogant, stupid fool. He ruined everything for all of us.* He realised he was clenching his fists and relaxed. *What good would being angry at the past achieve?* he thought, *I must prepare. If Dax were to return early he would find me here glum and sulking in solitude. No this will not do, it really will not do.* The King rose and rang the bell for his aid. *When Dax returns he shall find a proud and strong father. Not just a father, but a King.* There was a small knock at the door and Penthistle entered. His round, whiskery face as passive as ever.

"You rang, your highness?"

"Yes, yes, clothes, Penthistle. My finest attire."

"But sir, it's close to midnight."

"I'm aware of that, man, but my son is to return soon, and when he does he shall find me ready."

"Ready for what, your highness?"

"Anything, Penthistle, anything."

Chapter 58

Dax

Dax hadn't spoken since Papa's death. He had taken solace in the trees. Ingrid had approached him many times to talk him down but to no avail. He had watched Papa's funeral pyre from up high. Each dragon adding its flame. A beautiful song of whispering words and hums from the dragons had lasted well into the night.

"Dax, Dax, come down now!" Ingrid was irritated. The boy was not to blame but childish sulking was not acceptable. "I have given you time, boy, now my patience has run as thin as your skinny little legs. Come down at once or I will have no choice but to burn this tree down with or without you in it!" Ingrid stopped shouting and sank to the floor. Papa's death had been a blow not only to her but to every dragon on Babishmoore. A new blessed one will be chosen; a new era would begin. Mourning for too long was not the way of dragons. Ingrid heard a slow rustling above her. She waited. "Glad you could join me, young prince." Ingrid kept her voice soft as she didn't want to spook him back up the tree.

"Ingrid, I want to go home." Dax's voice was tiny and full of sadness.

"Well, boy, your wish is about to come true. What happened in the battle was always going to happen, Dax. It was written many years ago. Papa wouldn't have had it any other way. He knew his death would come at the hands of a young Sworn, and to be honest, most thought it would be your father. You have been chosen, Dax. Do not think of this as a tragedy, think of it as a progression, a step onto the right path."

"If that is true, then why do I feel so wretched?"

"It is because your heart is leading your head, boy. In battle your head must always lead. The path that lies ahead of you, Dax, is one full of danger. But we will face it together, we and the other Sworn and their bonded."

"I don't feel chosen. I don't feel ready."

185

"Well, this is just the beginning, boy, you will have to learn to reconcile your emotions and become the man who will do what is necessary for the good of all." Ingrid rose and stared down at her Sworn human. "Come, it is about time you paid your respects to Papa's pyre. Then it is time for you to leave. I will stay here until I am summoned, there is much to do." Ingrid walked slowly away, not looking back. Dax followed.

After a tearful visit to Papa's resting place Dax returned to the drinking well he had first come across when he arrived. He sat and leant his back to its cool brickwork. He thought of home, father, Lex. It all seemed so dream-like.

"Are you ready, young prince?" Ingrid emerged from the brush.

"Yes, Ingrid, I think I am."

"Very well. Dax, you will leave the island as you arrived."

Dax's eyes went wide.

"I know it is hard for you humans to see fire as anything else but death, but trust me, Dax, to you fire is yours to command. You just have to believe." Ingrid turned to leave.

"Very well." Dax also rose knowing his childish days were behind him. The death of Papa at his hand had changed him. The weight of responsibility was his to bear. He would not let Papa's death be a waste. He would serve him proudly and always do the best he could to honour his memory.

Dax and Ingrid made their way to the blessing circle, both deep in thought.

"The Deep Gate will need to be opened." Ingrid spoke with determination. "I will speak the blessing and breathe my hottest fire. You, Dax, will then walk straight into my flame." Ingrid braced herself for Dax's protest, his fear and pleading, but none came.

"As you wish." Dax felt no fear. He had seen and learnt things on Babishmoore that he couldn't explain. He trusted Ingrid completely and if this is what must be done then so be it. He would face it with courage.

Ingrid smiled. Her bonding complete. A Fire Sworn to be proud of. Her Dax, her Sworn. She spoke the words. She breathed her fire and Dax with head held high walked into the Deep Gate. Ingrid would wait to be summoned. Only The Mistress could summon her to the Holding Grounds. The palace of Meridien was not a place for a dragon to be seen. Ingrid was exhausted, she lay on the hot floor where Dax had vanished and slept, dreaming of Papa and his beautiful green eyes.

Chapter 59

The king had been making regular trips into Monmoo for days, every day hoping to find Dax. He had risen earlier than usual and slipped out of the palace and to the heart of Monmoo. He sat on the hot earth where he knew the Deep Gate would open and waited, half expecting to return to the palace disappointed and anxious. Just when he was about to rise he felt a slight tremor. Doubting himself he placed both his hands on the ground and again the earth shook. Max jumped to his feet, wringing his hands.

"Please, Please, I can bear the wait no longer. My son! Please let it be so." He screamed to the ground. He looked down as the earth crumbled, cracks spread out in all directions as he struggled to stay on his feet. A great booming sound echoed off the cave's walls as the earth fell away and the Deep Gate was revealed. The King dropped to his knees and held his breath. The sound and shaking became unbearable and Max screwed up his eyes against the dust. As quickly as it had started the unbearable noise stopped and the earth lay still. Max felt a gentle hand upon his shoulder and opened his eyes. In front of him stood his naked son, not the cheeky little boy who had left but a strapping, proud Fire Sworn. Dax smiled and offered his father his hand.

"Let's go home." Dax whispered.

The King and his son, now wrapped in a cloak, made their way through the winding streets of Meridien and entered the palace just as the suns rose. The King hadn't stopped talking, asking questions, eager for news from Babishmoore. Dax answered as honestly as he could, leaving out Papa's death. It was still too painful to talk about. They made their way to Dax's chambers, where The King ordered food and drink.

"Father. I know I have to leave again."

"Yes, son, you do. But let us not talk of tomorrow, boy, let us revel in your homecoming. My son, you look different, older, stronger. I am so proud of you." Feeling his cheeks redden Max snapped his mouth shut and busied himself with the plates and food.

Dax rose and walked to his father's side. "It's okay, Father. You don't have to say the words." Dax wrapped his now strong arms around his father and hugged him in the first embrace the pair had shared. No words were needed. They both felt the love only a child and parent could ever know. Max gently released his son and looked into his eyes.

"Watching you leave in the morning will be the proudest and saddest moment of my life, Dax. But always remember I am your father and if you ever need me I am by your side." Max stepped back and grasped his son by the hand. "Fulfil the dream and destiny that I could not, Dax."

"I will do my best with honour, father."

Father and son stood still, both knowing this might be the final time they could share a private moment, both wishing it would last. A sharp knock at the door had them both releasing their hands and turning away.

"Enter!" The King's voice was now royally harsh.

Lexion entered the room with his usual pomp and ceremony. "Brother. I see you have returned." Lexion's dislike for his brother obvious.

"Yes Lex, I have returned." Dax lunged forward and grabbed his brother in a friendly hug, much to Lex's displeasure. "And I see you haven't lost your stiff upper lip." Dax chuckled and winked at his father, who stifled a smirk.

"Well, err, yes my duties as you know here in the palace are of great importance." Lex strode to the fire and turned his back to them.

"Lex, your brother leaves in the morning for the Holding Grounds. Will you join us for supper?" The King knew this might be the last time he had his two sons together in the same room and wanted this opportunity to make a good memory he could look back on in his later years.

"As you wish, father." Lex turned and stared at his father and wayward brother, but something was different about Dax. He couldn't put his finger on it, but he didn't like it. But these things had to be endured if he wished to be King.

All three drank and ate and talked long into the afternoon, Dax's exhaustion eventually taking him to his bed. Lex had left his father dozing in his chair and made his way to his own chamber, making sure he was completely alone. Once inside he made his way to his dresser and opened a small, wooden box with great care. A tiny, black spider climbed onto Lex's hand and quickly crawled up his arm to his shoulder.

"What have you to report, your majesty?" The spider's voice was slow and hypnotizing.

"My fool of a brother is back, bumbling idiot! How dare he touch me with his filthy gloved hand?"

"Easy, your highness, don't take on so. Relax. I am here to help. What word does he bring from Babishmoore?"

"Babish what? What are you talking about? All I know is he is different, confident, defiant even. And he has my father's ears."

"Babishmoore is where his dragon comes from. Is he bonded? Is the dragon here?"

"No, no, he is alone and from what he says he is bonded."

"Good, good, my King. Do not fear. My Queen will deal with your brother when the time is right. And you shall be king, not just of Meridien but of all the Warm Realm." The spider had climbed into Lex's ear and was spinning a web of enchantment.

"Yes, you horrid little creature! I will be King and if Dax gets in my way, well, let's just say, Fire Sworn or not, my blade will slit his throat." Lex sniggered to himself, a slight black tint to his eyes and a tiny, black spider in his ear.

Chapter 60
The Mistress

The Mistress had been pacing the clearing outside her cottage for hours muttering and tutting to herself. Thistle had kept out of her way. Ever since the picking day The Mistress's mood had become darker and darker. Thistle bent down and lifted her small pup to her face and nestled her.

We'll just stay in here and cuddle a while my little Roo, Thistle thought. Thistle loved the pup like it was her child and the pup responded with long, wet licks to Thistle's face.

The cottage door slammed open and The Mistress flew in.

"It's nearly time, Thistle! I can feel it. They will be back any time soon. We must pack. We must be at the Holding Grounds and prepared when they come." The Mistress started fumbling through boxes and baskets. Thistle gently placed her pup in its basket and wandered over to The Mistress. She gently placed her hand on The Mistress's shoulder. The Mistress jumped and turned with rage. Thistle pointed to The Mistress's chair and started taking items out of the boxes and baskets herself.

"Yes, Thistle you know where our things are kept. You pack, but do it right, mind. Nothing is to be left behind." The Mistress slumped in her chair and gave a sigh. "There was a time I didn't need a serving goblin, you know, I was strong and managed my own affairs." Thistle just looked up and smiled at The Mistress all the time shoving bottles and bowls into carrying sacks. "But the one who ignores the turning of time is a fool indeed." The Mistress leant her head back and thought of all that would come. "I need rest and courage if they are to make it. Yes, rest and courage." With that The Mistress nodded off, for it had been weeks since she had slept properly and now the day was upon her, a little snooze could not hurt.

The Holding Grounds were at the centre of the forest, not easy to get to, surrounded by briar and thorn bushes. One path in and the same path out. It was forbidden to enter unless under strict instruction from The Mistress. The pack were the first in, charging with tails high in the air, a fearful sight indeed. The Mistress followed leaning heavily on her cane and bringing up the rear were Thistle and Roo.

"Come now Thistle, we must be inside the Holding Ground before dark. The briar and thorns will close the entrance off to hunting packs. We need no stray jackal or forest bear here tonight." Thistle quickened her pace and Roo followed.

The Holding Ground was a circular patch of flat earth at the base of a rocky hillside no plant or shrub grew there. It had a large cave to one side that had been hewn out of the hillside rock. The entrance was surrounded by large wooden cages, each with a lock and bolt. In the centre of the large clearing was a deep fire pit. Thistle rolled her eyes seeing it unlit. She knew her task for the evening.

"To the cave, Thistle! I want all the bags and carrying sacks emptied and arranged before we rest," The Mistress hissed at the pack, pointed to the fire pit and to the pile of sticks and logs next to the cave. The pack set to work building the fire. *Good,* Thistle thought, *less work for me.* She headed to the cave with Roo in tow. "Not you, Roo, you stay with me. I don't want half that bag of dried meat strips going to you, you spoilt whelp. These will be long days and your belly being fuller than mine is not an option." Roo slunk behind The Mistress, all thoughts of the meat strips in Thistle's bag gone from her mind, she crept over to the fire pit and curled up waiting for its warmth.

The rats had built the fire high and Thistle had lit it using her flints. The cave had been arranged to The Mistress's liking and Thistle had managed to slip a little slither of dry meat to her pup.

"Now we wait. All three should come tomorrow. Some at early dawn, some late at night. The pool will not be touched until all three are here." The Mistress sounded tired. Thistle fetched the sleeping furs from the cave and made a bed close to the fire. She turned towards The Mistress and gestured to the nest she had built. "Thank you, Thistle, I will sleep now but wake me at first light, I don't want them journeying here and finding me like a sleeping squirrel." The Mistress lowered herself to the furs and Thistle covered her almost completely. She turned to Roo and they curled up together next to The Mistress. The pack were also piled high, tails twitching in blissful slumber. A single owl called out across the forest and all was still.

The Mistress lay wrapped in her furs by the fire in the Holding Grounds. The events of the past weeks unfolding in her mind. *What kind of being could hold the power of both me and my sister? What dark craft has come to this land?* she thought, trying to plan, trying to see a path forward. *I must not fail. It is time to call upon my sister's favour and summon my token.* The Mistress pondered, *All must now be called to help.* Thistle and Roo snored and snuffled beside her. As she let sleep finally take her, she hoped that the Sworn children would come in time.

Chapter 61

Dax

Dax's leaving ceremony would be at sunrise. All the important people would gather to wish him well and shake his hand. Then a quick appearance on the balcony for the people to see their Sworn Prince. The King was fussing with his cravat when Dax entered the room.

"Here, father, let me help." Dax offered.

"I have dreamed of this moment, Dax, just as my father did before me and his father before him."

"I know, it does feel truly strange."

"The Lords and Dukes will try to ask questions and shower you with gifts for your favour. You must be humble but firm, son. We are pressed for time and she will not be kept waiting."

"She?" Dax pondered aloud.

"No, no, don't ask me, boy, I cannot say. You will find out yourself soon." Max finished dressing and turned to his son. "After you." The King gestured to the door and Dax smiled, drinking in his father's image.

"No, my King, after you." The pair left the room as friends, companions, not just father and son.

The ceremony was tiresome, and the people were greedy for Dax's time. He managed to fend them off with his charm and a few discrete promises here and there. Now he must face the people and declare himself their saviour. He stood beside his father and brother, the feeling of overwhelming nerves he had had at his hair-cutting ceremony were gone. Just a feeling of self-worth and pride filled him.

"Open the doors." Dax ordered and the doors to the balcony were thrown wide. The noise from the crowd was deafening. The King stepped out and all went quiet.

"My people! My Meridien! I present to you Prince Daxion, Fire Sworn." Dax stepped forward and the crowd went wild. Children threw small flowers of red and orange into the air, men shouted and whistled, women fainted. Nothing had ever been seen like this before. Acrobats dressed in red flowing costumes ran through the crowd. The breeze had picked up the children's tiny flowers and swirled them like dragon flames overhead. The scene had Dax dumbstruck. Lex on the other hand seethed with envy, his spider burying itself deeper and deeper into his ear.

"Dax! Dax!" The King was gently pulling on his son's sleeve.

"Oh! Yes, sorry, father." Dax coughed and cleared his throat.

"People of Meridien! Please, I ask for silence!" He leant closer to the railing. "I, Prince Daxion, son of King Maximillion, brother to Prince Lexion, promise to protect these lands. I promise to serve the people. But most of all I promise to do my duty to my father. I am Fire Sworn and for Meridien I will lay down my life." Dax raised his gloved hand above his head and allowed his dragon magic to turn the scales a dazzling red, that shone so brightly it hurt the eyes. The crowd gasped and then clapped and shouted themselves back into a frenzy. Dax turned to his father and gently guided him inside. Lex remained on the balcony waving at the crowd, lapping up their awe.

"It is time, father. Where shall I go?"

"My son, my glorious boy." Tears ran down The King's cheek. Dax quickly wiped them away and held his father by the shoulder.

"Do not fear. I shall return. It may not be soon, but I will return, father. You have my word."

Max gave out a long and slow breath, raised his chin and spoke, his royal voice returning. "You are to make your way to the forest edge, boy, a guide will be waiting. I can say no more. Your horse is ready. It is well provisioned for your journey across the Drylands."

"Thank you, father." Dax tenderly kissed his father's cheek and turned to leave. Lex stepped in from the balcony, his face looked pale, dark circles ringed his eyes.

"Safe journey, brother." Lex sneered.

"I wish you well, Lex. Look after father." Dax could bear it no longer and turned on his heels towards the stables.

The King turned to his remaining son, "Are you ill, Lex? You look pale."

"No, father, I am far from it."

Dax mounted his horse and stretched his arms and shoulders. It would be a hard ride to the forest edge but he had done it many times before when he was younger. He would enjoy the solitude the ride would bring. He dug his heels in and was off.

Chapter 62
The Grey

The Grey sniffed the air. *Blood,* he thought. He slunk low around the doorway of Kef's dwelling and entered, slow paw, by slow paw.

"May the Mother protect us all!" He gasped. The Grey approached the drying corpse of The Mistress's oldest friend. Throat torn out. Face etched with fear and pain. The Grey looked away. "This is the gravest of news. Dark days are truly upon us." The Grey quickly left Kef's home and made his way out of the city. He allowed himself a moment of grief as he sat on the sandy dirt that bordered Meridien and the Drylands and howled, the long, deep howl of a creature whose soul had been wounded. He would let the world hear of his pain. The Grey lay down in the soil and tried to make sense of Kef's killing. The Mistress would swear revenge, that much he knew. He must get to the Holding Grounds. This news was of the utmost importance. He would not fail The Mistress. Just as The Grey rose to leave, he saw the young Prince ride out hard across the sand towards the forest. "It has begun." He whispered to himself and set off to keep pace with rider and horse.

Chapter 63
Dax

Dax had been riding hard all morning. He pulled the horse up and reached for his water skin. He knew he was being followed by a wolf. He had not seen it but his dragon magic had sensed it and as long as it kept its distance it was of no threat. He sheltered his eyes from the suns and scoured the horizon, just making out the dark shading of the forest.

"Walk on!" He called to his horse, loud enough for the wolf to hear, curious as to why he was being followed.

The Grey was exhausted, his eyes dry with sand, his nose and mouth even drier. But he had no choice but to continue. He would serve.

Dax slid from his horse and let it drink its fill. He removed his pack and fastened it to his waist.

"Time to go home, boy." Dax whispered into the creature's ear, gently stroking its mane. The horse turned and slowly trotted away, for he was a desert horse and his life was on sand. He knew the drill, always home when his duty was over.

Dax ate a little bread and scanned his surroundings; the wolf was still there. Dax could feel its discomfort, its pain.

"Are you in need of water, friend?" Dax shouted over his shoulder. The Grey said nothing just hunkered lower into the sand. "I am no danger to you, just offering assistance." Dax waited.

The Grey's need for water overcame his need for camouflage. He slowly stood and made his way to where Dax had his back to him.

"I mean you no harm." Dax again assured him.

"I am The Grey. I serve only The Mistress I will not befriend or hinder you in any way, human. I only require water." The Grey kept a little distance.

"May I turn to face you?"

"You may." Dax turned slowly. When he lay eyes on the size of the beast his eyes grew wide and he held his breath. "You need not fear me, boy, it appears we both seek The Mistress." The Grey drew nearer.

When Dax found his voice he spoke with great respect, as Papa had taught him. "It appears we do, Great One. Here, I offer water." Dax held out the water skin and bent down to pour it into his ungloved hand. The Grey bent his head and lapped the water greedily.

"Thank you, boy. It would seem we have found ourselves unlikely companions for the rest of the journey. Will you allow me to accompany you to the forest?"

"It would be an honour." Dax replaced his water skin and turned for the forest, The Grey followed.

The suns were high in the sky as the two companions reached the forest edge. The Grey came to a halt and lay down on the cool forest floor.

"Our time together has come to an end, boy." The Grey could sense his brother and knew it was Jengo's task to lead Dax to The Mistress.

"Until we meet again." Dax gave a short bow and The Grey silently disappeared into the trees. Dax stood still a little bewildered at the wolf's ability to blend in to the forest so quickly.

"Welcome, young Prince."

The deep voice made Dax jump a little, he had been trying to sense The Grey and hadn't noticed Jengo slinking low in the undergrowth. Dax said nothing just re-adjusted his stance and slowed his breathing.

"I am Jengo, brother to The Grey, servant to The Mistress."

Dax relaxed his hands and opened his palms to shown he meant no harm.

"Please show yourself, wolf." Jengo made his way from the trees and sat just out of reach of Dax.

"I see you have met my brother. Any one he allows to travel with him is honoured indeed."

Dax gave a small nod of his head.

"I am to lead you to the Holding Grounds. Follow me, boy, if you will." Jengo turned and re-entered the forest, Dax followed, his thoughts swirling at the strange events of the day.

The coolness of the forest had Dax shivering. The hot air of Meridien and Babishmoore had not prepared him for the cold, damp shade of The Mistress's home. He found the thick trees and brambles fascinating and the many ferns and flowers of the forest drew his attention away from following Jengo.

"Keep up, boy, The Mistress is waiting." Jengo was growing impatient with this young Prince.

"Sorry, yes. What a beautiful place the forest is." Dax hurried to Jengo's side, a little embarrassed at his tardiness.

"We are here. The Mistress will not tolerate foolishness."

"Understood. Please, Jengo, lead the way."

Wolf and boy entered the Holding Grounds. Dax looked around with a sense of excitement. A fire was roaring and he could feel the heat making his dragon magic tingle.

"Wait here until she addresses you." Jengo crossed the Holding Grounds and bowed to a tiny figure behind the fire. Dax just stared with awe.

"Come forward, young Prince Daxion." The tiny figure's voice belied her stature. Another small figure had joined her. Dax froze.

"Now, boy, I have no time to waste."

Dax slowly rounded the fire and could see three cages lined up in front of him. He stared, confused and overwhelmed.

"For the love of the Mer, boy, come here. I cannot have this dilly-dallying, more will be here soon." The Mistress's impatience made Thistle retreat a little.

Dax drew his eyes from the cages and looked directly at The Mistress, her eyes held the beauty of the world in their blue swirls. Dax fell to his knees.

"Mistress, I am Prince Daxion. I vow to serve only you."

"Rise, boy, there will be time for grovelling later! Come closer." Dax rose. "That's it. Now, let me see your hand."

Dax shuffled closer to The Mistress, his breath held, his heart beating fast. He had never felt so much power, so much command. He held out his gloved hand. The Mistress grabbed it and brought it close to her face.

"Yes, Yes. Good. You have bonded well. Would you like me to summon Ingrid, boy?"

Dax swallowed hard. Hearing her name brought him back to the present, he hadn't realised how much he had missed her.

"Yes please, Holy One, please."

The Mistress chuckled at the boy's subservience. *He will be easy to bend to my will,* The Mistress thought with pleasure.

"Then step aside, boy. Let me do my work."

Dax stepped aside and was joined by the ugliest hobgoblin he had ever seen. She reached out a hairy hand and rubbed his arm making Dax shudder.

The Mistress walked to the fire's edge and spoke in soft tones.

"Open your gate, Babishmoore, open your gate." A gentle breeze stirred her robes. Her voice grew louder.

"I, Mistress of the forest, command you!" louder still. "By the power of Mother Nature, do as I command! OPEN!" The fire roared to life. Flames licked high into the air as Ingrid passed through flame to forest. "Welcome, dragon of Babishmoore! Welcome, Ingrid." The Mistress bowed her head and Ingrid did the same.

"It is an honour to be here, Mistress. I hope Dax has shown respect for your command?" Ingrid took a deep bow.

"You may rise, dragon. Your boy has shown no disrespect and I can see your bonding is strong. But is he strong enough for what lies ahead, I wonder?"

On hearing this, Thistle squeezed Dax's arm, making him shrink away.

"I am strong enough, Mistress." Dax stepped forward, not wishing to cause Ingrid any shame.

"Well then, boy. Into the cage!"

Dax looked at Ingrid, her eyes holding a deep pride for her Fire Sworn. He would not let her down. She knew he would prevail. She gave him a small nod of the head.

"I will not fail you, Ingrid. I promise. For Papa." he whispered.

"For Papa." Ingrid whispered back.

Chapter 64
Malya

Deep within the calm, wooded island a shaking started, gently at first then increasing to a rumbling. A small patch of soft earth started to split and crack. Birds and woodland creatures scattered and hid. Large cakes of mud fell inwards and the tiny tips of fingers, human fingers, started to claw upwards through the woodland floor. Malya, tribal witch of the Marshlands and Manuk, king of the cobras exploded upwards deep from the bowls of the earth. Both filthy, covered in dark mud. Both gasping for air. Both alive and full of the lust for life.

Malya shook her head and dropped to one knee. "Where are we? What happened to me?"

Manuk slowly coiled around her until his head was level with hers. "We are on the second island, child. This is where you start to become one with Mother Nature herself."

Malya looked around her. The trees were not like the ones in the dark forest or the marshes. These were broader, their leaves softer. She rose and sniffed the air. It smelt clean. As she scanned the woods she glimpsed a flicker of movement. Then another. Then another.

"Something's out there." She turned to Manuk who had uncoiled himself and now rose to his full height.

"I know, child. This is where it begins."

"Where what begins?" Malya shouted as she saw eyes and tails weave themselves in and around the trees.

"You will have to make them your pack, child. You will have to show them you are their leader." Manuk almost chuckled.

"How? Help me?" Malya screamed as she saw what made its way out of the woods.

Six hungry jackals snarled their way towards Malya, their eyes evil slits, their mouths slobbering with the thought of human flesh. Malya scrambled backwards behind Manuk, her eyes and head darting back and forth following the jackals slow crawl forward.

"Do something Manuk!" Malya begged.

"Use all you have learnt, little one. Use your beast knowledge." Manuk hissed and lunged at the closest beast. It sprang back but held its ground.

"I'm not trained for this. Please, Manuk. Help me!" But Manuk only lunged at another jackal.

"Whatever you are going to do, girl, best do it now." Manuk hissed.

The jackals had encircled the two and closed in quickly. Malya lowered herself to the ground and picked out the leader, not the bravest or the largest but the one who waited silently a little further back. *You,* she thought, *if I can take you down, the others will fall.*

With one last glance at Manuk Malya sprang. Fur and girl collided and Manuk new all would be well.

Chapter 65

Malya, or what looked like Malya crouched in the bushes. Manuk was at her side deeply coiled and silent. They had been stalking the three islands for six weeks, fighting and taming the beasts, surviving on what the islands had to offer. Now they had one last thing to do. Shamma the bear! No Sworn had ever tamed him. No Sworn had ever had his subservience. Manuk knew it was not a winnable challenge, but then again no one had swept as quickly through these islands as Malya. She had fought Jackals, hypnotized scorpions and drugged monkeys and birds alike with her herb knowledge. All now bowed to her. She could walk freely on all three islands uninhibited by beasts. Her plant knowledge had saved them many a time when they had become injured or poisoned. They fought and won as one, he and she, their timing and skill incredible. Manuk had never bonded with one so deep in Mother Nature's arms.

"Malya you have completed your bonding. You don't have to prove anything to me or yourself, child. Let us be away from here." Manuk hissed gently into Malya's ear.

"Do you think me not wise or strong enough, Manuk?" Malya returned, her eyes still straight ahead.

"No, small one. But no one has ever tamed the bear. He is mad, some say; mad from his solitary life here. Mad from loneliness is a deep kind of madness, Malya, one that holds no boundaries of rage."

"Then it is not battle or plant magic I will use to tame him. It is friendship. I will not raise one fist against him. I shall offer him a song." Malya rose from the bushes, sniffed and stepped forward. Her hair was a greasy mass of tangles. Her body covered in scars and bruises. The clothes she had worn on her first day on Vine Island were long gone; all she had around her were large swathes of moss tightened around her body with long roots. Her feet were hard and calloused, caked in dried mud. But her eyes shone bright and sharp through the filthy mess that was her face.

"A song? Have you also gone mad? Malya, come back here. Let us be away. You will fail." Manuk was hissing and spitting his complete shock at what she was about to do. He had bonded so well, all was finished. They could go home now. It was over. If she continued with this stupid plan they would both surely die. "Malya! Come back!" Manuk bellowed as loud as he dare. But Malya kept on walking, straight for Shamma's cave.

Malya kept her eyes ahead, seeing only the cave, its dark, foreboding entrance looming ahead. She sniffed the air and opened her ears. She smelt the deep male smell of a predator and the low, heavy breathing of that predator sleeping. She reached the cave entrance and did not falter. The earthen floor of the cave was cool and hard. She reached out a hand to trace the inside wall as she tip-toed forward, her breathing slow and steady. Deep within the cave Shamma slept. A giant of a beast his fur thick and matted. The Several teeth he had missing had given him a nasty snarling look and his chewed and battered ears were now lumpy with scars. His clawed paws were something to behold; the size of a man's head and as sharp as any blade.

He had heard the girl approach and chose to fain sleep. Malya knew he was not asleep. She sensed his slight eye flicker and nose snuffle; she knew he was ready to strike when she was near enough. This would become a battle of wills, they both knew it.

"Hello, Shamma."

Shamma opened his eyes and shook his large dusty head. "Hello, Malya, you came."

For what Manuk didn't know was Malya had been dream-walking every night since coming to the Vine island. And every night she would visit Shamma and sing to him. She would leave him with the promise that one day she would come in person and sing the song of dreams.

Shamma suddenly reared up and lunged at Malya pinning her to the wall by one large, clawed paw. His breath coming in huge roars that covered Malya's face with drool.

"How do I know you are not here to kill me, girl. Prove you are my dream songstress." Shamma had been tricked before and had nearly got himself captured by hunters from the North.

Malya started to hum, a small collection of notes. A simple little melody. Shamma lessened his grip, but only a little. Malya could now get more air in her lungs and was not about to stop. Now she had him. Her humming became louder and she added a few soft words here and there.

"You came! I thought you a dream my loneliness had conjured up. I have roamed these Islands for many, many years. All fear me. It is my way. But I'm old now; fighting has won me nothing but a solitary life." Shamma relaxed his body. "If you have lied, child, and this is to be my end then so be it. All I ask is that you make it quick. I have nothing left to offer this world."

Shamma released her throat and sank back down onto the floor. Malya gently slipped to the floor next to him and sang her dream song. A mesmerizing tune of old, her mother had sung it to her when she couldn't sleep. Shamma's breathing became slow and heavy as he laid his head to the floor. Still Malya sang. A beautiful song of soft notes and loving, calm words. Even she felt a yawn coming and rubbed her sleepy eyes. Malya lay down next to Shamma as the song came to an end. She was so very tired, it had been an exhausting six weeks and good, deep sleep had been very hard to come by. Now she felt she could sleep for a hundred years. She snuggled herself deep into Shamma's fur and the two of them drifted together into the welcoming arms of slumber.

Manuk had slithered to the cave's entrance and was listening intently. He had heard the soft tone of Malya's voice drifting from inside. He couldn't believe what was happening, no growls or screams. No roaring or sounds of a fight, just singing. He realised the song had ended and silently slipped into the cave. Ever alert and fangs ready, he reached the sight of child and bear wrapped together in deep sleep.

Manuk smiled to himself. *In all my days being reborn on this land I have never seen such a sight. The Mistress will be pleased. There has never been a Serpent Sworn like her before. I'm sure she will be my last.* Manuk slithered from the cave and coiled in the brush at its entrance. *Tomorrow I will take her home. She is ready. More than ready,* Manuk thought as he too slipped into sleep's embrace.

Chapter 66
Illiwig

Illiwig hugged himself with his one good hand. He sniffed and choked on the blood he had just swallowed. He was in a bad way, he knew it. The wound on his belly throbbed and his eye socket had crusted over and dribbled thick ooze. Illiwig started to cry, little sobs at first, then he racked his body with huge blabs and wails. The empty eye socket stung with every tear formed but Illiwig didn't care, it was his punishment, for he had told and he had told all: The Mistress and her rats, Selena being the Sworn Princess, the room with the carved door. Everything had come spilling out as soon as the blade bit deep enough into his stomach. It wasn't the pain that made him tell, it was the knowledge that death was just a whisper away if his guts where to be pulled out and Illiwig wanted to live. His life wasn't grand or wealthy, but it was worth something to Illiwig.

After crying himself dry and rocking back and forth for a bit Illiwig started to notice his surroundings. He had been dragged from his torturous chains and thrown in here. His first instinct was to curl into a tiny ball and hope he was left alone, but the mind has a habit of pushing you forward, even in the direst of situations and now Illiwig was peering round the room trying to get his bearings. His cell was large but not cavernous. Its walls where high, made from large chunks of rock held together by mud, moss and time. There were three slits high on one wall letting in grim slithers of light and from them trickled water to form a small pool in the corner. Moss and small ferns had grown down the wall and around the pool which gave off a dank smell. Illiwig tried to sit up but winced at the pain in his belly. He tentatively lifted his blood-soaked shirt to take a look at his wound. A thick, slimy puss had started to scab and the smell was that of rotten meat. "Not good." Illiwig whispered, "Not good at all." He lowered his shirt and examined his hand. Two fingers had been snipped off with such ease it had taken his brain a few seconds to realise what his eyes had witnessed. The bloody stumps were hot and swollen. "Two out of ten's not bad." He tried to cheer himself. He raised his good hand to probe his eye socket. The scab that had formed there was lumpy and fresh. "Leave well alone now, Illiwig, some things are best left." The feeling of his missing eye was too much to bear so leave alone he would. Illiwig managed after much pain and shuffling to sit himself up against the wall and swept his eye over the cell floor. It was hard-packed earth, mostly small rocks and quartz shards. He turned his eye to the corner that was farthest away from the meagre offerings of light from the window slits. There huddled so small was a bundle of sacking; brown and tiny it almost disguised itself as part of the floor. Illiwig peered a little harder. He used his good hand and reached forward then edged his body a little closer. Every shuffle was pain to his body but curiosity was his friend and neighbour so shuffle over he would.

After what seemed like an age he reached the farthest corner of the cell, he reached out and gently pulled a corner of the sack towards him, holding his breath with every inch. All of a sudden a tiny croak came from underneath the pile. Illiwig dropped the cloth and shrank back, his mind in dumb shock as to what could be under there. After a few moments the croaking stopped so Illiwig continued his coaxing of the sack.

Inch by inch Illiwig continued to pull away the stiff piece of sacking until he could make out a small shape curled into a ball on the floor. He edged a little closer. There on the floor was a tiny fairy, battered, broken and barely alive. Illiwig reached out a shaky finger and gently touched the creature's fuzzy, little head. *Warm,* he thought, *still alive.* With his hopes building that he was not alone in this nightmare he whispered a tiny hello.

The tiny creature responded with coughs and gasps, tiny sparks fell from its mouth and fizzled out onto the floor. Illiwig gasped in horror. "Merfolk have mercy! You are not a fairy, you are a firefly." Illiwig's father had told him tales of fireflies round the hearth. They were things to be frightened of, creatures that burned homes and fields just for fun. For if one was spotted at dusk, farmers and shepherds would place extra watches upon there dwellings in case of treacherous infernos. Illiwig had thought them tales for children, myths, and legends but here was a real firefly right before his eyes and it was very close to death. Illiwig peered at its little body, two wings bent and broken, small holes had been slashed into the delicate web of skin that covered them, its tiny legs had been beaten and one was bent at an awkward angle.

"Help me, please, friend." The creature suddenly spoke. Illiwig jumped with fright, for he didn't know they could speak. "Please, I'm dying." Illiwig could barely hear the firefly's tiny voice and he bent a little closer. The firefly shot out a little claw-like hand and hooked onto Illiwig's neck. He shot backwards and cried out in pain from his belly wound but the creature clung on. Illiwig shuffled back to the wall, all the time trying to shake the creature from its grasp, but it would not be parted, and in his haste he smashed his head and back against the wall and gave himself a winding. It took him a moment to recover and when he came to his senses he looked down at the creature which had curled itself into a ball in Illiwig's lap and seemed to be purring. Illiwig calmed himself and sent up a silent prayer, "Please, for the love of Merfolk, don't let this thing hurt me. Not old Illiwig. I mean it no harm." He looked down at the little creature, as tiny as a kitten, its chest rising slowly up and down. It felt warm and Illiwig suddenly felt comfort. Another living thing snuggled up to him meant he was not alone.

Illiwig must have dozed off for the clashing and banging of doors and bolts had him startling awake. The firefly was still sleeping in his lap and his belly wound shot new pain up his body. He listened intently to the noises. They were getting closer, he was sure of it. He quickly dragged the old sack across the floor and threw it over the snuggled-up stray and closed his eyes.

The door to the cell was dragged open with a piecing screech and the harsh light of a burning touch swept around the room.

"Wake up, dear Illiwig, we have a present for you." Illiwig cracked open his good eye, his heart was beating wildly and he could feel his bowls loosen.

"There you are, my little snitch, comfy, I hope." The torturer stood in the door way and Illiwig could make out large, heavy figures behind her, but he couldn't see their faces. "I see you have found your little cell mate." The torturer giggled like a child. "Well, have another; your days are numbered anyway with a wound like that." With that she threw another sack into the cell and heaved the door shut.

Illiwig waited until the noises of his captors had faded and then a little longer to make sure they had gone before he gently shifted the firefly from his lap. It was still breathing so Illiwig tucked the cloth around her lovingly, for he had always been a gentle soul and animals and birds alike had always flocked to him. He had a natural ability with them, preferring their company to that of people, and would always tend a hurt or distressed creature.

Once more Illiwig shuffled across the cell floor. His strength was waning and his belly was full of infection and he knew his days were numbered. But still he shuffled on. He reached the sack and fumbled to untie it, which was no mean feat with only one good hand. But after some improvising with his teeth he managed to remove the thick cord that bound the mouth of the sack, he leant over and peered inside. What he saw stunned him into silence. He could not make out what was head and what was body. Was it a creature, a plant? Was it even alive?

"H-h-h-hello." A small, shaky voice came from inside the sack. "Am I safe now? Please, tell me I'm safe?"

Illiwig leaned over and pealed the sack away from the being. Its head and body where covered in root-like tendrils and its face was as gnarly as tree bark and it was green, the same shade as leaves and plants.

"For the love of the Merfolk, what are you?" Illiwig stammered.

"My name is Grumble and I fear I have not long to live."

"You are safe friend, for now." Was all Illiwig could muster for he knew they were not.

Chapter 67
Koiya

Koiya had searched for Rubear for weeks but could find no trace. She could not shake the feeling he was in trouble and that something bad had happened to him. She lifted the large carrying-sack of fruit onto her head and turned to leave. A sudden change in wind direction had her stumbling to stay upright and the fruit sack fell to the ground, spilling its golden contents. Koiya looked to the sky as the clouds rolled in, blocking the suns. The wind whipped up and blew her hair around her face. Koiya dropped to her knees and prayed to mother earth. Large drops of rain began to fall, at first bouncing on the surface of the dusty, dry earth. Then making tiny rivulets that swirled the soil into small beautiful patterns. Koiya swept the hair from her eyes and started to gather the dropped fruit. The rain now streamed down, sheets and sheets of it flooding the field. Many of the women had abandoned their harvest and cowered under the nearby trees.

All of a sudden a crow appeared, black feathers drenched and slick with rain. It swooped down by Koiya's spilt fruit; it's black, beady eyes staring straight at her. Koiya shrank back in horror for a crow only brings bad news. The crow had something in his mouth and Koiya drew a little closer, intrigued. The crow dropped his token amongst the fruit and took flight squawking and fussing. Koiya scrambled forward and dug through the now rain-soaked pile. She froze when she glimpsed what the crow had dropped. The small, red ribbon lay tangled and torn, a cuckoo amongst the fruit.

"Malya." Was all Koiya could whisper to herself.

Koiya reached down and picked up the ribbon and clutched it to her chest. "She's coming home." She whispered. Then shouted. "She comes." Koiya was off racing through the field, pain forgotten, fruit forgotten, Rubear forgotten. She flew through the village, splashing ankle deep in the now muddy puddles that covered the pathway that led towards her hut. She knew she must prepare. She had been told what happens, when a Serpent Sworn returns, from her father and now she would hold her baby girl again.

Koiya burst into the hut and herded all the children outside. They complained and sulked, for the rain had not quite stopped but Koiya insisted and when their mother had her mind to something you might as well do as you're told. Koiya, like a woman possessed, started throwing everything outside, rugs, pots, stools, nothing gained favour, the hut must be cleared. The children stood around amazed at their mother's sudden madness but all too afraid to interfere. When the hut was empty, Koiya swept the earthen floor free from stones and rocks then set about scattering herbs and feathers in an intricate pattern in the centre of the floor. When she was satisfied all was in order she sank to the floor and prayed, to The Mother, to the Merfolk and last of all to The Mistress.

Chapter 68
Malya

Malya and Manuk had returned to the Vine Island. Their journey had been silent. Both sad to leave their feral life. Deep within the cave, deep below the stone henge they sat.

"I am proud of you, Malya. You have skill the likes I have never seen before." Manuk spoke quietly not wanting to break the moment.

"Thank you." Malya rose and rubbed her face. She wanted to see her mother and tell her all that had happened, for her mother to be proud. "Shall we leave?" Malya offered nothing more.

"Yes, child, there is nothing left here for us to do." The bond of nature was so deep between the two of them words were not needed.

Manuk slowly coiled himself around Malya and the two of them joined in spirit. The floor started to crumble, to open, and the serpent-bonded pair slipped silently into the earth's embrace.

Koiya had been chanting all day and night. Her back was sore and her legs were stiff but she knew she must continue. The children had sought refuge in a neighbour's hut and were quiet and fearful that their mother was losing her mind. As the suns' first rays hit the earth, Koiya's hut was transformed into an outbreak of carnage. Feathers and herbs swirled around in a relentless wind. The sides of the hut groaned and cracked under the pressure that was brought to bear by the shaking and shuddering of the earthen floor. Koiya covered her eyes with her shaking hands and continued to chant and pray. The floor around Koiya's feet started to crumble and cave inwards; she stumbled backwards and clung to the hut wall. Squinting her eyes against the debris Koiya watched in horror as her daughter and a huge Cobra fought their way up out of the earth. Malya collapsed into a heap, heaving in huge ragged breaths. The snake that had been wrapped around her body started to uncoil and Koiya fell to the ground, the shock and joy too much to bear.

"Do not fear me, witch, I mean you no harm. I am Manuk, Malya's serpent bond. Your child is safe, just exhausted. Leave her be, she sleeps now." The deep, slow voice of Manuk calmed Koiya's beating heart but her eyes could not believe the size of the snake before her. His scales perfectly shaped. The greens and browns melting into a shimmering coat of armour. His cowl was large and looming, but it was his blue, powerful eyes that held Koiya in a trance. The most compelling thing was the tenderness in which he wrapped his muscular body around her sleeping child, creating a safe cocoon.

Koiya rose and left the hut, not knowing what else to do and fearing her people had heard the noise and were scared. She owed them an explanation. The villagers had gathered on hearing the commotion and looked to Koiya for answers.

"It is safe, my friends. I have good news. Malya returns." Koiya knew she must lead with conviction; she didn't want her whole village running scared. The people just stared in confusion at the words. "A feast is in order. My daughter has returned and she has bonded. All will be well." She let her eyes roam over the elders and let the words sink in. The children looked around at each other for answers. At last an old, withered basket-weaver started to sing, the song of old to welcome the Sworn children home. It was a song unheard for many years but as the words started up the children joined in without thought or reason. It was a song deeply engrained in their people. As the song reached an end there were smiles and laughter as all joined hands and looked to Koiya for leadership.

"Malya has returned to us this day and we shall welcome her home with great happiness. She has been away many moons and we shall feast in her honour. Prepare the gathering fire for tonight we celebrate, tonight this village rejoices." Koiya turned to re-enter the hut amongst the cheers and hustling of her people.

Koiya busied herself trying to tidy her little hut, not an easy task with a sleeping, giant snake in the middle of the floor but she was quiet and slow in her movements. She had not allowed the children to come inside, much to their annoyance, but she could not explain away what slept before her.

The villagers had done themselves proud. A huge gathering fire had been lit and preparing food and drink had kept the people occupied. At last Malya started to stir. Koiya sat crossed legged close to her daughter and waited.

"Mother!" Koiya's voice was harsh and croaky from weeks of barely speaking. Manuk uncoiled and allowed Malya to fall into Koiya's embrace.

"My daughter! My beautiful child, you have returned to me!" Koiya could not hold back the tears that flowed down her cheeks and into Malya's hair.

"Oh mother! I have missed you with all my heart! Am I home, am I truly home?"

"Yes, small one, you are home." Malya and Koiya hugged and cried until Manuk approached them.

"We do not have much time, witch. You know what must happen." There was no spite in Manuk's voice just firmness.

"Not much time for what?" Malya sat upright and stared at her mother, her eyes still moist with tears.

"Now don't take fright, child. You journey is only just beginning." Koiya tried to keep her daughter in her arms but she had wriggled free and was starting to stand.

Manuk stretched himself to his full height and looked Malya in the eyes as he spoke.

"We must leave when the suns start to wane, child." Before he could continue Malya stumbled backwards and headed for the door.

"No! I will not leave again! I'm home now, I have completed my bonding! Please, mother, not again." Koiya quickly rose and blocked Malya's attempt to flee.

"Daughter, listen to me. Hear my words, child." Manuk had lowered himself and allowed Koiya to calm her child. "This is not my decision. It is the will of the world. You are chosen. You are special. What happens from here on will change the world forever, Malya. Please, come and sit and let Manuk have his telling."

Malya allowed her mother to lead her back to where Manuk waited with patience.

"Please Manuk continue." Koiya wrapped her arms around her daughter and prayed for courage.

"Malya, we are only one pair of Sworn, we are but only one part of the circle. Tomorrow we will travel to the Holding Grounds. There your learning will continue." Manuk paused waiting for the question that he knew would come.

"The Holding Grounds? I know nothing of this place. Am I to go alone?" Malya now in her mother's arms looked small and scared. Not the cunning hunter Manuk knew she was.

"We travel at high noon. I'm sorry that is all I can tell you." Manuk made his way to the back of the hut and coiled into the shadows. He would let the two grieve in peace.

"I'm sorry. It has to be so." Koiya held her daughter at arm's length and studied her mangled hair and body. "Manuk will guide you, child. You can do this, I know, because you are my daughter. You are witch blood. Now, off with these clothes! I will wash you and tend your cuts." Koiya's heart was breaking, her eldest and most precious daughter would leave her again and she knew she may never return. She had to give her strength and courage. It would be the hardest thing Koiya would ever have to do.

Chapter 69

Koiya stepped back to admire her daughter. Washed and tended, Malya felt at ease. The familiar surroundings of home were a welcome respite, even if it was fleeting.

"I have something for you." Koiya whispered. Reaching into her dress she pulled out the little red ribbon the crow had dropped.

"I didn't even know I had lost it." Malya replied reaching out to take the little token.

"Let me." Koiya reached up and plaited the tiny ribbon into a small strand of Malya's hair and gently kissed her forehead. "Ready, my child?"

"Ready." Malya slipped her hand into her mother's and they headed out into the light. Manuk stayed sleeping in the shadows of the hut. Fuss and people didn't interest him.

The villagers had covered the paths with flower petals and large fern leaves and laughter and singing could be heard far and wide. Malya and her mother walked among the people hugging and smiling. Each child graced Malya with a gift and soon she was struggling under the weight of them. At last they reached the welcoming fire. Food and drink was shared and enjoyed. Children ran and played. It was the happiest Malya had ever been. As the celebrations calmed Koiya rose to speak but Malya reached for her hand and pulled her back down.

"I will speak, mother. I am the Sworn daughter of the tribal witch. It is my destiny." And with that she stood, and all fell silent. "I am Malya. Daughter to Koiya." Her voice was pure and true. "It is my destiny to fight for this land. A place that our ancestors fought to keep sacred." All around her people held their breath. "With the power of Mother Nature I will fight for you, my people! I will fight to keep the Marshland's our home. But most of all I fight for the spirit of balance and love." Malya stopped suddenly and cast her eyes over her people. A low chant started. A series of hums and whistles. Malya took up the chant and built the crowed to a frenzy.

Every man, woman and child were on their feet. Malya raised her head to the sky and howled to the tune that Mother Nature had set.

As the fire died and people slept the afternoon away, Mother and daughter returned to their hut. They huddled together under Malya's blanket and spoke in hushed tones.

"You will be safe, my child. I trust in all the good things in this world. Manuk will guide and protect you." Koiya was trying to instil courage in her child, grasping at any straw she could.

"I know, mother, it's not my skills or Manuk's bravery that I doubt. It's the unknown." Malya sighed and stood, letting the soft folds of the blanket fall to the floor.

"The day is starting to turn. We need to start our journey." Manuk's deep voice came from the shadows.

Koiya fussed around the hut gathering a little food and water for her daughter. Malya picked up and hugged her mother's blanket, hesitating whether to take it with her.

"That will not be needed, Malya. You need bring only yourself." Manuk slithered over to Malya and coiled around her leg and waist. Malya placed the blanket on to her old sleeping cot and turned to her mother.

"Go swiftly. May the Merfolk protect you both, Return to me, daughter. I will always be waiting for you." Koiya gently hugged her precious child to her and Malya reached out and kissed her mother's cheek.

"And I will always carry you in my heart." With that Malya left the hut and made her way to the village edge.

"Where now?" Malya's voice was filled with determination and pride and Manuk puffed up with the knowledge he had done well, strengthening their bond.

"Now we make our way into the forest. Our guide will find us."

Malya scanned the horizon. The forest edge rose up green and lush, filled with dark shadows and hidden secrets. She turned to look at the Marshlands one last time, etching her homeland into her mind. She straightened and stepped forward. She was born for this.

Chapter 70

Manuk and Malya had been walking for a few hours, taking in the forest. Opening their awareness to all it had to offer when Malya came to a sudden stop.

"What is it child? What do you sense?"

"There. Just to the left. In the shadow of the trees." Manuk turned his head and caught just a hint of movement. He uncoiled himself and slithered in front of Malya.

"Do not be afraid. I am your guide." The soft, deep tone of Jengo's voice seemed to come from everywhere.

Malya crouched to the ground. She opened her ears and felt the ground for vibrations.

"Come into the light. Do not make promises from the dark." Malya was ready. She smelt wolf.

Jengo slowly padded out into the warm sunrays and waited. The girl was pack. She would have to be made to bow. *This forest can only have one pack leader and that is me,* Jengo thought, judging the girl's grit.

"It is I, Manuk. The Mistress is expecting us." Manuk knew he had to intervene. These two would fight to the death if need be and that was of help to no one.

"The girl is strong. I sense pack in her."

"I speak for myself." Malya had started to snarl and dug her finger and toes into the forest floor.

"We are bonded. She and I. If there is a fight to be had, mark my words, I will fall on her side." Manuk tried to sway the odds.

Jengo crept forward, hackles high, deep, blue eyes boring into Malya.

Manuk had to choose and quickly. Malya and Jengo circled each other, no one backing down, no one giving an inch. If he chose Malya, Jengo would surely die. The Mistress would want justice and they would both see the pit. If he chose Jengo, Malya's trust in him would be broken and these weeks of hard work would be for nothing.

He chose. As quick as a whip he flicked his tail out and wound his muscular body around Malya's. He held her tight and brought her down; he restricted her but not enough to cause her pain.

"You have chosen well, Manuk." Jengo had lowered his hackles and retreated. "I serve The Mistress. Only she can have me bow. We waste time here. Release the girl. We need to be away."

Malya could not breathe. She could not think. She simply stared Manuk in the eyes, a deep distrustful stare.

"Listen to me, child. Your beast sense is too strong. You think like them, act like them. But you are human. You must learn to use your judgement, girl. Not every battle is for the taking."

"Release me." Malya did not hear him.

"I will not. Not until you see my reasoning. I have been born many times to these lands and trained many Sworn. You are exceptional, Malya. The bond we have is the strongest I have known in many, many years. Do not undo our hard work."

"Why? Am I not a worthy leader? Does this wolf hold your loyalty?"

"My loyalty is to The Mistress and Jengo serves her, as do I."

"Who is this Mistress? Does she have a pack?" Malya's curiosity was starting to calm her.

"The Mistress is leader of all packs, Malya. All bow to her. All serve her. As will you."

Manuk slowly relaxed his coils and held his breath.

"Very well, wolf. It appears I acted too quickly. I trust Manuk's words. Lead us to this Mistress. I will judge her worth myself."

"As you wish." Jengo headed off, a slow smile appearing on his face. "The Mistress will have you bow, child, as easy as a spider catches a fly. Now this I will enjoy."

Manuk, Malya and Jengo made their way through the forest in silence. Malya greeting animals and birds as they went. All gathered to her and accepted her as their matriarch. By the time they reached the Holding Grounds quite a menagerie followed them.

"Follow me. The clearing is through the thicket." Jengo padded forward but Malya held back and turned to Manuk.

"What is to happen here?"

"You will be fine, child. Your bonding is complete."

"Are you to leave me?"

"Never, girl. We are to fight as one as long as The Mistress requires it." Manuk wound himself around Malya's body and they entered the thorn ridden path together.

The thorns thinned and the path opened up into a large clearing, a blazing fire burned high in the centre. Malya stood stock still and scanned the area. She sensed power, power like she'd never known. No beast she had encountered came close. On the far side of the fire stood two figures. Staring. Waiting. Jengo had crept towards them and was bowing.

So, Malya thought, *this must be The Mistress.*

Malya still didn't move. She crouched down and felt the earth. Sniffed the air. She had seen the cages and could sense one was occupied. *Human,* she thought smelling his fear.

"Malya. It is time." Manuk could tell she was still ready to fight, but his hold round her body was also ready to take her down again if necessary.

One of the figures gestured for her to come close and Malya rose, raised her head and stepped towards the fire.

"Closer, child." The Mistress's voice was clear and held no threat. Malya moved closer.

Jengo had rounded Malya and was ready from behind if Malya chose to take flight.

"Welcome, girl. I am The Mistress."

Malya inched closer.

"Do not be afraid. There is only learning to be done here."

Malya inched closer still. The Mistress drew back her hood and smiled.

"It has been a long time since anyone has challenged me. I quite like it. But for now, you will bow and you will do as I say."

Malya was mesmerized by The Mistress's swirling, blue eyes and nearly bent her knee. Nearly. Manuk uncoiled himself and lay flat on the ground, he wanted to show The Mistress something, some crumb of respect, and after all it was his Sworn child that brought the challenge.

"It's also been a long time since I have had to use force." The Mistress's voice was sharp, her patience thin.

The Mistress raised her cane and slammed it down hard against the earth. A wave of power and blinding white light washed over those who stood bringing them all to their knees, even Thistle.

"You will bow, child. I will have no discord here." The Mistress drew in close to Malya and grabbed her by her hair drawing her to her feet. "Do you serve me, girl?"

Malya was completely submissive to The Mistress. She knew she had met her leader. This was the power of Mother Nature herself and she would bow.

"Yes, Mistress, I serve. May the Merfolk forgive my disrespect!" The Mistress let go of Malya's hair and straightened her robes.

"Now that bit of business is out of the way, welcome to the Holding Grounds, Malya. Shall we begin?"

Chapter 71
Selena

Selena looked down at herself; she was in her battle armour, the sword of Balboar was in her hand. But instead of his crystal egg bound into the hilt, a plain lump of steel shone in replacement. She felt a strong wind in her hair and could smell blood and gore. Her eyes were wide with terror.

"Here is where we make history, little bird, here is where we fight." Balboar's voice rose with rage and passion.

Selena looked around. Men were slaying and hacking, weapons and shields crashing and scraping. Shouts and cries all mixed to create a scene of chaos, a scene of death.

Selena found her tongue. "But where are we, what's happening?"

"We are in the great battle of the swamp land. This will one day become the forest you know. But first it has to be won." Balboar swung his giant axe up into the air and spat at his feet. "He we go, Selena. Remember your training. Take courage, girl, they will show you no mercy."

Selena followed Balboar's line of sight. A large solider was charging their way, sword held high, a look of pure lunacy in his eyes.

"But I can fight him. I've never been in a real battle. What shall I do?" Selena felt like she was in a dream. All her senses were telling her this was real but her mind just couldn't catch up. "Balboar, please, what do I do?" Selena screamed, becoming desperate.

"Fight, girl, just fight."

Selena raised her sword and looked straight ahead. The soldier was just feet away. She took a deep breath and readied her body, feet planted, one back, one hard in front. She loosened her shoulder and gripped her sword. She sent up a prayer, "Please let this be a dream. For the love of Merfolk please be a dream." As she levelled her eyes he was upon her. She had no time to plan or worry. Her training took over. He swung his sword down. She blocked and stepped back. He swore and shouted and spat fury. Their swords clashed together as he swung again she blocked and jabbed, nimble of foot, her balance perfect. He faltered, flailed to the left and she struck out with both hands on the hilt of her sword. Her blade slipped right through his gut, the soldier hung there. Selena held her breath. They were eye to eye, both just staring, unblinking. Both surprised at the death scene.

"I had been told you were good, child, so what are you waiting for, finish him." Balboar seemed to revel in the violence, in the death.

Selena leant forward and pushed the man off of her sword. His blood ran down her blade and dripped onto her boots. She stared at her sword, the man squirming at her feet. *What have I done? How can this be?* Was all she could think. She felt Balboar's giant hand on her shoulder.

"Make it swift. Dying from a sword to the gut is no easy death."

"What? Me? You want me to finish him?" Selena babbled blinking wildly.

"Yes, little bird, just finish off what you have started. You never forget your first kill, so make it a good one." Balboar laughed out loud and turned to walk away.

Selena screamed out at him. "But how? Help me, please Balboar!" But Balboar just kept walking towards the battle. Selena looked down at the man who was nearly unconscious, his pale face was smeared with his own blood. She knelt beside him.

"I'm sorry. I'm not even meant to be here. I don't know what's happening." Selena realised she was crying and snot dribbled from her nose. She went to wipe it and realised her hands where covered in blood. "I'm sorry, I'm sorry." Was all she could say over and over. A great shadow loomed over her and the dying man. She felt a great sweep of wind as Balboar took the man's head off with one blow.

"Next time he's all yours. There's rules on a battlefield child. You kill what you maim." Selena looked up into Balboar's eyes. For a second, only for a second, she saw his kind heart. Balboar helped her to her feet. "Forward Selena, this will be a long night and there are many men to kill."

Chapter 72

Selena leant her arm across the filthy bar and raised her cup in the air.

"To battle, Balboar! To war! To killing!" Selena drained the whole cup of ale and slammed it down followed by a large belch.

"Indeed, little bird, indeed." Balboar gave a huge grin and followed suit, swallowing the whole cupful in three gulps.

Selena stank. She hadn't bathed in six weeks. No brush or oil had her hair seen. She was as dirty and blood-stained as the next man. Selena and Balboar had roamed the marshes and swamp lands fighting battle after battle, sleeping under hedges and in cow sheds. She had become brave, she had become deadly, she had become a warrior.

Selena stood and slapped Balboar across the back.

"The outhouse calls, old man, even to us girls." She laughed as she turned towards the door. Selena had grown, not just in stature but in strength. Her muscles were lean and solid. Her hands were calloused and blood-soaked. There was no mistaking that she was a girl but most now saw her as a warrior and she loved it. Being treated the same as everyone else. She revelled in the camaraderie of battle, even the friendship that war can bring.

Balboar ordered two more ales and rubbed his filthy face. *She is nearly ready,* he thought. *This has been a fine bonding, a fine bonding indeed.* As Balboar's thoughts turned the Holding Grounds he heard a loud crash behind him. He turned to find Selena with her blade to a man's throat. As he looked over the man he saw he had an assassin's knife in his hand.

"What in god's name do you think you are doing? You filthy coward?" Balboar flew from his stool sending it crashing to the ground. The tavern fell into silence.

"I caught this little wretch trying to stick you; I thought I'd better help an old man out." Selena said with a little smile.

"WHAT? You were trying to take my life with that little knife, like a pig at slaughter. Do you know who I am man?" Balboar was enraged at the insult of being quietly seen to. The assassin just shook his head. Fear had loosened his bowels and the tavern started to empty. "You will feel my axe, you lowly scum." Balboar started to raise his mighty axe.

"Let me do the honours." Selena said, as cool as ice. She slit the man's throat and watched him bleed out on the floor. Balboar roared with anger.

"That was my kill girl! My kill!" He looked Selena in the eyes. His breathing was hard and fast, his adrenaline finding no release, Selena held his gaze, blade ready. Eventually Balboar lowered his axe and leaned on the bar. "You are ready, little bird; it's time for us to fly away home."

Selena lowered her sword and stared at Balboar. She had waited a long time to hear those words. Now she wasn't sure she could do it. Go back, back to the palace, back to her grandmother and Jug and Minn. She swallowed and slowly sat.

"I've been waiting for this day Balboar. It feels like years since I've seen my grandmother. I've changed. I've grown. How can I face them like this?" Selena looked down at her armour. It was dented and stained. Her boots were filthy. She raised a hand to the nest on her head. Balboar let out a huge burst of laughter.

"You can always shave it off, girl."

Selena started to giggle, then laugh, then she couldn't control herself. She flew at Balboar. As they toppled over, they wrestled and grappled all the time laughing and swearing at each other.

"I'm going to miss you, you big, fat pig." Selena said whilst trying to get Balboar into a headlock.

"Me too, wench." Balboar returned, grabbing Selena around the waist and hurling her onto the bar. "More ale, inn-keep, for today we go home."

Selena and Balboar had stayed until the innkeeper had tentatively asked them to leave, then they had staggered up the lane to the edge of the marshes.

"It will be dawn soon, little bird, take a good hard look around. Here is where you had your first kill, here is where you cried, you fought and you found your courage. Don't ever forget these weeks Selena. I know I won't." Balboar turned away as he spoke, but Selena had caught the sight of the tears in his eyes.

"I won't, great friend, I won't." Selena whispered.

Chapter 73

Selena and Balboar had watched the suns come up and spoke of battles they had won and men they had killed. The suns were now high in the sky and Balboar knew it was time to leave.

"Up you get now, girl, it is time to leave this place." Balboar stood and offered Selena his hand. She took it and let him help her to her feet. There was no need, but it felt right. He had led her here, he should lead her home. "Now, hold onto your sword hilt. You know what is to come." Balboar gently lifted Selena's chin. "Come now, no tears, you are a warrior of the White City. A person to be feared and respected. We'll still be together, just not like... Well you know where I'll be." He smiled a big, toothy grin and Selena sniffed back her tears and raised her head high.

"Let's go." Selena said, staring straight into Balboar's eyes.

Balboar firmly wrapped his hand around hers and they both clasped the sword hilt. There was a flash of blue and they were away. Selena felt the spinning and turning but she held strong. She could no longer feel Balboar's hand upon hers but she knew he was still with her. Her vision was clouded with blues and whites and she was sure she was going to be sick. Selena slammed down onto a hard floor knocking the wind out of her and making her cry out with shock.

She opened her eyes. The room was gloomy, just as it had been before. She sat forward and coughed and spluttered and spat.

"Well," she spoke to an empty room, "home!"

Then she was up and off. She wrenched open the door and flew across the courtyard, sending chickens and washer-girls squawking for cover. She had no care for them. She was heading for her grandmother's chambers and she was hungry, so hungry. She thundered into the kitchen and strode past the cook and serving girls. They all screamed and hid under the table. Selena only laughed and grabbed a huge handful of cakes from the counter. She crammed them into her mouth as she lunged up the stairs, three at a time. She rounded a corner and froze mid-step. There walking towards her was Minn.

"Come here, my old friend." Selena hollered down the hall. Minn stopped in her tracks. Her hand flew to her mouth. The giant beast in front of her was rotten and smelt like sewage. She turned to run, thinking her life was in danger, but Selena ran after her.

"Get away from me, please! I have nothing worth stealing. Please get away!" Minn was screaming with fear. But Selena kept coming. She reached out a filthy hand and swung Minn into her arms. Minn scratched and bit and slapped and screamed, but Selena only laughed at her vain attempts at violence.

"Hello Minn." Selena's voice was low and quiet. She looked Minn straight in the eyes.

"Oh! My goodness, Selena." And with that Minn fainted in Selena's arms.

Chapter 74

Philamo was racked with nerves. Selena had been gone six weeks and keeping Jug and Minn away with lies was becoming unbearable. She had kept herself busy with palace business nearly pruning the roses to death, she had ordered new bedsheets, pillow covers and spreads. The whole palace had been cleaned from top to bottom and now she had run out of things to do. She sat by the fire in her bed-chamber and sent up a silent prayer.

"Please, god, protect her, help her bond fully and come back in one piece. She is a kind and happy child." Philamo bent her face to her hands and cried huge sobs of worry. "What will I do if she is hurt or worse? I cannot be alone again." Philamo whispered to herself.

A scream had Philamo jumping to her feet. That was Minn screaming, she was sure of it. She flew to the door and heaved it open, and there in front of her was an unconscious Minn and a giant, rotten soldier.

"What happened here? What's going on?" Philamo demanded.

"Hello, grandmother," Selena replied.

Philamo heard the voice. It was so familiar, she could almost make out who it was. Philamo stared into the crystal blue eyes for a moment longer then gasped and clutched her chest.

"For the love of Merfolk, Selena! How? Where? What happened to you?" Philamo had started to step back into the room, she wasn't sure whether through fear or shock.

"It's okay, Grandmother, I will explain everything. Can I just get to your bed to put Minn down. I think I was a bit too much for her." Selena made her way to Philamo's bed, crashing and thumping as she went. Her week's fighting in the Swamps had made her bullish. She tried to gently lay Minn down but ended up throwing her onto the bed. She looked at the soft and colourful bedlinen and pillows and was suddenly aware of her appearance. *Bath time would have to wait,* she thought. *A rumbling belly comes first.*

"Grandmother, is there anything to eat? I'm starving and I need a full belly to tell my tale." Selena hollered as she headed for the fire to warm herself.

Philamo was shocked to silence. She couldn't believe her eyes. This creature, this rotten, filthy creature was Selena her granddaughter, the princess. She was big and loud and manly.

Selena turned to find Philamo, staring at her with large, fearful eyes.

"I know I've changed." Selena said, staring down at her armour and patting down her hair. "But the things I've seen, the things I've done." Selena had a faraway look in her eyes as she spoke. "Oh yes I was scared at first, terrified even. But I learned. How to fight, how to battle charge, how to kill! I've never felt so alive!" As Selena spoke, Philamo became more alarmed, more scared, scared of her own granddaughter.

Selena realised that Philamo hadn't spoken and looked up. Philamo was backing up to the door as pale as milk.

"Grandmother, what's wrong?" Selena asked edging towards her.

"Food, yes, food. You said you were hungry, I shall order some food." And with that Philamo fled out of the door.

Selena stared at the closing door and slumped into a high-backed cushioned chair feeling it groan under her weight. She hadn't known comfort like it for weeks and it felt so good.

"I guess coming home's not going to be as easy as I thought." Selena stretched out her legs and closed her eyes and sleep came quickly and soundly and before long she was snoring.

Philamo paused for breath and clutched the wall. *My god, what has happened to her,* she thought. She rounded the corner and hurried down the stairs towards the kitchen. *Food, I must order food,* was all she could think, her mind racing with possible reasons why Selena looked and acted like a wild thing. She blundered into the kitchen and halted when she realised all eyes were on her. The cook and the stable boys, scullery maids and horsemen where all gathered at the table.

"Your majesty, what are you doing here? We saw the arrival, well, the return. We didn't want to disturb you, but is the Princess well? Is she okay?" Cook looked very embarrassed when she spoke and blushed bright red on seeing Philamo's distress.

Philamo lowered the hand that had clutched her chest ever since she had opened the door to her bedroom and steadied her breathing.

"Yes, yes Selena is fine, just a little ragged from her journey. But she's home now and she's hungry, so you know what that means. If she is not fed, we will not hear the end of it, so to your duties, please. No gossip to be had here. Cook, a full spread, please, to be served in my bedchamber and spare nothing. Selena has been away long enough and we need to show her she is welcome home." The whole kitchen staff just blinked and stared at Philamo. She feared she had raised more questions than answers but one step at a time. "Now, please people, quick to it!" Philamo sharply clapped her hands and bodies ran in all directions until only cook remained.

"Are you sure all is well, your majesty?" Cook stepped closer to Philamo and spoke in a whisper. "I don't mean to speak out of turn but Selena looked, well…wild." The cook stepped back as Philamo's face snapped up in anger.

"Yes, cook you speak out of turn! Selena is fine. Nothing a hot bath and a hair weaving won't solve. Now, food, cook or I will have to look elsewhere for kitchen help." And with that Philamo swept from the room. *I must be strong, I must be gentle. Who knows what she has faced out there in the last six weeks,* she thought.

Philamo returned to the bedchamber and gently pushed open the door. Selena was asleep in the fireside chair and Minn was awake, crouched at her feet and gently stroking her hand. Minn looked up as she heard Philamo slip through the door.

"What has happened my lady? What has she been through? Oh! My little bird!"

"I don't know Minn, but I intend to find out."

Chapter 75
Grumble

"My name is Grumble. I fear I have not long to live." The gentle voice that was returned allowed Grumble to open his eyes.

"It's okay, friend, you are safe for now." Illiwig peeled back the remaining sack and allowed Grumble to roll out.

"What are you?" Illiwig's shock at the creature dissolving any scrap of manners.

"I am a tree elf. And I think I have been kidnapped." Grumble eyed Illiwig and noted his missing eye. He could smell the infection on him and judged him gravely ill.

The pain returned to Grumble's hands and feet, the chains biting and burning.

"Please, kind friend, my hands and feet, if you could." Illiwig stared down dumbly at Grumble's body and snapped into action. He reached out a tentative hand and tested the chains. The touch of Grumble's hard knobbly skin startled him and he quickly withdrew. Seeing the helpless look in the little creature's eyes, Illiwig knew he must try. He gently scooped the tiny, strange being up in the sack and held him to his chest. Illiwig started to shuffle back to his corner and into the light to get a better look at the chains.

"Now, don't scream or shout. This will hurt some." Illiwig cautioned Grumble as he set to untying the chains. The rusted metal had dug deep into Grumbles skin, but to Illiwig's relief had not cut him. After much hissing and fainting from Grumble and wiggling and apologising from Illiwig, the chains around his hands and feet were finally off. Grumble felt the blood return and he rubbed the life back into himself with tiny strokes and licks.

"Thank you, friend." Grumble started to cry.

"Come now, little one, none of that. They will be back soon and we need to stay silent." Illiwig knew they were not safe but he would comfort this little thing with kind words.

"I'm sorry." Grumble sniffed and raised his face to Illiwig's. "Where are we?"

"As far as I can make out we are in some kind of dungeon. We have been here only one day. My name is Illiwig."

Grumble reached out his hand and slowly ran his tiny fingers over Illiwig's missing eye. Illiwig was so startled by the soft, bony caress it silenced him. Grumble continued to touch Illiwig's scabs and bruises working his way down to the stomach wound. He slowly lifted Illiwig's shirt and revealed the festering wound.

"I know. I'm done for. Leave it be." Illiwig's sad voice settled over the little cell.

"Me help." Grumble offered.

"Nothing to be done here. I know the smell of rot. Seen it many a time, has old Illiwig." He started to lower his filthy shirt when Grumble stopped him

"Me, help. Watch." Grumble rubbed his battered hands together and started to swallow loudly. He coughed and spluttered until a thin, silver liquid dribbled from the side of his mouth. Into his hands he spat a blob of the liquid and made to rub it into Illiwig's wound. Horrified Illiwig swatted his hand away.

"What in Mer's name are you doing?" Illiwig gasped. A disgusted look on his face.

Grumble attempted to rub the gooey blob onto Illiwig's stomach again.

"Me, help. Me, heal." Grumble insisted. Illiwig protested no more. The events of the last few days had left him dumbstruck and with the creature's spit applied he fell into an overwhelming stupor.

Grumble had spread two more handfuls of spit onto Illiwig's wound while he slept and had squeezed the yellow puss from his scabby eye hole. Now he tended his own wounds. His back was tight where his root had been cut and his head was lumpy and bruised but looking at Illiwig he thought he had got away lightly. As he was covering Illiwig's stomach with the empty sack he heard a coughing sound, tiny and squeaky. He shrank with fear. Just behind Illiwig and huddled in the corner something moved. Grumble stared deadly still. From the shadows crawled a tiny thing, smaller than himself. Grumble was intrigued, he leant closer. A tiny fluff of hair followed by two pale hands made their way into the light.

"Praise be! A firefly."

Illiwig stirred from his stupor and sat up rubbing his face. He looked at Grumble's frozen face of shock and spotted the little fire fly crawling out from the shadows.

"Grumble, meet our cell mate." Illiwig scooped up the firefly and curled her in his lap.

"These are truly strange times, friend. Do you think we are going to die here?" Grumble whispered.

Chapter 76

Selena

Selena opened first one eye then the other, she felt the warmth from the fire on her face and smelt the delicious wafts which only roast pheasant can bring. She leapt up, coughed, spluttered and almost spat in the fire. Minn and her grandmother were sitting opposite her and had shrunk back with fright.

"Oh sorry! I'm not used to being indoors when I wake." Selena swallowed loudly and turned to the table. It was loaded with all her favourite hot meats, pies and cakes. She could bear the smell no longer.

"Please, dear, help yourself." Philamo said, seeing Selena's hungry stare.

Selena dived for the table. She crammed in whole sweet cherry pies. She ripped meat from bones and glugged down wine like it was water.

"Selena, please, slow down! You will make yourself ill." Minn was by her side holding a plate and fork in the air. Selena stopped and dropped a half-eaten pear.

"Minn, I'm so sorry. Where are my manners?" She let out a loud burp, laughed, snorted and carried on stuffing her face.

"That's enough! Selena! I can see you have been through a lot but this is out of control. I didn't bring you up to scoff like a pig at a trough. Now put down that food and be seated." Philamo held her breath. She couldn't tell if she had just made things worse.

Selena swallowed her mouthful, wiped her mouth with her hand and sat down hard on one of the gilded dining chairs.

"Sorry" was all she could manage. She had spent so long fighting over scraps and begging coin for meals, she had forgotten what it was like to be in the presence of a feast.

"Now, Minn, you take the chair to the left and I shall sit at the right." Minn sat and gingerly put a few morsels of food on a plate and Philamo did the same. Selena pushed her chair back and looked at the floor. She felt ashamed. She wanted her return to be glorious, to fall into her grandmother's arms and tell her tales of adventure and mystery, for Minn to ooo and ahhh at the stories of battles and wars. But instead, she had scared everyone half to death and embarrassed herself eating a simple meal.

"Selena, it is obvious that your time away hasn't been easy." Philamo's tone was soft and encouraging. "But we love you and we are here for you. So just eat, take your time and you can tell us everything." Selena smiled at her grandmother and picked up a plate.

After hours of eating and talking, Selena was plain tired out. Philamo had cried and shouted, cursed and laughed at all that Selena had to say. Telling her grandmother of her bloody battles had not been easy but Philamo had insisted on hearing every twist and turn so Selena had left nothing unsaid. Minn had not said a word through the whole telling.

"I think a bath and hair weave is in order, little bird, not to mention some clean clothes." Minn had heard enough. Selena was home and it was her job to care for her.

Selena turned to Minn and smiled. "What would I do without you? I always say your hands are magic."

As Selena rose, to follow Minn to her bathroom, Philamo grabbed Selena's hand.

"There's just one more thing, my dear." Selena lowered herself back into the chair and turned to face her grandmother. "Tomorrow will be your leaving day. Selena, we did not expect you home so soon. Nothing has been prepared. Jason was away for ten weeks, I thought I had time to plan." Philamo was rambling and getting in a fluster.

"Why? Grandmother! I have only just come home what could be so important that I have to leave again?" Selena looked at Minn, panic starting to rise.

"Tomorrow you leave for the Holding Grounds."

Chapter 77

Jug had risen early. He had heard that Selena was back but he couldn't get anywhere near the castle. He had to try today. Everyone in the city had been told that today would be Selena's leaving day, that she was to make her way to the Holding Ground, whatever that was. He would have one chance to see her and that was before sunrise at the old oak. He knew she would be there waiting for him. It had always been their meeting place and he would not let her down.

Minn crept into Selena's bedchamber to wake her just before dawn as promised. Last night had been a whirlwind from terror, to excitement, to fear and now she was losing Selena all over again. She had eventually got her in the bath and washed her from head to toe. Selena's body had been covered in bruises, cuts and scabs. She had tried to turn a blind eye but Selena had laughed and said they were her battle scars and she was proud of them. Selena's hair had taken an age to tame, filled with twigs, dirt and full of lice, but Minn had worked hard with comb and oil and had tamed the beast. Now she would have to say goodbye all over again.

"Little bird, time to wake up." Minn kept her distance. She didn't need a fist in the face for waking her. Selena stirred, turned over, then sat bolt upright.

"Where am I?" Selena croaked through sleepy fog.

"You are in your bedroom, my lady. You are home." Selena started to cry, at first small sobs, then huge loud wails. "Oh, little bird, all will be well." Minn perched on the bed and took Selena into her arms.

"No, Minn. It won't. I've only just returned, now I am to leave again and search out the Holding Grounds, I've never heard of them. Where am I supposed to go?" Selena cried and sobbed until she was hoarse and Minn rocked her until she was calm.

"Come now, Selena, isn't there a certain person you were meeting this morning before sunrise?" Selena jumped up.

"Oh, yes. Jug. I nearly forgot. Help me to dress, I must be away before Grandmother wakes." Minn helped Selena into soft leggings and a smock. She had tried a dress, only to be laughed out of the room. Selena tied the last lace of her riding boots and was out the door just as the suns peeped over the horizon.

Jug had been at the oak for a while and had started to have doubts that Selena would come.

"Hello, Jug." Selena's voice whispered from behind the tree.

"For the love of Merfolk! You startled me!" Jug turned to see Selena leaning against the rough bark. She was dressed for riding.

"Come here, old friend." Selena lunged forward and grabbed Jug in a huge embrace, smacked him on the back and nearly sent him sprawling.

"Woo there, little bird. That's quite a hug you've got on you." Jug really was shocked at how Selena had grown. She seemed taller, stronger but she was just as beautiful.

"Race you to the stables!" Before Jug could answer, she was off, leaping over hedge and flower beds, skidding through puddles and dodging chickens. *And she's got fast*, was all Jug could think as he raced after her.

Philamo had been making arrangements all day: food, banners and the royal musicians had been called. It would have to be an evening ceremony but that can't be helped. Her gown had been steamed and pressed and all the serving staff assembled. *Now to find Selena,* she thought. She had been missing half the morning but Philamo knew where she was. She had been at her window. Sleep had deserted her, when she had seen Selena and Jug race towards the stables. She was glad Selena was finding a little time for fun. It would be hard to let her go again but let her go she must. Philamo crossed her bedchamber and sat in the fireside chair. The fire was burning low. A little nap couldn't hurt. *Everything is in order*, she thought, as she drifted into sleep.

She dreamed of walking through the forest. She came to a clearing where a crow was scratching in the dirt and it looked at her with beady, black eyes

"Hello, your majesty, I have a message for you." The crow spoke with a rusty cackle.

"For me?" was all Philamo could say.

"Yes. It is from The Mistress." Philamo suddenly felt panicked. Was this a dream? Was this a nightmare? "You broke the vows, Philamo, you must pay your penance." Philamo tried to turn to run but her feet felt like they were weighted down.

"Please, it was a mistake. Tell her I'm sorry." The crow just stared, its little eyes like small, black pearls.

"Selena will endure an extra day in the cages because of your mistake, your majesty, because of your broken promise."

Philamo screamed "No! Please! She has been through enough! Take me, please." The crow just laughed.

"Now that would be no penance at all, would it?" The crow spread his wings and took to the air. "You will not speak of this, Philamo, remember your vow." And the bird was gone.

Philamo woke on the floor wrestling with a pillow, covered in sweat. "What have I done? Please, God, have mercy. What have I done?"

Chapter 78

Selena and Jug had been riding all morning. They had made their way to the west side of the kingdom and had followed the path to the harbour and then down onto the beach. The tide was out and they were sitting side by side on the rocks dangling their feet into the rock pools.

"I know you've got questions, Jug, I can almost see them worming around in your head." Selena laughed and turned her face to Jug.

"I have. But I figured you'd tell me in your own time."

"Oh Jug, it was amazing. At first I thought I couldn't do it, I cried, screamed, begged to go home but then I felt the pure rush from it. The skill it takes to win. It's all I ever dreamed it would be." Selena's face was glowing with joy. She was throwing her hands around, she had jumped up and the pool was up to her knees.

"What are you talking about, little bird?" Jug was smiling at Selena's play acting; he didn't have a clue what it all meant.

"Killing, Jug, battle. I've seen some things, let me tell you." Selena was so enthralled in her tale she hadn't noticed that Jug was not smiling in fact his face had become hard and angry, Jug rose from the rocks and turned for his horse. "It was everything we always talked about, Jug. You should hear my battle cry." Selena paused and looked up. "JUG! JUG! Where are you going?" But Jug was already mounted and was preparing to leave.

"We were meant to find out together, Selena. You promised."

"I know, Jug, please, it's not my fault, I never asked to go away. I never planned it. I didn't agree to any of this." Selena lowered her arms and stood in silence.

"I'm glad you had fun, Selena. Some of us were actually worried about you." And with that he rode off leaving Selena standing alone in the rock pool.

Selena looked around her. *The beach, the harbour, it's all so tranquil, so beautiful. Why hadn't I noticed before*, she thought. She made her way back to her horse and sat down in the sand.

"I guess I truly have grown. Out-grown Jug, anyway." She spoke aloud to no one. She picked up a piece of driftwood and started making lines in the wet sand. "And now I have to leave again and I want to try and explain to Jug I didn't have a choice. I'm Sworn, it's my destiny. Balboar always said." Selena sat bolt upright. "Oh God, Balboar!" Selena quickly mounted her horse and raced along the sand. She took the grass verge in one huge leap and was away up the harbour road towards the castle, she slid from her horse and threw the reins at a bewildered stable boy. She strode over the cob-bled courtyard and slipped behind the hay wagon, crouched down and calmed herself.

"He has to be there. I was so caught up with coming home, I didn't even look for him, let alone pick him up. Oh God! He hates being on the floor. He's going to be furious." Selena whispered to herself. She crept towards the tower and slipped through the wooden door. There on the floor, where she had returned was Balboar. Not the man, but the Sworn Blade. He was back in his crystal and glow-ing a deep, brilliant blue.

"Balboar, forgive me! I hadn't thought. I just ran. I'm sorry." Selena slowly stepped closer.

"GET OVER HERE NOW AND PICK ME UP!" Balboar was so angry, he thought he might crack his crystal home.

Selena bent down and swept up the sword.

"Oh Balboar! Please forgive me."

"I don't want your pity, girl; don't ever leave me behind again. Do I make myself clear?"

"Yes, Great One I won't." Selena and Balboar stared at each other. Their bond was strong, they both knew it. They felt it.

"Now, take me with you to your grandmother. I have a gift for you."

"But people will see you, well, see the sword. There will be talk." Selena felt very protective of Balboar and it made him chuckle.

"I shall keep my glow to a minimum. Any way I shall be in your hand so everyone will think of me as just a sword. Now come on, forward, young warrior, there is much to do."

Selena made her way back across the courtyard and through the castle, after a few alarmed stares and a little whispering she made it to her grandmother's chambers.

"Now what?" Selena whispered seemingly to herself.

"Knock and enter, girl, no time to delay." Balboar instructed.

"I scared the living Merfolk out of her and Minn last night. I think a talking sword will be a step too far." Selena imagined her grandmother's face when Balboar spoke. "I think it will scare her half to death."

"Your grandmother knows more than you think, little bird. Now come on. Courage child." Selena knocked on the door and waited.

"Oh God." Selena whined.

"Come in." Selena jumped when Philamo answered.

"I am a warrior, I am Sworn, I can do this little thing," Selena told herself. She slowed her breathing and pushed open the door.

"I see you finally returned for poor old Balboar." Philamo said eyeing the sword.

"Grandmother! You knew. You knew I had left him behind. Why didn't you say something? Why didn't you remind me to go back?"

"I am forbidden from interfering, Selena. I have broken my vow once already when I said her name, I was not about to make a second mistake. Your path is your own. You must make your own choices."

Philamo crossed the room and gently took the sword from Selena's hand. Seeing the look of fear in Selena's face, Philamo halted.

"It's okay, Selena, give the sword to me." Selena dropped her hand away and stared in silence. "Hello, old friend." Philamo's voice was soft and gentle.

"Hello, Philamo." Balboar was glowing beautiful hues of violet and blue. "It's been a long time, a long time indeed." Balboar turned his face to Selena. "Your grandmother and I have been introduced before, when Jason came home from the bonding." He turned back to Philamo, she looked pale and sad. "Jason was a fine warrior, Philamo, you know that."

"I know. It's just that seeing you again has stirred up old memories, painful memories." Philamo sat by the fire with Balboar in her hands. "Is it time for the gift?" Philamo asked, quiet as a mouse.

"Yes, my lady, it is time." Balboar spoke as if to a grieving mother, his words soft and kind.

Philamo rose and gave Selena back her sword. She crossed to a large, wooden chest under the window and knelt to unlock the lid.

"It won't fit. It was made for Jason." Philamo's hand paused on the key.

"It will fit, my lady, it always does." Balboar encouraged.

Philamo nodded and lifted the lid, a gentle, glistening light lifted from the box and Selena gasped.

"This, my child, is armour made from Shanzzy. It is a rare metal, fired in the volcano of Meridien, it moulds to the body like silk, yet if struck by blade, arrow or knife is as hard as diamond." Philamo stood and held up the armour. Selena's mouth was hanging open with awe.

"I know, girl, it is truly beautiful." Balboar chuckled

Chapter 79

Minn had been fussing over Selena all afternoon and it was starting to get on her nerves.

"Minn, please, I don't need any more poking and prodding! I swear I shall go mad."

Minn stopped mid-poke and lowered her hand.

"Sorry miss, I'm just nervous. This is a big day for you, for your grandmother. All the folk from the city will be here, all looking at you. It makes me feel sick just thinking about it." Minn started to pale but Selena had her in a quick embrace.

"I know, Minn, it's a lot to take in, but like you always say, all will be well." They both started to laugh and hugged each other closer.

"I'm proud of you, Selena, real proud." Minn rubbed her eyes to hide the forming tears and Selena turned away and stared out of the window.

"I know you are, Minn. I can do this, it's what I've been born to do."

There was a knock at the door and Philamo entered.

"How are things going in here?"

"Good, your majesty." Minn turned to wipe her face and compose herself. "We're all good here. How's things outside?"

"As organized as a prize pig show in the square." Philamo snorted a large laugh and all three gasped in shock at Philamo's fall from grace, then giggled at the scene they found themselves in. Soon the giggling turned to roars of laughter that had them clutching their sides with pain.

"Grandmother, where are the Holding Grounds?" Selena's question stopped the fun in its tracks.

"I cannot tell you, my child, all I know is that you have to make your way to the edge of the forest and wait." Philamo wanted to tell all but the crow's nasty message had been clear and it silenced her tongue.

Selena sighed her defeat and turned to stare back out of the window.

"One hour, my love, you need to be at the door in one hour." Philamo crossed the room to stand by Selena's side. "I will miss you very much, my dear, I know you have only just returned but there are greater things happening in this world than we can ever know and you are part of them. Selena, you are a very important part." Philamo placed her hand on Selena's and gently squeezed. "I am so proud of the woman you have become and whatever you face out there, know that you are loved and cherished." Philamo kissed Selena on the check and slowly turned to leave.

"Grandmother," Selena's voice was barely a whisper, "I love you."

The banners were flying, the market square was packed and bustling, hawkers and stallholders hollered for trade, the smell of fresh pies wafted on the breeze.

"It's time, Selena." Minn said, holding up the Shanzzy armour, its silver sheen dazzling.

Selena reached out and tentatively stroked her fingers down the sleeve.

"It really is beautiful."

"Here, miss, let me help you." Minn gently coaxed the silver skin onto Selena. As if the armour was alive it moulded and slunk its way over Selena's body to form a perfect fit. Selena turned to the mirror and smiled. She really had grown up. "Let me finish your hair and help you with your boots, little bird, then we must be away." Selena sat at her dresser and Minn did the final weaving. The little, red ribbon still plaited into the single strand looked a little out of place now but Selena thought she'd keep it as a reminder of all she had been through.

Minn stepped back. "Perfect, my love, just perfect."

Selena stood and walked over to the window.

"I must say," Balboar chuckled, "that Shanzzy looks better on you than it did on Jason."

Selena turned to where Balboar was propped up by the fire.

"Thank you, Balboar, now it's time to put on the show."

Selena, Balboar and Minn made their way down the stairs. The banisters had been looped with flowers and the smell was heavenly. They crossed the entrance hall to where Philamo was waiting.

"Selena, you look beautiful."

"Thank you." Selena reached out her free hand and held on to Philamo.

"Thank you for all that you have done for me, Grandmother, I know it hasn't been easy for you." Selena turned to Minn. "Do I look the part?" she said with a smile.

"Magnificent." Minn smiled and dabbed her eyes with a handkerchief.

"Right then, let's go." Philamo nodded to the guards and they heaved open the heavy main doors.

As Selena strode out on to the deep, worn steps of the great castle with the sword of White City in her hand, the cheers that went up were deafening, hundreds of people surged forward to see the Sworn Princess and her famous sword. Selena walked to the top of the stone steps and halted, silence fell and thousands of eyes and ears waited. Selena lifted Balboar aloft, took a breath and shouted.

"I am Selena, granddaughter of Queen Philamo. My family has promised to protect this castle and this city with our lives." She paused for breath. She could feel Balboar's warm glow against her palm. "I am Blade Sworn and with this sword I offer my life to you. I promise to fight for this city and uphold the laws of this land." The crowd started to clap, slowly at first then faster and louder until its rhythm consumed everything. Selena looked around at the people, her people, and raised Balboar higher, she screamed at the top of her voice, "For the White City!" She lowered Balboar and drew in huge gasps. *I've done it*, she thought. *All the training, the blood and sweat, the weeks with Balboar fighting and crying, it's finally over! I am Selena, the Blade Sworn Princess of White City and I am ready.*

Chapter 80

Selena re-entered the castle doors and collapsed against the wall. She couldn't breathe, she was sweating and she couldn't breathe.

"Now, child, hold yourself! The hard part's over. You did well out there. Let's not spoil it with girly tears." Balboar was glowing a soft, sky blue and Selena looked into his eyes.

"Everyone expects so much, Balboar, even though I've done the hard part I can't shake the feeling that this is only the beginning."

"That's because it is, child. This right here is the beginning. We must be away soon, the suns are low, we must reach the Holding Grounds before midnight."

Selena straightened herself and turned to her grandmother.

"What now?" she asked, the look of a lost child on her face.

"Now you leave." The sadness in Philamo's voice was almost alive. "Your horse is saddled and waiting in the yard. A bag has been packed with food and drink enough for one day." Philamo faltered on her words but swallowed down her fears, her sadness.

"Oh." Selena looked down at Balboar and smiled. "At least I have some company. Well, if you can call him company." Selena's attempt at a joke fell flat and they all just stared at each other, no one wanting to be the first to move.

Philamo broke the silence.

"Well, why we are all dallying here? Let's be away!" She turned and headed for the yard, Minn and Selena followed in silence.

The yard was empty except for a lone stable boy holding the reins of Selena's horse. He looked terrified. Philamo stepped forward and gently took the leather straps from his hand.

"Thank you, boy, you may go now." The boy flew from the yard as if his shoes were on fire.

"Poor boy!" Selena chuckled.

Minn slipped next to Selena and slid a hand around her waist.

"Now take care, little bird, don't look for trouble where there is none, do you hear me?"

"Yes, miss." Selena turned and gave her the bravest smile she could muster. "Now go on in, Minn, this is no time for tears. You have done your job well, I'm fit and clever and brave and that is all thanks to you." Selena softly removed Minn's arm and stepped away. Minn fled from the yard and was gone through the kitchen door as quickly as the stable boy.

Philamo held the reins as Selena mounted her horse. Balboar was at her side and the food sacks bound securely to her saddle.

"Go swiftly, Selena, nightfall is upon us. You must make your way to the forest edge and wait. Dismount your horse and send him home, he won't want to leave, but you make him. He knows the way, don't fret." Philamo handed the reins to Selena and stepped back.

"Will I be gone long, Grandmother?" Selena asked, hoping for an answer.

"As long as it takes, child, as long as it takes." Selena looked ahead to the courtyard gates. The suns were setting behind the trees and the sky was a brilliant shade of orange.

"Grandmother?" Selena turned back but Philamo had already gone.

Selena took up the reins and pressed her heels into her horse and headed for the gates.

"When we clear the castle, Selena, put some wind in your step, we don't have long." Balboar spoke with determination and grit. "This will be a long night, a night when your eyes are opened to all things in this world. Take courage, Selena, and remember all you have been taught."

Selena had galloped her way through the city and was swiftly through the fields and orchards. She was hungry and reached down into the carrying sacks for a snack.

"Balboar, the forest is not far ahead. Shall I dismount now and cover the rest by foot?"

"No, child, every step counts. There is a long walk ahead. Use this speedy beast while you can." Selena just nodded, finished her apple, threw the core and urged the horse on.

After another hour the fields started to thin, the fruit trees were few and far between, thicker, bushier trees started to crop up and the ground became hard and stony.

"Stop here, child. Now's the time to send the horse home. We need to cross the Black Road."

Selena dismounted and unbound the sacks. She knew of the Black Road and what it could do to the mind.

"Go now, my beauty. Off you go home!" The horse didn't move just nuzzled Selena's neck.

"You'll have to do better than that." Balboar laughed.

Selena had never struck a horse before and the idea didn't sit right.

"GO, NOW GO, GO!" Selena shouted.

"You'll have to give him a whack girl, he won't take it personal, I promise."

Selena raised her hand and gave the horse such a smack it rose up and kicked the air behind him, then he was off back across the field from where they had come.

"Poor thing, it carried me here only to be turned away."

"For the love of Merfolk you can kill a man with your bare hands but smacking a horse brings you to tears." Balboar chastised.

"May be my work is not done here!"

"Oh, your work is done, old man and if you were here in body I'd show you a good beating." Selena stared at Balboar grinning from ear to ear.

"Well, maybe you're right, Selena, that left hook of yours is certainly a belter."

Selena slung the sacks over her shoulder and started forward. The Black Road was not sleek and smooth. It did not lie in a straight line with defined edges. Huge chunks of black crumbling rock poked up from the ground like rotten teeth. Selena picked her way through them, eyes wide. Years ago the palace guards had built a bridge across it connecting the Kingdom to the Forest; it still stood but had seen better days.

"Easy now, Selena. It will hold. Just take your time."

Selena held her breath and with gentle steps crossed the ramshackle bridge. Once she had crossed she realised that the earth beneath her feet felt different from the ground on the other side of the Black Road. The air was cooler and she could hear the sounds of night creatures starting to emerge.

"How do I tell exactly were the forest begins?" Selena looked around. Darkness was falling and the landscape all looked the same.

"Look, straight ahead, my girl, that is what you seek."

Selena screwed up her eyes and tried to look straight ahead, then she saw it. Only a glimpse at first, then as she walked forward they became clear, two glowing blue eyes. She followed them through brush and rocks, blindly stumbling forward.

When the blue eyes were just ahead, Selena stopped, lowered her sacks and waited, her breath in short gasps, her sword hand on Balboar.

"There's no need to fight here, Selena, he is our guide." Balboar tried to reassure his charge.

There was rustling ahead and Selena stood stock still stretching her senses for any danger. Slowly and like the slip of a shadow, a large forest wolf made his way out of the thicket. Selena held her breath, she had heard there were wolves in the forest but the size of him had her in awe.

"Balboar, Selena!" Jengo kept his voice calm, his animal senses could feel the fear in Selena and he didn't fancy a sword at his throat, for her skills had reached The Mistress's ear and all now knew Selena as lethal.

"Don't come any closer, wolf, speak your name." Selena had found her voice and wasn't going to give up her ground.

"My name is Jengo. I serve The Mistress. You and Balboar are to follow me to the Holding Grounds." Jengo inched forward as sleek and smooth as tar.

"Selena, he is friend, not foe. Lower your weapon!" Balboar intensified his voice, he knew Selena was ready, ready for the fight.

"How do I know you are not a trickster, a falsehood, wolf. Where is your proof?" Selena had been here before other warriors pretending to be fighting for the same side then trying to slit your throat in the night.

"You are very wise in these uncertain times, girl, very wise indeed. Let Balboar see me. He will be my proof."

Selena slowly unclenched her hand from around Balboar's crystal and held out the blade, her feet still firmly planted ready to strike at one false move.

"Jengo, old friend, you have grown." Balboar's hues were almost white and shone a path to Jengo's feet.

"Balboar, you have bonded well. She is highly trained. I can smell it on her. She is ready to fight even me."

"My money would be on her. She'd have you skinned and hanging before you could even blink." Balboar let out a huge roaring laugh and Selena relaxed her shoulders and released her breath.

"Very well, wolf, it appears you are friend. What happens now?" Selena was tired and alone at the edge of the forest. It was pitch black and she wanted answers.

"Now, Selena, you follow me. Balboar can light the way. The brush will be thick and thorny. I hope you don't mind a hike." Jengo had an edge of humour to his voice.

"Please, wolf, I am Selena, Blade Sworn, lead the way!"

"As you wish, girl. This way."

Selena and Jengo covered the ground quickly. He led her through brooks of ice cold water, over rocky hummocks and through thick briar patches. There were less dense and treacherous ways but Jengo felt a little humble pie wouldn't kill her. She seemed too arrogant for his liking.

"How much further, wolf? I have a thirst on me." Selena's warrior ways were starting to return. This wolf had had her traipsing through the forest for too long.

"We approach now, your majesty." Jengo's voice was syrupy, sweet but with an insulting edge that Selena didn't miss.

Selena smelled the smoke before she saw the fires glow. Balboar had been silent the whole journey and now he spoke.

"Behold, Selena, the Holding Grounds." His voice was not the hollering boom it usually was. He sounded small and humble.

"This way, Selena." Jengo led Selena to the entrance. The briars and thorns had almost completely covered the path and the thorns bit and scratched at Selena's limbs but the Shanzzy brushed them aside like they were petals on a rose. Eventually the path opened up and Jengo and Selena emerged into the clearing. Selena quickly scanned the area looking for trouble. She saw none. There was a large fire in the middle of the clearing and she could make out two figures standing by it. Jengo crossed to the shadowy side of the fire and bowed to the larger of the two figures, then he turned and left the way they had come. Selena could make out some kind of cages arranged around the fire. She screwed her eyes up to get a clearer look. She could just make out huddled figures in two of the cages. One was empty.

"Forward, Selena, it is time to meet The Mistress." Balboar kept the fear from his voice. The last time he had been face to face with The Mistress she had been brandishing threats of the pit. He must instil courage in the girl. She must do well. Selena tentatively crossed to the other side of the fire, every fibre in her body ready for the unexpected just as Balboar had taught her.

"Welcome, Selena, to the Holding Grounds. I am The Mistress." The voice was cool, calm. Selena couldn't tell if it was old or young, welcoming or frosty. "Relax, child, all is well. I see Balboar has kept his oath and bonded with you well." The Mistress was secretly pleased. *She shall be an asset to the group*, she thought to herself.

"Don't be afraid, girl, there is nothing here but work to be done." Selena felt a little mesmerized by the voice. Its gentle commands felt in control and safe. As Selena moved to the side of the fire pit, The Mistress stepped forward. A large, green robe covered her body, in her hand she clasped a long, thin cane, its top a large, blue crystal much like Balboar's, only jagged. The Mistress lifted her hand and removed the hood of the robe. Selena gasped. The Mistress's eyes where pure blue. No white or black. Just shimmering, swirls of azure. They were beautiful and her face radiated life and knowledge.

She is a goddess here, Selena thought, *a goddess.*

Chapter 81
Three Lost Souls

Illiwig, Grumble and the little firefly slept. A ramshackle group of three, all injured, all fighting for their lives. Their cell was cold and damp and at the end of a long corridor of empty cells. Deep in the bowls of an abandoned fort. Ivy and thorn bushes strangled its walls and fog and mist covered its entrance. They had no chance of being found. No chance of rescue. But hope springs eternal, my friends, and fate was about to give them a fighting chance. For hacking his way through the undergrowth, a warrior came. The Oracle had pulled upon his heart strings and The Mistress's token that lay there. Driven by the need to find what has been hidden. Young Jug was a saviour made.

Chapter 82
The Mistress

The Grey crouched low in the bushes, waiting for The Mistress to complete her tasks. He had wanted to talk to her and give her his grave news before Jengo and Dax arrived but they had made good time and interrupting The Mistress in full flow was unheard of.

The Mistress cast her eye over the three cages, all three Sworn were hunkered low, she sniffed the evening air. She needed to stretch her legs and remove herself from Thistle's constant fussing. A little stroll around the Holding Grounds was in order, she thought.

The Mistress set a slow pace, taking in the forest smells, glancing at the three moons now high in the blackened sky. She came to a sudden stop and waited for her guest to make himself known.

"Mistress, may I approach?"

"Yes, Grey, you are a friend here. You know that."

The Grey slunk his way from the dense brush.

"Mistress, I have grave news, very grave indeed."

The Mistress felt the cold tingle of fear sweep across her body. She swallowed but kept her tongue, allowing The Grey to find the right words.

"Speak on." The Mistress finally whispered. The Grey could not. He lowered his head afraid of what his news would mean. Afraid that on hearing of Kef's death, The Mistress's oldest friend, she would rise to such grief and anger she would not be contained. "Grey, please. Your report." The Mistress could not hide the tremble in her voice.

"It's Kef, Mistress, he is dead."

The Mistress's eyes flew wide, her jaw slackened as she inhaled an almighty gasp.

"Report! Grey, report! How has this happened. Was he ill? An accident perhaps?" She was frantic, blinking and shaking her head as if trying to erase the truth.

"Murder, your Holiness. It was murder."

The finality of his words left a silence so overbearing The Mistress could take no more. Her knees buckled as she slumped to the floor. Her head hung low as a deep groan escaped her mouth. A single tear ran down her cheek. The dancing light of the fire caught it and it shone like a tiny jewel upon her face.